The Clacking of Mandibles

Monk was sti
him in, but his
now; they were
anything. There
and he clutched
the most precious
body trembled
verged on seizures ... closed
again and again though he seemed to have little control over it or the word that he kept repeating over and over and over and over again. Just one word. It took Wheatley a moment to distinguish the syllables and differentiate the word from the rolling *clack clack clack* of sound: *Glaaki Glaaki Glaaki.*

Clack clack clack...

Like mandibles...clacking...

He had heard that sound—that word—before. Realization sent a cold shiver down the ladder of his spine one bone at a time...

The Sign of Glaaki

by Steven Savile and Steve Lockley

This one's for Marie, who makes me a better man than I ever thought I could be.

This one is for Becky and Sam—two constants in an ever-changing world.

Paperback edition published in 2014.
Printed in the United States of America.

Cover illustration by Rafal Hrynkiewicz.

ISBN: 978-1-61661-714-1

Fantasy Flight Publishing, Inc.
1995 West County Road B2
Roseville, MN 55113
USA

The Sign of Glaaki

Trailer

A ship's horn cried forlornly into the thick fog.

It was like some lost animal calling out, desperate to be heard, to be found. It was one of the loneliest sounds in the world.

But the ship didn't *want* to be found. Not by the *things* out there…

Tom Sanders had heard the stories, they all had. There were more things down there in the deep water *The Dunwich Ghost* sailed upon than most men could dream of.

They were only one day from land. One day. Tom knew he must remain calm and vigilant tonight of all nights, so close to home. He braced himself on the railing and stared out into the fog. The paraffin lamp barely penetrated a few feet into the heavy peasouper.

He kept glancing at the dark shapes out there, sure they were moving.

The night could play tricks on the mind in conditions like this, but the truth was that even so, that didn't mean there weren't *things* out there.

The liner plied its trade across the Atlantic, running between the docks of Liverpool and the coast of Massachusetts, carrying its passengers in what would once have been considered style. Now the staterooms, dining halls, and ballroom were threadbare, but beauty was ever in the eye of the beholder. Most of their passengers were swept away by the destination and the journey itself, blinded to the worn-out upholstery and cigarette burns in the carpets. Below decks, the band was in full swing. The passengers danced and laughed, oblivious to the danger all around them.

Heavy footsteps echoed on the iron deck behind him as two men struggled with the burden they carried between them.

Here be monsters, Tom thought, not turning his back on the water.

He only had eyes for the fog and the things he thought he imagined within it.

The pair worked in silence, shifting the weight of the long box as they shuffled toward the prow.

The light from Tom's lantern barely reached them.

There was no one else on the deck to witness what they were doing.

They couldn't have hoped for better conditions for this kind of work; on a clear moonlit night there would have been passengers taking a turn around the deck, suitors smiling at the ladies in their sheer dresses, dancing in the moonlight, and widows looking out toward the new life they hoped to make for themselves come landfall. Not tonight.

The pair paused, adjusting their grip and lifting the box smoothly up so it rested on the guardrail.

Tom didn't feel the need to watch the coffin slip over the side. There was a splash, itself swallowed by the fog as the sea swallowed it.

The heavy iron sea door *clanged* closed.

He was alone again.

Tom doused the lantern and moved away from the railing as an alarm rang out. There was an odd moment of calm before the meaning of the alarm registered with the passengers, and of course the band played on.

Crew and passengers alike came rushing to the deck. Then a cry of "Man overboard!" filled the foggy night. He recognized the voice. It was one of the hands that had pushed that peculiar passenger over the side in the first place.

The powerful searchlight blazed into life, its beam turning slowly onto the ocean. The light cut deep into the fog, but it didn't reveal any more than his lantern had. The coffin was gone, the passenger consigned to the depths.

Feature Presentation

Reel One

Chapter One

The dapper young man stopped at the top of the gangplank, savoring the moment. Kingsport, USA. To a man, everyone who had disembarked before him had done the exact same thing. It was a unique moment; the first time they'd set foot on foreign soil. Dennis Wheatley fully intended to remember it. It wasn't every day you braved a new frontier.

"*Wheatley!*" came a cry from the crowded quayside.

It was one voice amongst hundreds, but it carried all the way up the gangplank.

He scanned the mass of waving arms—there were pretty girls and grinning grandparents and expectant friends down there, their smiles infectious, and amid all of that happiness, the man he was looking for: the Great Houdini. "Dennis! Over here, man!"

Despite the fact they had only corresponded by letter—well, many letters, actually—Wheatley was utterly fascinated by the man, by the deceptions around him and the persona he presented the world. Face-to-face for the first time, there was no mistaking the man, even in a crowd of thousands.

Wheatley waved in his direction and started down the plank.

So this is it, he thought. *America.*

It didn't look so different. The fashions of those waiting on the quayside were a little stiffer, but people were people the world over no matter what they wore.

At the bottom of the plank he presented his passport to the Immigration officer.

The man took it, bent open the card cover, and unfolded the single page document inside. It was still crisp, unused before this trip. Wheatley knew every word written on it. The personal description detailing his height, weight, age, and coloration, sections including his name, nationality, and a grainy photograph along with orders that the bearer be afforded the same rights and privileges that would be offered to His Majesty the King. It was his life reduced to a few words.

The Immigration officer said, "Everything seems to be in order. Welcome to America, Mr. Wheatley. Enjoy your visit," and folded the document up before handing it back.

"Thank you."

Slipping the passport back inside his pocket, he took his first step on American soil. The next passenger was already on his way down the gangplank and the waiting crowd jostled around him.

He pushed and wriggled his way through the crowd toward the piles of luggage trunks and the waiting Houdini. "Mr. Houdini," he said, holding out a hand. Close up, the magician looked considerably older than he had in the movie reels Wheatley had seen, but still physically imposing all the same. He smiled, thinking of all of the hours he had spent watching those great escapes, building a dossier on the tricks, trying to predict what wondrous deception Houdini might conjure next. He loved the theatricality of it all. But looking at him now, he seemed...*reduced.*

"Harry," the man replied, matching his smile. "Harry, Harry, Harry." He seemed intent on repeating the name until it stopped making sense. "Houdini's a character. A piece of theater for the great unwashed." A character he lived and breathed. He *was* the character he'd created, and the world was in awe of him. "Besides, you made the damned journey without drowning, that's got to be enough to earn you the right to call me Harry hasn't it? I figure we'll head straight to the set. Ulysses is like a kid on Christmas morning, he can't wait to meet you. It's all Wheatley this, England that. I warn you, he can be a little…intense. That's a good word for it. Odd, even. You know what the artistic temperament can be like, but still, he's a likable enough sort. And he's paying the bills."

"Is this when I'm meant to wonder what I've gotten myself into?"

"Oh, we're well past that point, my friend," Houdini grinned. "But we will have fun. And that's what life is all about. Come on, let's get your luggage and get out of here."

Wheatley followed Houdini through the crowd to the waiting bags.

He had his reasons for making the trip—and meeting Houdini was only one of them. Another one was simply to be anywhere but home right now. The last twelve months had been hell. Not only had he lost his best friend, Eric Tombe, brutally murdered by his pet thug, he'd found himself blackmailed into giving the killer an alibi. Everyone knew he was lying, but no one could prove it. That didn't stop things from being uncomfortable. Questions he did not want to answer were being asked far too often. On every corner he was sure he saw policemen shadowing him, in every doorway he was sure he saw private investigators dogging his trail.

The timing of Houdini's invitation could not have been better, no matter how curious the offer it contained.

It had given Wheatley the justification he needed to make his excuses and move on without seeming to be running away; two birds with one metaphorical stone.

The offer?

Houdini had finagled a deal with the young filmmaker Ulysses Monk that saw them employed as consultants on his new project which had just begun shooting in Dunwich. Though what, exactly, they were supposed to be consulting on was sketchy to say the least.

He grabbed his suitcases.

"The car's this way."

Wheatley followed Houdini as he wove a path through the crowd people, always two steps behind him. As they reached the car he asked the question he'd been wanting to ask ever since the invitation arrived: "Why me?"

"Ah," Houdini said with a mischievous grin. "What can I say? Personally, I find there is nothing quite like exposing fakers and charlatans. Call it an obsession with the truth, but in my defense, I ask you: How can anyone willingly live in a world of lies?" Before he could answer, Houdini answered for him. "They can't. Obviously. No one can. That is why the world of the motion pictures is so fascinating. It is all about painting lies on a moving canvas. Selling the drama. Our stories are always melodrama, deliberately manipulating the heartstrings instead of working the mind." He tapped two fingers against his temple. "It's all up here. The mind. It's a beautiful thing. Monk wants to show the truth in his film, or at least as much as he is able to. We're here to make sure he can."

"The truth about freaks?"

"A harsh word, I know, but yes."

And if he was being honest with himself, he was looking forward to seeing some of these people in the flesh. It wasn't just morbid curiosity. There was something eerily fascinating about the underside of society, the notion of disfigurement versus beauty, and the perceptions around it. He could see why Monk was drawn towards it. In Wheatley's experience, people were willfully superficial when it came to valuing others. They would talk to someone with physical abnormalities as though it was their brain that was twisted, not their bones.

Even so, he wasn't sure how either of them were supposed to know just by looking at them if they were the genuine article, honest-to-God freaks, or if their disfigurement was the result of accident, or worse, tricksters using prosthetics and stage makeup to alter their appearance.

But that was the job he'd traveled four thousand miles for.

Monk wanted everything in his picture to be *real*.

Of course, none of that really explained why Houdini had reached out to him.

* * *

"The strangest thing happened last night," Wheatley said, somewhere between Kingsport and Dunwich.

"Oh?" that caught Houdini's attention, as he knew it would. "Just how strange is the strangest thing?"

"I'll let you decide," Wheatley said, baiting the hook of the story. "There was a passenger in the cabin next to mine. He kept to himself, but I heard him moving about often enough. Only caught a glimpse of him once when his door was open as I walked past. A most peculiar chap. Gaunt, like one of the walking dead, without a trace of a hair on his head."

"Well, he does indeed sound strange," Houdini laughed. He signaled to take the next turn toward the outskirts of the town even though there was no other vehicle on the road.

"And that's before we get to the interesting part: he *disappeared* last night."

"Ah, a mystery. Excellent."

"We were caught in a terrible fog. As far as I can tell he either fell overboard...or *jumped*."

"It happens."

"Ah, but this was the *first* time he had left his cabin in the whole trip!"

"So he was either damned unfortunate, or the victim of something more sinister, is that what you're suggesting?"

Wheatley nodded beside him. "It makes no sense that he'd choose the one night to venture on deck when the passengers had been instructed to stay below."

"Okay, *now* you have my interest, Wheatley. Ask yourself this: Why on earth would the passengers be told to stay inside? It isn't all that likely they'd fall overboard just because of some fog, is it?"

"I've got no proof, but I listened and watched. I got the distinct impression the crew was afraid that there was *something* out there..."

Houdini looked across at him for a moment, not watching the road. He stared at Wheatley without so much as blinking. He didn't seem remotely surprised by the notion. Quite the reverse, in fact. It was almost as if he *expected* it.

"All right, you asked 'why me?' I owe you the truth," Houdini said, finally. "It was no coincidence, I'll admit that. You were recommended to me by a mutual friend. It was suggested you were a man with an open mind and an understanding of the *peculiar*. To be frank, weird things happen in this part of the world. And by weird I mean things that are not easy to explain."

"Like sailors being terrified that there is something out in the ocean deep?"

"Precisely like that, yes. There are more things in heaven and earth and all that malarkey. I was assured you were open to the uncanny, where others would be inclined to simply deny the possibility of it."

"I'm flattered. I think. 'Uncanny'? Does that mean you suspect something of a *supernatural* nature is going on here?" It was the obvious conclusion to draw; it was, after all, the one thing they had in common—an almost unhealthy interest in things that did not belong and could not easily be explained.

"I'm suggesting nothing of the sort—*yet*—but I will go so far as to say I believe there are things that science isn't in a position to rationalize, and those things seem to happen more frequently here than anywhere else I've been. But, and this is the crux of the matter, events don't need to be supernatural to be weird. Take this picture of Monk's. It is beset by tragedy almost daily. The latest may even have put the whole enterprise at risk, but Monk is relentless. People are calling it cursed; yet he refuses to be stopped. He will carry on through hell and high water as long as he has the coin to do so."

Wheatley was about to ask what he meant by "latest tragedy," because it sounded like there was a story to tell there, too, but before he could the sky was lit by a sudden fork of lightning that hung in the road in front of them. It was followed by an ear-splitting crash of thunder.

The rain came from nowhere. It was just suddenly there, a solid sheet that divided the road in two.

The deluge transformed the road ahead of them into a river in a matter of seconds, too much water for the canted surface to drain away before it flooded. The wipers couldn't keep the windshield clear for more than half a second. It was incredible. Biblical.

"Now I understand what they mean when they say the heavens opened," Wheatley said. It was a lame joke. The ferocity of the storm was frightening. He made poor jokes when he was frightened. "Unbelievable." He shook his head. He had to shout to be heard over the fury of the breaking storm.

The rain drummed on the roof of the car.

He could smell the tang of electricity in the air.

"Should we sit this out?"

"If we wait there's every chance we'll be stuck here for the night, and as much as I like you, I don't particularly fancy sleeping with you on a first date, no offense old chap, but Bess is more my type." Wilhelmina Beatrice Rahner—Bess Houdini to the rest of the world—was Harry's wife and the center of his universe. The pair were inseparable. She'd been his beautiful assistant for as long as he'd been the lord of illusions, up on the stage beside him night after night.

"Speaking of Bess, is she in town? I'm looking forward to meeting her."

"Ah, alas, no. She and Monk don't exactly see eye-to-eye. As I said, he's a little...*odd*. She thinks he's using me, trading on my reputation to add notoriety to his 'little film' as she calls it. We're meeting in a week for rehearsals. So until then it's just you and me."

Wheatley nodded. "This is *ridiculous*," he said, peering into the storm. "Is it normally like this?" The sky had turned black in the time it had taken them to cover three hundred yards. He could barely see two feet beyond the hood of the car, even with the headlights on full beam.

The rain drummed against the hood, bouncing back six inches high.

"Depends on your definition of normal. I've seen storms like this bring half a hillside down and block a road for weeks. I've seen floods grow so deep that they become impassable without a rowboat."

"I'll take your word for it," Wheatley said. "Maybe staying at home, warm by the fire, wouldn't have been a bad way to spend the autumn after all."

Houdini laughed—and then stopped laughing abruptly as the car slipped and slewed in mud and rain.

Panic gripped Wheatley. He felt for something secure to cling onto. Anything. Beside him, Houdini seemed to take perverse pleasure in it all; man and machine versus the elements.

"This guy that went overboard?" Houdini said, bringing them back to his story. "Anything else worth knowing about him?" He fought with the wheel, eyes straight ahead, somehow able to make small talk.

Wheatley had no idea how the man could do it. It was as though by distracting himself he was leaving less space in his brain to worry about driving. However it worked, it *was* working. If he'd been in the driver's seat they would have ended up in a ditch long ago.

Lightning flashed again. Within it he saw the road, and just how close they were to the grassy verge. He saw the rainwater cascading down the side, bringing mud and debris with it. And then the darkness returned. But not soon enough for him to miss the roots of the trees exposed as the mud slipped, or the bare stone where the foundations of the bank had been ruthlessly exposed. To take his mind off it, he tried to think about *The Dunwich Ghost*'s peculiar passenger. "I'm not sure that there's that much to tell. I only saw him once."

"But an observant man can see a lot without *thinking* he is seeing anything. For instance, what about his meals?"

"They were all served in his cabin. Always by the same steward."

"See then, that is something. A detail. There must have been talk about him. A mysterious passenger who never ventured out of his cabin, who only accepted food delivered by the same steward, day or night? People talk. It is human nature. They gossip. And with someone behaving so oddly, that gossip must have been rife? So think: did you happen to overhear the crew talking about their mysterious passenger? Did you hear the steward complaining about having to work all hours just to be sure the gaunt man with no hair didn't go hungry?"

"Well," Wheatley said, drawing it out slowly so the word seemed to last one, two, three heartbeats, building the anticipation. He smiled, knowing this was the detail that would reel Houdini in. How could it not? "I did happen to overhear one of them saying that he had a *coffin* in his cabin."

"A coffin?" Houdini barked out a laugh. "And that didn't strike you as peculiar? That, my friend, is what newspaper men call burying the lead."

"I did say he was a most peculiar guest," Wheatley grinned, almost managing to forget about the storm for a moment. "I thought given his appearance he may have been suffering some affliction, and with his days numbered, intended to be buried here, hence bringing his coffin with him."

"How very practical, and *English*. So, the sixty-four thousand dollar question: Was it still in his room after he had disappeared over the side?"

Wheatley had no idea. He hadn't even thought to look. "No idea," he admitted, cursing himself for ruining the end of a good story. It would have been perfect to say that no, in fact, it was gone and that the man had been thrown over the side in his coffin. That sort of detail had a delicious quality to it. The door of the cabin had been left open when the search began, and he'd walked past it several times during the search, but hadn't thought to look inside the room.

"It couldn't have been there," he said eventually, trying to think it through. It was useless. He was inventing memories. Wheatley rubbed at the stubble on his chin. "Do you think I should tell the police?"

"Why ever would you want to do that? I'm sure that they will interview the stewards and, if as you say, there was a coffin and then there wasn't, then one of them will mention it. So I don't think you need to worry about getting involved."

"Technically I'm already involved; they questioned me this morning before we docked."

"Oh?"

"Officers from Kingsport came on board in a launch before we dropped anchor. They wanted to be sure our details logged with the captain were correct and establish that I hadn't seen anything. Which I hadn't, of course. I gave them your name as point-of-contact; I hope that was all right?"

"Of course."

"They didn't believe me at first," Wheatley admitted. Houdini laughed again; it was an easy laugh with no sign of nervousness being created by the storm. "Actually, I'm not entirely convinced they believed me at all."

"I am sure you're not the first to offer my name as their sponsor when arriving in the country. They must think I'm assembling my own little pool of slave labor. Ah," he said, affecting a thick brogue, "Tis a mercy you weren't Irish or I'm sure they'd have sent you back where ya came from." It was an awful impersonation.

In the distance Wheatley could just make out the lights of a town fighting to make themselves seen through the deluge.

"Well, here we are." Houdini brought the car to a halt in front of a boarding house a few minutes later. He pulled up on the handbrake, hard. "Ma Mocata has a full house, but I used my charms to convince her to let you have the last room."

"Then I owe you one."

"Don't be so sure," he chuckled. "She's not a fan of the 'movie people' but I promised her you weren't one of those, so you better be a good boy and not be causing her any problems now, Wheatley."

"Wouldn't dream of it."

"Good man."

Wheatley peered out through the rain at the big old clapboard house. The place had seen better days. A hand-painted sign in the front window declared "no vacancies" in an awkward scrawl.

"You're not staying here then?"

"Heavens, no. Monk *insisted* that I stay with him in the house he's rented. It's just outside of town. I could hardly say no, now could I? Not that he has room for me up there. He's sleeping on the sofa so I can have his bed. But, between you, me, and the steering wheel, it's never easy for me to get any peace in a boarding house. There's always someone who wants to have their 'Houdini moment' so they can go back home and tell the folks all about it. Not that I begrudge them, it is the price of fame, and if I'm honest, it's one I rather like paying most of the time. But sometimes it's nice to just rest, you know?"

Wheatley could only begin to imagine what it must be like for his companion, who was surely one of the most famous men in the world. There could be no privacy—no anonymity—he would always be the Great Houdini, never just Harry.

Chapter Two

"Annnnnd *action!*"

The clapperboard came down with a snap.

Filming had begun at first light. The crew had assembled a makeshift studio and soundstage in-situ to help control light and sound so they could shoot well into the night if need be. The storm had cleared, leaving behind a clear blue morning sky and the kind of wonderful autumn light that was a cinematographer's delight.

Wheatley and Houdini stood in silence, watching the scene evolve. This was Wheatley's first exposure to the magic of cinema.

They were in a mocked up graveyard. A man stood in the middle of the stones, hunched over a shovel, digging.

"Cut! Print that! Good job, Ephraim!" A man Wheatley took to be Ulysses Monk barked through a bullhorn. He watched with fascination. It was like spying on another world. Even so, he couldn't quite believe that the magic was so *straightforward.* He'd imagined scenes having to be done over and over again to make sure that they mated with the director's particular and precise vision of them, not just run through once and banked. But perfectionism cost money, and looking around, one thing was for sure and certain: this was being put together on a shoestring. The set was actually *flimsy*. Without the windbreakers, the tombstones would have toppled like dominoes if one of the stagehands had so much as coughed. But that was all part of the illusion.

"It's not always like this," Houdini said. "Sometimes it's actually quite *boring*."

"Hard to imagine," Wheatley said, still feeling like the poor country relative brought to the big city for the first time. "So what's your role in this? I mean, aside from consulting?"

"Ah, nothing too taxing this time. I'm playing myself in a few scenes." It was easy to see why Bess might have been skeptical. "But mainly they wanted me on board to help with the mechanics of the underwater filming. The camera time's just to flatter my ego. Monk knows how to appeal to my vanity," and then he barked, "Ulysses, my man!" catching the director's eye. "You have a visitor!"

Monk pushed himself up out of his seat. To Wheatley's untrained eye he appeared to have had very little actual input into the performance beyond shouting three words, but perhaps there was some unseen magic to it all he didn't quite grasp? Perhaps by giving them their freedom, the actors were rising to the challenge, or maybe it just didn't matter given that this particular film seemed to be more about shock value than artistic merit?

If he remembered right, Monk had made something of a stir with his first talkie. Now it seemed he was hell bent on ending his career with a horrific film that was very likely to fall foul of the Motion Picture Production Code. Houdini said he was odd. He wasn't odd. He just relished the prospect of ruffling feathers. That wasn't odd, it was contentious, which told him all he needed to know about the filmmaker.

"Even if the picture never sees the light of day in the US, Monk will still secure distribution for it elsewhere. The more controversial it is, the more likely it is to light a spark within the public's imagination. That's just the way people are," Houdini explained as the filmmaker crossed the set to join them. "Monk's plan to make a film about freaks and degenerates using real disabled and deformed people is as controversial as it comes. It's a goldmine. Believe me. It's one thing to see the freaks in sideshows and carnivals, but quite something else to see them larger than life up on the big screen." Wheatley shuddered to think.

"Is this your young English friend?" Monk said, reaching them.

"It certainly is," said Houdini. "Dennis, meet Ulysses Monk—one of a kind, finest filmmaker of a generation, a name you'll be hearing for a long time, believe me. Uly, Dennis Wheatley—be gentle with him, he only arrived yesterday, fresh off the boat."

"Yesterday? Well that must have been an eventful landfall." The filmmaker extended a hand and shook briskly with Wheatley when he clasped it.

"We were lucky to get through. The road to Kingsport is closed again, and more than likely it'll be a few days before it's cleared—assuming that it doesn't rain again."

"Mercifully everyone who is in, or at least hoping to be in the film, is already in town," Monk said. "I just need a little help in sorting the wheat from the chaff, so to speak. Isn't that what you Brits say?"

"I suppose we do," Wheatley agreed.

"I've given Harry a list of the names and addresses of people who claim to be unusual enough for my needs. Whether they are or not, well that's for you to say, but to my untrained eye they certainly have the look. Check them out; tell me what you think. I need to know that the bearded lady really has a beard and that it's not just stuck on. I want to know if the baby with six toes really has six and can wiggle them all, if you get my drift? I don't want anyone accusing me of making people look like these sideshow freaks when the real thing is out there. This isn't about exploitation, it's about authenticity, you understand?"

Before he could say yes or no Monk turned away and barked an instruction at one of the crew, his attention clearly elsewhere already. Houdini put his arm around Wheatley's broad shoulders. "Let me give you the grand tour; you might as well meet the cast and crew while we're here. Then we can get started."

Wheatley found himself being dragged around from one

technician to another, each of them seeming to perform more than one task on the movie: the electrician helped build the sets, the cameraman was handy with a paintbrush, and the actor stepping out of the fake graveyard also happened to be in charge of catering. From what he could tell, there weren't that many people working on the project—certainly not as many as he would have expected. Even so, after meeting a few the faces and the names of each began to merge with the next.

They seemed happy enough to risk the wrath of the director to take a few moments away from their work to say hello, though, and tell him a little about what they did and how they fit into the grand scheme of things. He noticed the way they kept glancing toward Monk, making sure they weren't overstepping some invisible boundary. It was illuminating. And considering the nature of the picture, they all seemed remarkably—disappointingly, even—normal.

The two leading actors were different.

Wheatley could see immediately that this was where the budget had been blown.

Each had their own well-appointed trailer, and Wheatley counted three attendants for the pair, so no doubt every whim was amply catered for.

Houdini reminded Wheatley of their names as they approached, whispering both, and although the man's face was vaguely familiar, he wasn't star material, not an icon like Harold Lloyd, Valentino, or Douglas Fairbanks, even if he was being treated like one. Taylor Andrews had been around for long enough to accumulate an interesting if somewhat eclectic list of credits, but even edited together it was unlikely they would clock up an honest-to-God hour of screen time. That didn't prevent him from acting as though the sun shone through his sphincter though. It amused Wheatley to see him strut and preen like a peacock, demanding everyone jump when he snapped his fingers, even Houdini, whose name was the draw that would lure viewers into the cinemas.

The woman was different. She had the beauty of a leading lady. She was breathtaking, though it was a porcelain statue kind of fragile beauty. She was fresh-faced, raven-haired, and couldn't have been out of her teens, but she had presence of star. Poise, bearing, glamour. She was born for fame. It almost hurt to look at her, she burned that brightly. Wheatley was in no doubt that Collette Verney could easily be next year's Gloria Swanson or Mary Pickford, all it needed was for the public to see enough of her. She had that illusive quality they all craved. Maybe this film would be her big break, maybe it wouldn't. It would happen, though, he was sure of that. It was fated.

Unlike Andrews, she was happy to stop and talk, letting him bathe in her aura, before Andrews dragged her away, insisting that they had lines to rehearse to be ready for the afternoon's scene.

"Believe it or not, that beauty wasn't the first choice for the part," Houdini said conspiratorially. "I mentioned troubles around this picture? The actress Monk originally cast *disappeared*. You might have read about it? No, no, of course, you'll have been at sea. She was last seen leaving home to begin principal photography, but she never arrived. It's almost as deliciously sinister as your gaunt passenger and his coffin, wouldn't you say?"

"Perhaps she got a better offer."

"If that were the case, dear boy, explain to me why no one has seen hide nor hair of her since the day she left home?" He blew into his fingers as though making her disappear. "No, believe me, this—this whole place, this film—it's beset by so many tragedies and misfortunes it could have a man flapping his bed sheets at the aurora borealis and mooing like a cow."

"Eloquently put, I think," Wheatley said wryly. He found himself liking the escapologist more and more, even if he didn't quite understand everything he said.

Set apart from the main hubbub he saw a ring of brightly colored gypsy caravans, and around them a clutch of equally garishly clad people. The freaks. Dennis Wheatley had never seen anything like them. There were midgets and incredibly tall, desperately thin men side-by-side. He caught a glimpse of a boy—at least that's what he thought it was—the poor soul looked more like an animal, and holding his hand a woman who was so incredibly fat that rolls of skin overflowed from gaps in her clothes. Beside her he saw a man who appeared to have no backbone being supported by two grotesquely deformed and conjoined twins. It was impossible to look away.

"Welcome to Darke's Carnival," Houdini said. There was something in his voice—Wheatley could have mistaken it for pride if he hadn't already spent some time around the escapologist and grown at least a little familiar with the nuances of his personality. It was obvious the man felt some sort of affinity for the afflicted. Perhaps it was because, in their own way, they were showmen like him?

The remainder of the tour consisted mainly of them walking between a number of trailers that seemed to form avenues along the back of the set. This was where the crew and actors lived and rested when they weren't working. The trailers offered a cheap way of providing accommodation. They were no doubt leased by the week.

Then it was on to the prefabricated workshops. They were a couple of buildings built in sections that could be taken down easily and moved to another location when the work was completed. They housed everything from scenery and props to huge steel catering trays.

The final workshop was a curious one.

It contained something Wheatley hadn't expected to see: a large glass tank filled with water. He thought of the escapologist's famous "Chinese Water Torture" trick, and wondered if that was what Harry had meant when he'd said he was helping with some underwater filming?

"Now *this* is my domain," said Houdini, coming around to join him beside the huge tank. "My idea. So much more controllable than trying to film anything of worth in the murky water of the lake."

Wheatley walked around the tank, placing his hands against the glass. It felt surprisingly cold to the touch.

"Do the cameras work underwater?" he asked.

"We've got one that does. Incredible technology, really, watertight to a depth of thirty feet! But every time I get my hands on it they're on at me not to drop it like I'm some sort of hopeless klutz. Me, the Great Houdini!" It might have sounded pompous, but he delivered the epithet with just the right balance of self-deprecation and self-awareness Wheatley knew immediately he didn't mean a word of it. It was all one endless performance with the man. "There's one tricky scene where someone else has to use the camera while I fight off a dreaded sea monster." He shrugged as though to say how could the outcome ever be in doubt, but before Wheatley could offer any sort of agreement, a piercing scream came from the direction of the trailers.

"The sound of some fresh tragedy befalling our production," Houdini said. And while he'd said it half in jest, all humor was gone as the concerned voices were silenced by a second scream.

Houdini took off like a shot, Wheatley close on his heels, dreading what they might find as they rounded the corner into the alley of caravans. Others chased after them, help coming from all sides.

The next sound they heard was a cry for help.

Suddenly everyone was moving toward the trailers, some running, others edging tentatively toward them, fearful of what was waiting for them in there.

Even so, the door of the nearest trailer was jammed with people trying to see inside.

"It's Collette," someone cried. And a chorus of voices told Wheatley all he needed to know as he tried to push his way to the front.

"Oh my Lord!"

"Oh, God, no…"

"No."

"She's dead."

Chapter Three

The police kept them waiting around far longer than Wheatley would have expected them to, but he was an outsider. While it might have appeared logical to grill him first and try to work a confession or clue out of him—especially as the murder had happened a few hours after his arrival in town—breaking a suspect took time, so saving him till last made a grim kind of sense to him. The questions were all the same: "Did you know the victim before today?" "What brought you to the United States?" "Are you or have you ever been involved in a criminal investigation in your home land?" That one he couldn't answer for them, not truthfully. Questions, questions, questions. But, despite his reticence to share his past he was exactly what he appeared to be, as Houdini had so eloquently put it, fresh off the boat. He couldn't have committed the crime; they both knew that even if the police didn't. He had been in Houdini's company when the actress—still very much alive—had begun screaming. There was no better alibi in all of America.

Before they got to him, the detective, true to prejudice, focused his enquiries on the people traveling with the carnival: the freaks first, and then their ringleader, the illusive

Mr. Darke. Darke gave them short shrift, and they got no joy from the freaks, so finally they came looking for the foreigner.

There was the inevitable comic double-take moment as the detective recognized Houdini and, flustered, seemed to be on the verge of asking for his autograph instead of asking the hard questions, but then the seriousness of the situation hit him and his face changed. He was all business. "I need to ask you and your friend here a few questions, sir."

"Be my guest," Houdini said amiably. "Terrible business. Anything we can do to help. Anything at all. Don't hesitate to ask. Poor woman."

"Indeed," the detective agreed. "You were together the entire time you were on the set?"

"Absolutely. Monk was eager to meet Dennis here, and then we did the rounds."

"Right, Mr. Whateley is it?" the policeman asked eventually, starting a new page in his notebook.

"Wheatley," Wheatley corrected him.

"My apologies," he said. "I'd assumed that you must be related to one of the people with the carnival. My mistake." He thumbed back through the pages of his jotter. "We have a Mrs. Whateley listed as traveling amongst them." He nodded in the direction of a white-haired woman who was clutching a glass jar to her breast.

"Easy mistake to make," Wheatley said. "Wheatley, Whateley, pretty much the same thing."

"Ah, yes, but she's a bit of an odd sort, that one."

"Is she?" Wheatley started to ask, but Houdini gave him a sharp dig in the ribs with an elbow to stop him going any further. The detective took a surreptitious look around them, and then nodded, but only when he was sure the old woman wasn't looking their way.

The detective offered a forced smile, and again made a note in his jotter. "And you were with Mr. Houdini at the time of the murder?"

"I've been with Harry from the moment I set foot in America," Wheatley confirmed. The detective nodded, satisfied. As he'd suspected, the man wasn't about to question Houdini's trustworthiness. He made another note in his book.

"And you talked to Miss Verney this afternoon?"

"Not fifteen minutes before she was killed," Houdini said.

"Which would make you one of the last people to see her alive, then." It wasn't a question. Wheatley had had the same thought.

"Apart from her killer," he said.

"Of course. Of course. I didn't mean to imply anything else. Did you perhaps notice anyone hanging around her trailer when you were there? See any of the crew in the vicinity?"

Wheatley thought about it, but no, he hadn't seen anyone loitering around the actress's trailer. There had been plenty of people moving about the set, though, and any one of them could have been the killer. He said as much.

"Indeed," the detective made another note. He seemed resigned to the fact that there would be no easy solution.

"If you'd be so kind," he suggested, "I'd be most interested to hear your take on the scene, Mr. Houdini?" The request rather amused Wheatley. It wasn't as though escaping from handcuffs and locked boxes gave you any particular insight into the criminal mind, did it? Still, Houdini took it in his stride and smiled one of his winning smiles.

"Of course you would—and it would be a crime for me to deny you access to a mind as powerful as mine, wouldn't it?" Houdini said with more than a trace of sarcasm in his tone, which the detective wasn't sharp enough to catch. The criminal fraternity must have trembled in their boots when he was on the case, Wheatley thought grimly. "By all means, lead on. I will tell you all that I see; perhaps it will help bring this ghastly killer to justice. I will do my best. The dear girl deserves no less from any of us."

The detective took them to the actress's trailer, but not inside.

Her body was being prepared for transport to the morgue. The detective placed a hand on the shoulder of one of his colleagues, causing them to pause for a moment as they emerged, bearing Collette Verney away from the bright lights one final time. "Mr. Houdini?" he asked, pulling back the sheet to reveal her face. Her star had most definitely burned out.

It was strange to see the absence where only a few minutes

before life had blazed so brilliantly, and sadder still to think that the world would never get to know this stunning woman. It was everyone's loss, Wheatley thought. He turned away from her. He had seen enough bodies after life had abandoned them and did not wish to spend any great length of time looking at any more. He suspected Houdini was committing every aspect of her corpse to memory. The human body was his business; no one knew it better. Finally, her body was carried away.

They went inside.

They might just as easily have stepped into an abattoir as the actress's trailer.

There was a strange smell in the air.

He breathed it in, trying to place it, but couldn't quite put his finger on what it was. He half-expected Houdini to turn around and proclaim with surety that in fact it was this rare intoxicant from the Middle East or that incredibly uncommon herb that grows only in the shade of a certain mountain in rural Vermont or some such. He didn't offer any opinions. Perhaps he trusted the professionals to do their job? Or not, if his expression was anything to go by. His lips pursed. His nostrils flared. He picked over the evidence offering an occasional sigh, obviously less than convinced by the methodology of the murder investigation.

They made their way through the caravan, looking curiously at trinkets and necklaces, at makeup and mirrors and everything else imaginable that a young woman could accumulate. And as they did, Houdini stopped every now and again to point something out. "Do you see the powder in that makeup brush? Curious don't you think that it's a different shade to the powder in the case beside it. The one is coarser than the other. The coarse one in the case is for the harsh light of the camera. The one on the brush—suggesting it was the last she applied—is much finer. I'd hazard that she had taken the time to make herself look beautiful for a gentleman caller."

"Fascinating, Mr. Houdini," the detective observed, making a note in his jotter.

A strand of greenery hung from the dressing table. Upon seeing it, the escapologist took it between thumb and forefinger, then rubbed it before taking a tiny bite and suggesting, "Spinach, I think. Check her meals with the caterer." The detective nodded and made another note. He pointed out a damp patch on the carpet—just inside the open door—which had no doubt been caused by the rain. But Houdini had other ideas. "Had it been down to the storm, it would surely have dried out by now and left little more than a dark stain, so it in and of itself is a curious anomaly that does not fit with the scene. Check the victim's shoes, see if they are wet."

After that Houdini offered no more observations, despite the fact that he stopped from time to time to examine something else that piqued his insatiable curiosity.

"Well, my thanks for your help, gentlemen. Not the kind of welcome to America we like our visitors to experience. I hope the rest of your stay is less eventful, Mr. Wheatley."

"Amen to that," Houdini agreed.

He waited until the detective was well out of earshot before he gave Wheatley a conspiratorial look that, if Wheatley read it right, seemed to suggest things were about to get interesting.

"Well, the good detective isn't looking particularly closely at the evidence, is he? He's made his mind up that the murderer is hiding out inside the gang of freaks."

"Isn't that a reasonable supposition?" Wheatley asked.

"It's only a reasonable assumption if you're a half-wit. He barely exchanged a handful of words with Andrews—one of the last people who saw her alive. We know that for a fact. We saw the pair of them walking back toward the trailers together. Surely that's a line of investigation he ought to be following, don't you think?"

"You think he's the killer?" Wheatley was surprised by that.

"Not at all, my dear chap. Not at all. You'll recall he was there when we all gathered at the caravan as the murder was discovered. There was no sign of blood anywhere on him and the logical conclusion looking at the scene is that whoever did kill Collette Verney would have been covered in blood. There couldn't have been more than fifteen minutes between the time we met them and our hearing the scream, no time for him to clean up, and he was still wearing the same clothes as when we spoke. No. I can categorically say he cannot be our man. Impossible."

"So who then?"

"How should I know?"

"Ah, so you're as in the dark as the rest of us mere mortals then, Harry?"

"Not quite, my young friend. It's never quite as dark in my head. However, I wouldn't mind another look inside that caravan without the flatfoot keeping an eye on me, if you catch my drift?"

"How do you suggest we accomplish that, given that it's a murder scene?"

"I have my ways," the escapologist said with a smirk. "There isn't a lock that's been built that can keep me in or out, my friend. I hardly think a cheap rented trailer is going to pose much of a challenge, do you?"

"I know it won't, but don't you think its rather inviting trouble to break into a crime scene?"

"The good detective isn't interested in us. He's not even interested in any actual physical evidence we might unearth unless it points directly at one of the carnival freaks. He's made up his mind where the blame lies, he just wants to apportion it before the story is splashed all over the newspapers. It's all about maintaining the illusion of safety. If he can say New England's finest have got there man, everyone will sleep easy. No one wants the general public to panic, and murder, especially of a celebrity no matter how minor, has an unfortunate ability to put the cat amongst the pigeons. The difference between us is that we want to find the real killer, not just someone to blame."

"We?"

"Sorry?"

"You said 'we.' 'We' want to find the real killer?"

"Well, of course we do! You do say the damnedest things, Dennis. Why wouldn't we want to find the real killer? Do you intend to see an innocent man locked up? Surely not."

"I didn't say that."

"You might as well have! And I won't be able to make any inroads into the investigation without your help, Dennis."

Houdini said his name again. Wheatley had noticed the magician only seemed to use his first name when he wanted something. It was a curious habit, but made him readable, like a poor poker player holding his cards too close to his chest. "So yes, 'we.' You and me, my fine foreign friend. We might not find out who did it, but I would be most disappointed if between us we lacked the wherewithal to stop an innocent man being fitted up by an incompetent officer of the law."

Wheatley nodded. It wasn't unreasonable. And despite his reticence, he couldn't help but think it might actually prove to be *fun*. Houdini was renowned for exposing fakes and frauds in the spiritualist world; was it such a stretch to imagine him applying the same inscrutable logic and eye for detail into the world of crime?

"There is something most peculiar going on here, believe me, something most peculiar. No single project can be so beset by troubles. I don't know the root cause, but I will get to the bottom of things. And who cares if I upset the local constabulary? Not I. This place has secrets, Wheatley." Back to his surname now he'd got what he wanted. Wheatley smiled. "And we're outsiders, so who better to dig around in them looking for the truth? Our minds are the keys that set us free. With them we are capable of great things. Now, we might well only succeed in scratching the patina off the surface, but if the meat is rotten, that's all we need to do." He made it sound noble, like they were truth seekers, the pair of them in a unique position to hold the guilty accountable and set the innocent free. "Besides," he offered with a grin. "I'm not sure I could stop myself from asking a few questions here and there. So, after we see to the trailer, how about we start by making friends with some of these people who've come out here for the film?" He patted his jacket pocket where the list of possible extras had been tucked away. "After all, that's why Monk brought us here, isn't it? Two birds and all that."

Wheatley couldn't argue with that.

No one stopped them as they returned to the actress's trailer.

Surprisingly, the crime scene was left unguarded and the door still hung wide open. Wheatley took a furtive look around but couldn't see any tell tale signs that they were being watched. When he turned back he saw that Houdini was on his knees examining the three short steps that led up to the door. His face was only inches from the wood; he appeared to be sniffing it like a dog. He made his way up one step at a time, sniffing, until he reached the damp carpet, which he touched yet again with his fingers, then held their tips up to his nose.

"What do you make of this?"

He pushed himself up to his feet and stepped inside to allow Wheatley to take his place on the steps. He pointed down at the damp patch just inside the door. "Well?"

Wheatley had accepted the presumption that it was rainwater without question. The storm had been hellish and there were puddles everywhere. It was logical that either the actress or her killer had been soaked and traipsed it in. But as he crouched down and smelt the stain, he wasn't so sure. Rainwater, after all, would carry no smell. At best he should have been hit by the faintest earthy tang from the carpet, given that people regularly scuffed their feet on it as they came and went, but there was more than that.

"It smells brackish."

"It does indeed."

"Rainwater doesn't smell like that."

"Again, correct. Your conclusion?"

"Pond water. Not sea water."

He started getting up and looked to Houdini for approval. The man slapped him on the back. "You're already a better detective than our friendly policeman." He walked across to the strand of spinach caught on the dresser. "Now this," he said, offering it to Wheatley. Wheatley took it from him and held it up to the light coming through the doorway. It didn't feel like spinach. It was cold and slimy to the touch. He lifted it to his nose. It carried the same slightly stagnant smell as the water in the carpet.

"Pondweed?"

"Of some variety, almost certainly."

"But that makes no sense," Wheatley said, shaking his head. "How the devil would pondweed get in here?"

"And there, I think, lies the answer to the riddle of who killed our young starlet. How indeed?"

Wheatley thought about it. "Is it possible she'd been swimming?"

"In the fifteen minutes since we made our introductions and she left this world? Unlikely, I think."

"Hmm… Is there a lake nearby, then?"

"There is indeed. In point of fact, we will be filming there in a couple of days. That's why we've got the tank for the underwater shots."

"Well that explains it then, surely? An early morning dip."

"I'm not sure it does," Houdini said, unconvinced. "But we have no other hypotheses at the moment."

"Hello, there!" came a voice from outside. Wheatley put the pondweed back where it had snagged as Houdini stuck his head back out through the doorway.

"Oh, hello again, detective," Houdini said, smoothly, like poking around the crime scene was the most natural thing in the world for him to be doing.

"I'm afraid you can't be in there, Mr. Houdini. I need to lock this up now before I head back to the station."

"Ah, of course. Sorry. We weren't thinking. I just wanted to have a quick look, see if anything else leaped out at me."

"Quite all right, but just this once, and only because it's you," the detective said, producing a key to lock the door. "Best we just keep it between us, though, eh? I'll be back later if you need another look," he said, and turned his back on them before walking slowly away along the avenue of caravans toward the garishly painted Mr. Darke's wagon and the way back out of the set into the real world.

Wheatley remained by the caravan, not entirely sure what they should do next. He rather hoped Houdini would make the first move, as the man seemed to have a plan.

"Well, that was a shame," the escapologist said quietly once the policeman was out of earshot. "I wouldn't have minded a little longer in there. Ah well."

He was rather surprised the great man hadn't suggested picking the lock and sneaking back inside. It seemed like something he would do.

"So what now?" Wheatley asked.

"Well, quite frankly, I think it's about time we started to listen to the dead, don't you?"

"A séance?"

"Hah! I didn't suggest we talk to her, only listen. People do so love to gossip. It's human nature. The carnival folk will almost certainly have closed ranks, so talking to them will be like trying to wring blood from a stone. But the locals who are hoping to ingratiate their way into the film? Make a few promises, grease a few palms. If anyone has heard any rumors, I'm sure we can encourage them just enough to share. After all, who wouldn't want to impress the Great Houdini?" Again with the self-deprecating smirk. This was a man who knew the way the world turned.

"Perhaps we should start with that woman... Whateley, wasn't it?"

"Oh yes, Mrs. Whateley. She's something of a character around here."

"So, I'm not really sure how to put this, but...well...why is she here?"

"You mean what makes her think she's a freak?"

"Rather indelicately put, but yes."

"It's not her, it's what she has in that glass jar she carries around with her all the time."

"Okay, you've got me. What's in the jar?"

"I think it's probably better if you take a look for yourself and make your own mind up. I wouldn't want to color your first impressions of the good lady. And, as luck would have it, she's on our list, so I'd say that makes her a good place to start."

The woman sat by herself. They saw her as they reached the freak's encampment on the far side of Darke's caravan.

Most of the others had either made their way back into town, assuming the filming was done for the day, or were huddled together around their caravans talking amongst themselves. It was only as they grew closer, though, that Wheatley realized her hair was not the only thing about her that was white. Her skin was almost completely devoid of any pigment and her eyebrows and lashes the same. The woman was an albino. Now he understood why she would assume Monk would want her. Albinism was by no means a common affliction. Peering from beneath her heavy eyelids were a pair of the most disconcertingly pale pink eyes he had ever seen. The woman refused to look directly at them. Shame?

"Hello, Mrs. Whateley," Houdini said as they approached her, his smile broad and genuine. He didn't offer a hand in greeting. Wheatley studied her, realizing there was no way she would have relaxed her grip on the jar to take his hand. "Do you know who I am?"

"I've seen you around some. You're tight with the man in charge," she said, like that was all there was to Harry Houdini. Perhaps she genuinely didn't recognize the most famous man in the known world? Was it possible she could have lived this long without at least hearing his name? *Well, in this place it feels like anything is possible*, Wheatley thought.

Houdini smiled, clearly hoping to relax her, but it didn't make any difference. She refused to make eye contact with either of them.

"As you say, Monk and I, very tight. In fact, he's asked me to speak to everyone who wants to be in the film."

"Well, I don't want to be in the film, so you needn't trouble yourself on my account."

"If you don't mind me asking, why *are* you here then?" Wheatley asked.

"My daughter," she said, getting quickly to her feet. She moved awkwardly because she absolutely refused to so much as shift her hold on the glass bell jar. She stood and started to walk away, her stride threatening to break into a run at any second. The speed and suddenness with which she set off, the look of terror in her face as she glanced back at them, jar clutched to her breast, and the complete disinterest shown by the freaks gathered around their caravans made Wheatley want to go after her.

Houdini took hold of his arm. "Let her go," he said. "She will be back."

"Okay…but what *does* she have in the jar?"

"I'm not sure if I believe it myself, to be honest, so I think it's only right and proper you have the chance to see and decide for yourself."

"Well, let's hope the curiosity doesn't kill me first then, eh?"

"I'm rather counting on you staying alive. One dead body at a time is more than enough."

Chapter Four

Dennis Wheatley had been staring at the ceiling for hours. He had woken from a strange dream feeling cold and clammy.

In a strange bed in an even stranger town, he couldn't get back to sleep no matter how hard he tried to just surrender. He tossed, he turned, he lay on his side and on his back, he stared at the ceiling, he stared at the skeletal shadows cast on the wall by the denuded tree in the yard outside. He listened to the wind as it whistled through the eaves and rattled the panes in their frames. He rolled over again. He couldn't unwind. He couldn't shake that dream and that vague nagging sensation that something had woken him from outside the dream. Some other noise. Not the wind. Not the windows. Something else. It had sounded like...*mandibles clacking?*

He tried to work his way through it, to find it in his memory.

Back to the beginning when they'd parted after dinner: a thick fog had descended on the town, making it almost impossible to maintain his bearings. There were turns that seemed to lead nowhere, there were buildings that all began to look the same. Unfamiliar streets filled with unusual people. He wasn't sure he would want to stay here if it wasn't for the case.

And that thought concerned him; it wasn't his case. He wasn't the law. And yet someone had to speak for the dead girl, didn't they? Because that detective surely wasn't.

There was nothing there that might have fueled his nightmare—and nothing that might have dragged him from it.

So then, thinking it through, back to his room.

He had lain there on his too-hard mattress and had drifted into a restless sleep laden with dreams of the albino woman and the jar she clutched to her chest, and the dead girl in the trailer who wasn't fated to be a star after all...

And now there were strange noises in the house, the creaks and settlement of an old, unfamiliar building. For a moment, groggy, he wondered if he wasn't hearing the shuffle of someone moving about. He drifted around the edges of sleep but couldn't seem to give himself to it for more than a few minutes after that, so rather than lie there growing frustrated, he decided it would be more productive to try to rationalize his thoughts and put them down in the notebook he always carried with him. Point by point. Methodically. Think it through, map it out like a plot line. From some angle it had to make sense. It just depended whose point of view he was seeing the story from—and that was what it was, in a way. Every murder was a narrative. It had means, it had motive, it had to have opportunity or else it fell apart. He had ambitions to become a writer one day, and as part of that, looking to develop the discipline it needed to study people, to understand how they worked, what drove their emotions and the difference in physicality of each person he met. He kept meticulous notes about such things, trying to find different words to describe the people he encountered, how different people phrased things, snatches of overheard conversation, unusual sights he glimpsed on his travels, the names of places and people that might one day provide inspiration. In other words, anything and everything. It was the way his mind worked. He liked to look at life written down. It made sense on paper.

So he started at the beginning, making a list of the people he could remember who were actively working on the film: the director, obviously, the actors, minus one, and the technicians and the rest of the crew.

But why would any of them want her dead?

That was what he couldn't see. He liked order in his chaos. He liked there to be method lurking in madness. There were no women on the list who could benefit from her death, no jealous B-list actresses looking to rise. Collette Verney had only just joined the cast, a late addition after the original leading lady had failed to arrive on set, according to Houdini. Could that be it? Someone else who had been hoping to get the call? *No one on this list*, he thought, scanning through the names again. Apart from the wardrobe woman who doubled as light technician and half a dozen other odd jobs, the list was bare—and even in her wildest dreams she couldn't have imagined herself as leading lady material. She was the wrong side of fifty and had sacrificed her figure for—he hoped—a happy life. So scratch professional jealousy, unless it originated outside of this group of disparate characters.

The next name that stood out was Taylor Andrews. Her leading man was the one person who seemed to have at least a clear opportunity to kill her, even if there was no obvious motive. He had been one of the last people to see her alive. So to the question of motive—why would he want to kill her? Wheatley pondered the variables, running imaginary stories through his head. Fame must be a weird beast, he reasoned. So many people thinking they owned you or knew you or wanted something from you. So many people who would give anything to be you. So many people who would do anything to be with you and have some of the glamour rub off. Was that it? Had Andrews become so enamored with the heartthrob lifestyle he was just used to starlets bending over for him? He didn't know the man well enough to judge if he expected all of the legendary Hollywood excesses to be his by divine right, but it was easy to imagine fame changing a man—even a good man. Had Collette mocked his advances? How would a man like Andrews take that? Would he answer with his fists and take what he wanted? It was not impossible but—no matter how insufferable the star appeared from first impressions—it seemed unlikely. Just because the man acted as if he was the most important person in the room didn't make him a killer. *Only a pompous arse. Or ass,* he corrected himself with a wry smirk.

And, logically, if she had been killed because of some kind of sexual motivation then there were any number of men in the crew who could be put in the frame—she was an attractive woman, vulnerable in this world of men—but as far as he could see they'd all seemed to be so busy trying to keep the production of the film in motion.

That left the freaks and carnival folk who had borne the brunt of the police's attention thus far. They really were the obvious suspects, but again that didn't make them guilty, did it? Innocent until proven and all that. He couldn't remember all of their names so instead started to make a list of them by physical descriptions. It was a motley crew indeed: the bearded lady, the Siamese twins, the animal boy, the obese woman, the midget... The list went on until he had filled a full page when he eventually added the name of the albino woman, Mrs. Whateley. She was certainly a strange bird, but that hardly meant she was capable of murder. *Unless*, he thought, *the actress tried to take the jar from her?* She was more than just protective of that jar. Was that it then, something to do with the contents of her jar?

No matter how much he stared at the list there were no obvious suspects in there—or they were *all* obvious suspects. Of course there were other people working on the set he'd not so much as seen never mind been introduced to, and even then there was always the possibility that it was none of them. It wasn't as though it was a closed set surrounded by guards to keep people out; anyone could have walked up from the town onto the set unnoticed.

He started another page, titled it "curiosities," and made a note about the damp patch on the carpet and the strand of green weed. What did they mean, if anything? He had absolutely no idea. And it was driving him mad. Houdini clearly saw some sort of connection between all of these disparate clues, but he wasn't sharing.

So that left Wheatley back at square one.

He had a list, not that he could do anything with it.

He was desperately tired but there was no way he could fall asleep now. The sun would be up soon, even if the fog diffused its light. Even so, his head lolled, and he caught himself drifting as sleep stole up on him.

He was still staring at the list as the flame of the gas lamp flickered; it wasn't just a slight breeze, a gust almost put it out. The sudden guttural hiss and the momentary near dark startled him out of his contemplation. The lamp roared back into glorious flame. The suddenness of it sent his heart racing. The sound of his blood pounding in his ears masked another sound, but as the *thump, thump, thump*, slowly subsided, he caught it; not the clacking mandibles of his dream. Voices.

He scrambled out of his seat, trying to locate the source of the sound. He couldn't be sure what they were saying—the tone rose and fell in a steady rhythm. Like music. Chanting? Singing? He strained to hear it better, moving toward the window thinking it must be coming from the street. He couldn't make out a single word. But there was no doubt that these were human sounds, not the *clack-ack-i* of mandibles scissoring away. The street was empty. He moved toward the wall, wincing at the slight creak of one of the floorboards beneath his feet, and pushed his ear up against the flower-patterned wallpaper. The wall felt cold and damp against his cheek.

Almost as though they sensed him listening, the room on the other side fell silent. Perhaps he'd been mistaken? Could it be rats in the walls or just water banging in the pipes? Some early riser running off a sink of cold water to shock themselves awake? Or had the noise been coming from somewhere else and he'd confused himself?

Wheatley held his breath, sure that there was someone on the other side of the wall, inches from his head, listening to him.

He counted to forty silently, then the air gasped from his mouth.

The voices began again.

He listened but couldn't *hear*.

There was a pattern to it.

He pressed his ear harder against the wall, as though by doing so he could amplify the sounds. All it did was increase the sound of his own pulse.

After a full minute of listening he went back to the desk, and his list, but he couldn't concentrate on it, so he lay down again, and without realizing what was happening allowed the sound to lull him into some kind of fitful sleep.

He jerked awake when he heard a door close.

He had no idea how long he'd been asleep. A minute, an hour?

He stumbled out of bed, looking around. He saw a slice of light beneath the bedroom door leading out into the hallway, and padded toward it, determined to discover who had been in the room next to his. He wasn't a fan of his own fecund imagination at times, so it was always better to put a face on the nightmare—name the creature, kill the monster, and all that. He slipped his jacket on over his pajamas and, leaning ever so carefully on the doorknob, opened his door just a fraction. There was a light on in the narrow hallway, but where he expected to see his neighbor there was no one, and nor were there any sounds of footsteps on the staircase.

He was about to close his door and return to the list when he realized something that had been nagging at the back of his mind; he looked along the hallway to confirm what he already knew. His was the last door on that side of the passage. There was no room beyond his.

He returned to his bed, head spinning, and lay there, trying to make sense of it all.

The only conclusion he could come to was that the voices must have been part of his dream, some lingering part of his sleepy mind playing tricks on him as he fell into some sort of partial waking sleep hunched over that damned list of names.

The sounds had all gone now and he was fully awake. Was that a coincidence? It couldn't be, could it? He listened, but the house was silent. Eventually his mind stopped long enough to allow him to drift back to sleep and when he woke the sun had risen. Instead of bright shafts of sunlight his room was filled with a dull grey light. Even though the curtains were still drawn he knew that the fog had not lifted during the night.

They were in for another dour, damp day.

People were already starting to move through the house, though no sounds were coming from beyond the wall at his head. He could smell breakfast, rashers of bacon, eggs, caramelizing onions, burning toast, and realized he was starving. He rolled over onto one elbow and froze, hearing a strange scratching and scraping and for one disorientating moment thought it really was down to rats in the wall, and then saw that a piece of paper had been pushed under his door; the sound had been the paper scraping along the carpet as it was pushed through.

He got out of bed quickly and opened the door, ignoring the paper on the floor, hoping to catch sight of the bearer. A shadow scuttled away, followed by the heavy clatter of footsteps on the stairs. He ran to the landing, but they were gone. Wheatley returned to his room and picked up the piece of paper. He unfolded it and read the blunt message that had been scrawled out on it. It took him a moment to digest the meaning of what was written on it, despite its childish simplicity.

He held the paper up to the window but the meager light did little to illuminate it.

He studied the words.

They were written using a pencil with a childlike hand. The writer was no scribe, but they had a certain way with words: "*Keep your nose out or you'll be next.*"

He dashed to the window and looked out. Down below he heard the front door slam, then saw someone running down the street. The fog made it impossible to see clearly—it was a real peasouper already—but it was a clearly a man. A man, he had the distinct impression, whose limbs were a little too large for his body. He moved quickly, but awkwardly, in long strides. It was as ungainly a gait as Wheatley had ever seen. No step seemed to take the man in quite the direction he seemed to be heading. It was as if he were zigzagging a path through the fog.

The man paused once and looked back up toward Wheatley where he stood at his window, his wide brimmed hat covering most of his face, then he scuttled into the cold grey mist and was swallowed whole.

Chapter Five

Houdini pulled his car to a halt across the street from Ma Mocata's Boarding House and peered through the fog to see if there was any sign of Dennis Wheatley. The fog was already so thick he'd essentially driven blind from Monk's place. Mercifully, Dunwich wasn't exactly a thriving metropolis, so he hadn't had to worry about people stumbling into his path.

The streets of Southside were eerily quiet even though the working day had already begun for most of the town's residents. He was pretty sure which window corresponded to Wheatley's room, but there was no sign of light coming from inside. He couldn't imagine that young Dennis would have ventured too far—he wasn't exactly the exploring type—so he decided to sit tight and wait for the wanderer's return.

Through the shroud of fog he saw the faint glow of a cigarette. It flared red for a moment before fading again. Houdini flashed his headlights in case it was Wheatley, hoping that it would attract his attention, but there was no movement. Reluctantly, Houdini got out of the car and stepped into the fog. Three steps away from the car and it enveloped him like a damp blanket.

He tried not to shiver, but it was hard not to.

"Wheatley? That you, old chap?" he called toward the man with the cigarette, and almost laughed at just how awful his "English" was. *Old chap*? He shook his head, half-mocking himself.

There was no reply.

The air felt utterly dead. Sound couldn't travel more than a few feet in any direction without losing all shape and becoming meaningless to the mind. He crossed the road and walked toward the man. He used the light of his cigarette to guide him.

"Mr. Weiss?" the man said a second before Houdini stepped out of the fog before him. It was rare to hear his real name spoken these days, especially in a town where so few people actually *knew* him. He was Harry Houdini. That was what people called him. Hearing his real name from a stranger lurking in the street intrigued him. "I've been hoping that I would bump into you." The inference was: *on a deserted street.*

The man flicked his still glowing cigarette butt to the ground. He didn't grind it out beneath the sole of his shoe, though; he let it burn. Instead, he moved with ruthless efficacy, his hands closing around the escapologist's lapels and spinning him around, slamming him bodily into the side of a building, and pressing his face up against cold, damp brickwork with one hand while the other pushed up against his back. It was a street fighter's move. A good old brawler's play. Houdini grinned, ready to have some fun. He could quite easily dislocate his shoulder without any real pain, and slip out of the hold, turning the tables on his assailant, but he thought it would be polite to ask who he was about to beat to a pulp, and what it was that the man wanted. If it was money, he could pay his way out of the fight. If the man wanted to humble the Great Houdini, that was a different matter.

"What do you want?"

"Just a quiet word."

"And you think it's necessary to slam me into a wall and almost break my arm in the process? I'd hate to see what you do when you want to get serious with a fellow."

He felt the man's grin as he said, "Sorry about that." The grip on the back of his head relaxed. "It's fairly rare someone actually wants to talk to me. I'm used to having to encourage them."

"I'm not sure I'd count shoving their face into a brick wall encouragement."

"Well, it incentivizes things."

The man released his hold on Houdini so he could turn slowly to face his assailant. Houdini rolled his shoulders, stretching the muscles of his arm, his back still close to the wall. The man had the look of someone accustomed to scrapes; both giving and receiving them. He had a boxer's nose, in that it had been broken more than once, and a hero's square jaw, which, Houdini thought, looking at it, just begged to take a swift right hook.

"The name's Diamond," he said, lifting the brim of his wide-brimmed fedora a fraction. "Joe Diamond, PI."

"Well, I'd like to say that it's a pleasure to meet you *Mister* Diamond." He emphasized the *Mister*, making it clear that he viewed his status as below that of a real police detective. "But I'm not a masochist. Getting my face plowed into a brick wall gives me no pleasure at all, so let's just say you've not exactly made a great first impression, unless you count the pebble dash on my cheek."

"Okay, how about we shoot for second impressions?"

"I'd rather not be shot, if it's all the same with you, Mr. Diamond."

"Touché. I promise not to shoot, or smash your face into the wall again, in return we get to start again and I get to ask a few burning questions?"

"There will be no burning, I trust?"

"None whatsoever."

"Excellent. Then ask your questions. If I know the answer, I'll tell you, if not, you're just going to have to strong arm someone else."

"You've been hanging around the film set lately, haven't you." It was more of a statement than a question, and fully aware of this, the PI didn't wait for his answer. "My client is concerned his wife might be having an affair."

"Ah, and that's the crux of it. You think that I'm the adulterer?"

"Well, what is it they say about fame being a powerful aphrodisiac? What with you being the self-professed most famous man in America, I would have that that made you—"

"A walking aphrodisiac?"

"I might not have phrased it quite like that, but, well, to be blunt, yes."

"And who do you think I'm having an affair with?"

"I didn't say..."

"Of course you didn't. But I'm asking you, man to man. I'm not asking you to make accusations, I'd just like to get to the bottom of it sooner rather than later given the amount of dark alleys there are in this town. So let me put it another way: Who is your client?"

"I'm sorry, client confidentiality, you understand? It's important my clients can trust me with their secrets."

"And I would have thought that if it's important enough to have you out in this weather, waiting for me, you don't actually need to betray that trust, just nod when I say her name. After all, there are not a lot of possibilities, are there? You've said it's relating to Monk's motion picture, so logic dictates you are working for the husband of the unfortunate Miss Collette Verney. That no one knew Miss Verney was in point of fact Mrs. Verney is interesting, but in no way a crime. However, I could see why her husband might feel jealous if he was being hidden away from the world while she chased fame."

"I didn't say that."

"You didn't have to. There are no other women working on the film whose husbands fit the bill: well-off enough to be able to pay for the services of a private dick, attractive enough to be a temptress. It's only natural your boy was looking to protect his interests."

"I didn't ask why he wanted to hand over the greenbacks, I just folded 'em over, slipped 'em into my billfold and set about doing the job I was asked to do. He wanted to know if she was having an affair. If she was, he wanted hard evidence to prove it."

"And now she's dead."

"That she is," Diamond agreed. He wasn't a man of many words if a few would do. And he obviously had no problem billing Verney's grieving husband until he got word he was off the clock. Death was no obstacle. "He paid up front. I want to give him closure."

"Prove she was faithful?"

"Or that she wasn't. Either way, he gets an answer. I think that's all he wants."

Houdini considered it. In the cuckold's place, would he want to know? Of course he would, but not for any healthy reason. "Well, in answer to your question, I was *not* having an affair with the delightful Miss Verney. I won't deny she was a pretty girl—pretty enough to tempt a man, for sure—but there's only one woman for me. Only my Bess holds the key to this heart."

Diamond nodded.

"But?" Houdini offered for him.

The PI shook his head. "No buts."

"Then, pray tell, why the whole production? The dark alleyway, the strong arm tactics? Why not just ask me?"

"Because I had to be sure. I'm sure you understand, Mr. Houdini." He noticed the PI was no longer calling him Weiss. He'd obviously passed the test and established some sort of trust bond. "I had to hear it from your own lips."

"And you're happy to accept my word for it?"

"Absolutely. Besides, I'd know if you were lying. It's my thing. So many years in the business surrounded by liars and thieves, you get to know the smell of truth."

There was no question that he believed that he could; some people had talents that were hard to explain, Houdini included. Being able to read someone well enough to spot a lie didn't seem out of the question. Indeed, it seemed like a pretty useful talent for a private detective.

The possibility that the young actress could have been partaking in a little extra marital loving put an entirely different spin on the circumstances around her death; the spurned lover, the jealous husband, the lovers' wife, they all immediately became suspects, even if they lacked names or faces. What they did have was motive.

"So, if I might be so bold, who else is on your most wanted list?"

"Just the two names, now you're discounted, Mr. H. Both working on the film."

"And let me guess, they're the kind of people who were in

a position to help her with her career?" It didn't take a lot of imagination to figure out who the two men were. Unfortunately for Diamond, he could dismiss them both at a stroke, not that he was about to do the PI's job for him; at least not without something in exchange.

"That's about the sum of it, yeah. Good old-fashioned motives: sex, revenge, money, broken promises. My kind of motives. Human ones, you know? Stuff that makes sense."

"So, if I may ask, how come you haven't been able to eliminate these two yet?"

"It's all the damn freaks; since they rolled into town in that carnival sideshow of theirs you can't move on that film set without them watching you. They give me the creeps. It's like they have eyes everywhere. Hell, I wouldn't be surprised if some of them *have*, if you get my drift? They are everywhere, Mr. H., and, you ask me, most of 'em ain't here for the damn flick, either."

"Really? So why *are* they here?" Houdini asked, rising to the bait.

Diamond was about to tell him when a dark shape filled the diffuse light of the alleyway's entrance, taking with it the little light there was with its long shadow.

"Everything all right in here?" the newcomer asked.

Chapter Six

So what the devil was all that about?" Dennis Wheatley asked the escapologist as the car pulled away from the curb, leaving the third man alone on the street corner as he lit another cigarette. The headlights of the car barely pierced the fog. Houdini didn't push the car beyond ten miles per hour, happy to crawl along. It would have been almost as quick to walk.

"The guy's name is Jim Diamond, or Jack or Joe, something like that. He's a private dick—detective," he amended, seeing Wheatley's confusion. "Seems young Collette was actually married. Diamond was hired by a jealous husband to see if she was playing away."

"He thinks she was having an affair?"

"But she wasn't," Houdini said with surprising authority. Wheatley cocked a curious eyebrow his way. "I spent enough time in her company to know. Everyone's got tells. You just need to learn how to read them. It's how spiritualists draw their marks in. They're gulls. Gullible. They tell the mark what they want to hear, and they know what they want to hear because they read their tells."

"Fascinating. How does it work?" Wheatley asked, curious.

"Well, for instance with Collette, I spotted the mark where her wedding band should have been—it was a faint discoloration around the finger, but the indentation had faded, meaning it had been off for a while. She clearly didn't want anyone to know about her marriage, but that wasn't because she was being unfaithful. One might surmise she was unhappy in her relationship, but that didn't mean that she was finding comfort in the arms of another man."

"How on earth can you be so sure, Harry? If she was having an affair, that would change everything."

"Well, for a start, I was his prime suspect." He offered a little shrug as though to say "*Who could possibly believe that?*" "And then there's the field of opportunity—if she was indeed having an affair it had to be with someone involved with the film."

"Why not a local?"

"She was career-driven. She was calculating enough to hide the ring, as it would almost certainly have reduced her broad-base appeal to the amorous young men of the Heartland. In other words, she wanted to be a star. She wouldn't throw everything away for someone who couldn't help her career."

"That's callous."

"Indeed it is. Calculating, even."

"And you're sure?"

"I know people," he said. Which, Wheatley realized, could easily have been parsed as *I know how to manipulate people*. That wouldn't have been entirely wrong, either. He did know how to manipulate people—or at least their expectations. He was a master of misdirection.

"That leaves Andrews and Monk, then, surely? The only two men who could help advance her career."

Houdini laughed this time, but gave no indication as to what he found quite so amusing. To Wheatley they were the obvious choices for the dead woman's paramour, assuming such a beast existed at all.

And he didn't think an awful lot of the actor, truth be told, so he found it easy to believe Taylor Andrews *could* be a nasty piece of work. He had something about him Wheatley just didn't like. But would he take advantage of a young woman with stars in her eyes? Wheatley grunted. The question didn't even warrant thinking about; of course he would. He'd encountered men like that before. He had served with some in the war. He didn't enjoy their company. Backs to the wall, they weren't the kind of people you wanted on your side. But did that mean the actor was capable of killing the young woman?

Wheatley found his mind wandering back to the trenches, the things he'd seen there, the things he'd done and suffered and somehow survived; remembering the whistle of shell-fire and the crack of rifles; the mud sucking at his feet as he slopped and slithered and tried to run; the smell of mud and cordite and the choking sting of the first trace of gas and the yellow fog that obscured the battlefield…

You could take the man out of the war, but you could never ever take the toil of the war out of the man.

The fog seemed to be enveloping the car again. He could have been right back there, in Hell.

He had no idea how long he had sat in silence, but Houdini hadn't interrupted his thoughts or intruded on his private fears.

It was only when the car lurched to a sudden halt and the constant chug of the engine died that he returned to the real world. They were outside the set. The lights were dim, and the entire place was utterly and eerily silent. It wasn't right. Wheatley didn't like it. Not one bit.

He clambered out of the cab and closed the door quietly behind him. It didn't feel right.

There was no sign of activity anywhere.

They walked side-by-side toward the empty set.

It was as though they had stepped into a genuine, honest-to-God, ghost town.

"I don't like this," Wheatley whispered. He could barely see Houdini even though he knew the man was right there beside him.

"I can't say that I'm all that partial to it, either. Come on, let's—"

A shocking *crash* came from the direction of one of the workshops.

They started to run, blind. But in a matter of seconds they heard more crashes and bangs coming from the workshop and realized it wasn't trouble breaking out—far from it, it was the first hint of life going on as usual. The fog was too thick for the crew to work outside, so they were improvising, building a controlled indoor set for the upcoming shots. He realized that he knew next to nothing about the film that was in production, or about the film business itself, for that matter. It was very much outside of his wheelhouse.

They walked in on Ulysses Monk; the young director was hunched over a typewriter in the partitioned office that annexed the workshop. He was working away feverishly, hammering at the enamel keys only to tear the sheet free of the bar and add it to a growing stack beside him. A tower of steel film canisters were piled in the corner. They each had labels Wheatley couldn't read, but assumed they were cuts from the work-in-progress. Almost every inch of the floor was covered with more pages of typescript. Most of them had been utterly defaced with red pencil: entire passages cross-hatched out, frantic inspirations scrawled into the margins to replace words only for some of those to have been struck through, too.

"Harry! Good to see you!" he said, seemingly oblivious to Wheatley beside him. He was getting used to being invisible in the great man's presence.

"Uly, have you been here all night?" Houdini asked.

"What?" The director rubbed his eyes, answering with body language long before he confirmed it with words. "Yes, yes, of course I have. Where else would I be? No time to lose, Harry. Not now. Too much at stake." Each line was staccato, like Tommy gun fire rattling from his mouth. "I'll be damned if I'm going to be beaten. Not now." He tapped his temple. "I've got it. I know how to save this cursed film!" There was an edge of madness to his triumphant declaration. Wheatley studied the man. He seemed quite different from the cultured filmmaker he had met only the day before. His eyes glittered like pennies at the bottom of a wishing well. There was something utterly disconcerting about the manic change in his behavior.

"But you're not filming today?"

He shook his head, feeding a fresh page into the typewriter's carriage and moving it on two lines. He rubbed at his chin, and then seemed to pause, as though he couldn't quite recall what he was doing—or thinking. "A couple of policemen managed to make it through from Innsmouth to take full statements from the cast and crew. Bit of a nuisance, obviously, but it seems that the detective we had blundering about the set all afternoon was a bit of a no-hoper. These two at least seem to know what they are doing, which is a big step in the right direction. Obviously they'll want to speak to you two at some point."

Houdini nodded. "Anything I can do to help." It had been a statement as opposed to a question, but Monk took it as one.

"Actually, yes, the list. The list I gave you yesterday. Have you got it with you?"

Houdini reached into his pocket for the page and offered it to Monk without even looking at it. The filmmaker unfolded it and spread it out on the desk in front of him. He took the red pencil from behind his ear and began to cross some of the names off the list, striking through each one with a single harsh slash and mumbling to himself as he did so.

"These," he said, handing the truncated list back to Houdini. "Concentrate on these first. They are the ones most likely to fit in with the new script if I am going to be able to resurrect the film. I can't afford to start again with another leading lady, so it's either work with what we've got in the can, improvise around it, and find a way to make the storyline hang together without her being around for new scenes, or throw away everything we've got in the can, and frankly I'd rather face down the barrel of a Colt, thank you very much."

Was it really possible to do that? To rework a film that was already partially complete so that the leading lady could simply disappear and yet still give it a solid resolution? He couldn't see how—a body double perhaps? Like writing a novel, it wasn't necessary to film each part of the movie in sequence, but to build a new movie out of parts of another? That beggared belief.

"Why these? What's special about them?" Houdini asked, looking down the list again.

"They fit. It is all falling into place. It came to me in a dream, or maybe it was a nightmare. I heard the voices and they showed me how I could save this. I can't begin to tell you how empowered I feel, my friend! It's so close to genius. So close to perfection. I was blind, but now I understand what these freaks *really* are, but it's imperative they're real, no fakes, there can't be any fakes. These freaks are *special*. They are not less than human, they are *more* than human. They are as much children of gods as Hercules was. I didn't understand, not at first. I had no idea. But now I do. Don't you see?"

He didn't. What he saw was that the man was growing more agitated as he talked, and Wheatley found himself fearing for the filmmaker's sanity. For some types of people it didn't take a lot to push them over the edge; he had seen it firsthand with the sights and sounds of war. Strong men, warriors, could fight day after day, only to break at the sight of a severed limb lying disconnected in the mud of a battlefield or something as seemingly innocent as a child's doll lying on the side of the road. It was all about what the mind does when it sees these things.

"Is he all right?" Wheatley said softly, hoping that Houdini would hear but his words wouldn't penetrate the madness that seemed to be brewing around Monk.

"Out, come on," Houdini urged, ushering him out of the room. He closed the door behind them, then blew out a heavy sigh.

"Lack of sleep, possibly alcohol, coffee, and cigarettes—they make a potent cocktail in the body. Add stress and fear to the mix and it is no surprise that it's having a marked effect on him. He needs food and sleep, but will he even listen given the obviously manic stage of creation his mind is in? I wouldn't. I know myself well enough to admit that. When I'm working on a trick and inspiration strikes, I can go three or four nights without sleep until I am sure that every kink has been worked out, and even then my mind won't let me rest until it is close to perfect. That's the white heat. He has to work. He has to get everything planned out. Stop him now and all that stuff he's got inside his head, all of the lines that connect to give him the big picture and show him how to save his precious film, they go, they come undone. And there's no guarantee they'll come back, ever. He could dry up. That would leave him in a worse position than he is now. All we can do is let him have some peace and trust in the creative process."

"Are you sure?" It didn't sound healthy to Wheatley, but who was he to question the Great Houdini?

Houdini nodded.

"Let's go do something useful, rather than sitting here twiddling our thumbs. Uly needs his freaks. If he's convinced himself there's something special about them, then who are we to argue?" He unfolded the page and read through the names and addresses that had not been crossed out by the filmmaker. "Hmm, well, well, would you look at that?" He held out the sheet for Wheatley to see. The first name left on the list was the jar woman, Whateley. She had given her address as Ma Mocata's Boarding House.

Chapter Seven

Chief Constable Martin and Constable Ropes had spent the entire morning taking statements and cursing at the sheer damned incompetence of the officer who had taken them initially. The man was an embarrassment to the force. Looking at his notes, he had quite literally done no more than take names. Most of the addresses he'd written down consisted of two words: Darke's Carnival. As far as the crime scene went, he'd given it little more than a cursory examination, and allowed all and sundry to trample all over it and gawk at the corpse like she was one of the freak show's damnable attractions. It just wasn't good enough.

He was also operating under the assumption that the killer was living among the strange people who had come to Dunwich to try to exploit their own deformities for financial gain. Again, it was not an unreasonable assumption, but to discount all else was to ignore the basic tenets of policing. Gather facts, work the leads, throw out the dead ends, arrive at the truth. You didn't start an investigation by ignoring sixty percent of the available suspects simply because they weren't deformed sideshow freaks. Martin had no great problem with the freaks; putting their deformity on celluloid was no different from sitting on the midway and letting gawkers look for a few coins. Their livelihood depended upon people being shocked and disgusted. But that didn't make them killers.

"So, Ropes, first impressions?" Martin asked as his constable came into the supply closet they'd converted into a temporary interview room and placed a lukewarm coffee in front of him. In Martin's experience it was hard to mess up a cup of coffee, but Ropes had a particular skill when it came to that. His defense was that he was more of a tea man. That in itself confounded the good detective. Who would willingly partake of a poisoned leaf when there were good Arabica beans on offer? Ropes had been gone a little longer than it should have taken to fill a couple of cups, but given the oppressive atmosphere of the set, he had most likely stuck his head outside for a little fresh air before plunging back into the miasma that was their unfolding case among the freaks and sideshow geeks. "Bit of an odd bunch aren't they, these film people?"

"The whole setup is weird if you ask me, sir, but then, what do I know? It's not like this is my world. Maybe they're all like this over in California?"

"I'm sure they are, Ropes."

"There is one thing that bothers me, though."

"Tell me."

"The English guy, Wheatley."

"Just because he's a Brit doesn't naturally make him suspicious, Ropes. Well, I suppose it does: never trust a Brit."

"Two days ago a ship called *The Dunwich Ghost* was heading toward Kingsport when a passenger disappeared overboard."

"Okay, and this ties in to Wheatley how?"

"He was a passenger on the same ship, in fact he was listed as being in the next cabin. Now, I'm not saying it's linked, but let's be honest: it's a hell of a coincidence that someone dies on the ship he was traveling on and the first day he appears in town the star of the big city motion picture being filmed gets killed, wouldn't you say?"

"I would indeed." Martin pushed himself back in the rickety old schoolroom chair, tipping it onto its two rear legs. The wooden joints creaked alarmingly with the change in weight distribution. "Now you know how much I love a good coincidence, don't you, Ropes?"

"I do indeed, sir."

"I think we're going to need to keep a close eye on our Mr. Wheatley. Has the body of the missing passenger been found yet? If there's any hint of foul play, then this guy's going to be on his guard. He'll be expecting to be under the microscope. Let's not disappoint him."

"Nothing as of yet, but given the tidal charts we got from the harbor master, it could be days before it washes ashore—and even if it does, there's no telling where it'll turn up. The undercurrents here are pretty strong. It could end up as far away as Innsmouth. And every hour it's in the water it deteriorates. Who knows how much of it will be left by the time we find it."

"What a pleasant thought." The last time he'd seen a body that had been in the water for a few days almost half of its flesh had been eaten away by bottom-dwellers, leaving only rags of clothes hanging from bones and shreds of organs. It wasn't pretty. And, apart from anything else, it made his job impossible because there was nothing left to identify the body with. It wasn't like it was some army grunt with his dog tags still snagged between vertebrae.

Martin leaned forward, lowering the chair so that all four legs were on the ground again. "Anyway," he said at last, "Dennis Wheatley just earned himself a spot at number one on our most wanted list. I think it's time we had a little chat with him, don't you, Ropes?"

"Either he is following trouble, or trouble is following him."

"Or," Martin offered, "he's causing it himself."

"I like the way you think, sir."

"Find out what he's doing here. The real reason. Get in touch with Scotland Yard. I want to know everything there is to know about our Mr. Wheatley."

"Sir."

Chapter Eight

The man lay inside the wooden coffin, glad beyond words that the carpenter had the skill to craft a watertight box. It could have been a very watery demise if the coffin had sprung even a single small leak.

Once it had risen from beneath the churning waves after the plunge from the deck, it had bobbed back to the surface, buoyed by the special air bags he'd had designed and fitted, and begun to float on the churning waves, riding them as they rolled in to break on the shore. He had waited before unplugging the two wax-filled ventilation holes in the lid to ensure that he could still breath if he pressed his face up against the wooden surface.

He felt the immense press of water and the power of the ocean as the coffin pitched and rolled with it. He was helpless. A plaything of the elemental forces of nature, tide, and time. It didn't take long for him to lose track of how long he'd been trapped or how far it had carried him, but eventually he felt the boards at his back scrape against rocks and sand as the coffin finally ran aground.

Time returned with that scraping sound. He was aware of his heartbeat, of the thinness of the air that remained to him, and of the weakness in his muscles that came with having been pinned motionless for days.

He began counting in time with the beat of his heart against the cage of bones in his chest. He had thrown his hand in with the mistress of chance, and now all she had to do was deliver a savior to release him before the tide dragged him out to sea again and carried him away to where, surely, this time he must drown.

There was no point in crying out—the padding in the coffin that allowed for the ballast bags that kept it afloat would muffle any sort of call he made. His voice wouldn't carry above the crash of the waves, never mind reach all the way up to the road beyond the beach—assuming there was a road and he hadn't washed up in the middle of nowhere.

The salt of the sea mixed with the thin layer of earth that filled the bottom of the coffin created an unusual—and unpleasant—aroma. It filled the narrow space. He longed for the open air. Pressing his mouth up against the tiny holes was no substitute for real, deep gulps of breath. He wanted to look up and see the sky, the moon and stars the only things above him, not a heavy plank of wood nailed above his head.

At last he heard the crunch of footsteps on the shingle as people moved toward him. Pebbles shifted and rolled against the side of the coffin. The percussive effect was amplified inside the box; excitement mixed with fear inside him as the coffin was dragged away from the surf toward dry land.

He imagined them cracking open the lid and seeing him; his gaunt white face and sallow features scaring the life out of them, and smiled. It was deliciously perfect.

"Let me out!" he cried, beating his hands on the lid over and over until the coffin bearers lowered it back to the shore.

In moments his rescuers were attacking the lid feverishly, splintering the wood as they prized it open by brute force alone.

He was ready to show himself to this new world just as his ancestor had done on the shores of England.

Ancestor? Was it his ancestor? Was it another aspect of him? It was hard to recall. His mind had blurred the identities together inside his head so that he no longer knew where he ended and that other one began.

He felt his long front teeth pressing into his lower lip as he prepared himself.

They would be afraid of him; they would worship him.

Yes.

Yes. Yes. Yes.

And finally, at last, the lid was teased away from the coffin and grey light flooded in with fresh air.

He blinked hard even against this half-light, glad that the sun was not there to beat down on him. Overhead he heard the call of gulls and the crash of waves. It was idyllic.

Right up until the moment the near quiet was shattered by a single terrifying scream.

It was only when he ran out of breath that he realized the scream was his own.

Instead of being terrified at the sight of him, his own mind was in turmoil at the sight of the four faces looking down at him.

Hands with webbed fingers reached in to touch him.

He felt them, cold and clammy against his skin as he tried to shake them off.

Four fishlike heads with lidless eyes and mouths that were too small—slits lined by hundreds and hundreds of razor sharp barbed teeth behind thick, sea-slick lips—filled the space above him.

He gasped for breath as the gills on the sides of their necks vented open and closed, unable to comprehend the nature of his rescuers. The last fragments of sanity that he had clung so desperately to slipped away in a heartbeat as the creatures pulled him out of the coffin.

His last rational thought: *sometimes dead is better*.

Chapter Nine

Despite the list, Houdini appeared reluctant to approach Mrs. Whateley first.

There were others Ulysses Monk had named who were both closer to their location, and more obvious suspects for police investigation, so he wanted to get to them before the law did. Instead, he suggested that they start with a few of the members of Darke's Carnival who had set up camp on the Common for the duration of the film shoot.

According to Monk, it was a happy coincidence the Carnival had rolled into town just when it had. He'd placed some advertisements in local broadsheets listing his needs, though, so Houdini was inclined to think it was no coincidence at all. Monk's people had told the carnival people they needed to be on hand at a moment's notice if they wanted a part—the light and shooting schedules were tight, and they didn't have time to wait for the freaks to get organized and traipse in to the set from town, so the Common offered the most logical solution as it allowed the carnival to take place every evening, filling Dunwich with laughter and tunes as the barkers swaggered down the midway shouting "Roll up! Roll up! Come and experience the wonders of Mr. Darke's Carnival! Experience the greatest show on earth! Revel in the wonders of the world's strongest man! Gasp in admiration at the exquisite beauty of a captive siren who has lured many a sailor to his doom with the seductive lure of her song! See Guerin, part man part bear!" and on and on, into the night, drumming up business, offering the locals the chance to go toe-to-toe in the ring with their prize fighter for a pot of gold. It was pure theater.

"So who first?" Wheatley asked. It was beginning to feeling like something of a grand game now that a full day had passed and there was some breathing room between seeing the body and hunting the killer. It wasn't just that they were getting down to work, or that they were distracting themselves from Collette Verney's death, or moving in and out of range of the murderer, they were part of it. They could go where the police couldn't, ask questions they couldn't and get answers, in no small part because of Houdini's fame. People just naturally wanted to please him.

"Well, I've always had a thing for the ladies, especially those with a healthy amount of facial hair, so how about the Bearded Lady?"

"She should be an easy one to cross off the list," Wheatley agreed. "Anyone can stick on a fake beard after all. It shouldn't be too difficult to tell if it's real or not."

Houdini laughed but didn't pass any judgment beyond that short, sharp bark of humor. Wheatley was getting used to his friend knowing more than he did but not sharing. It was infuriating, and wasn't helped by the fact that Houdini seemed to enjoy watching his puzzled expression.

A stick thin man answered the door when they knocked. He looked at them blankly—as though they were speaking different languages.

"She does live here, right?" Wheatley asked again. "The Bearded Lady?"

The man gave a toothless grin in response and stepped out of the caravan, forcing them back down the steps. "Round the other side, lad," he said. "Just give me a minute and I'll make sure that she's...presentable."

As the man left, Houdini clearly struggled to keep the smile from his face. He was enjoying this far too much.

"Stop yanking my chain," Wheatley grumbled. "Isn't that what you say over here?"

"The gold miners in Colorado might, but it's not one of my chosen phrases, colorful as it is," the escapologist grinned like a boy.

"Come on, tell me what's so amusing?"

But before he could press any further, the toothless man returned. "This way," he said, motioning for them to follow him to the far side of the caravan. Wheatley admired the other caravans as they followed, marveling again at how each caravan seemed to represent the personality of the owner with colorful images painted on the sides.

Wheatley wasn't sure quite what he had expected to find, but it certainly wasn't this: the "woman" sat in the corner of a cage that had been disguised with the not-so-subtle use of a curtain that ran on a rail all the way around the outside. With the right lighting—or lack of lighting—it *might* have been impossible to tell that it was a cage if the door was open. Might.

"Madam? May we have a word?"

"She's had a bit of a heavy night," the stick man laughed when the woman failed to move in response to his question.

Wheatley looked at her properly: the dress was too small for her. Rolls of fat threatened to burst the seams of the yellow print. The nails of her hands, both of which rested in her lap, were dark and uncared for, but one thing was clear, even from outside of her cage: the hair on her face was real. She was genuinely bearded.

"You seen enough?"

"We wanted to ask her a few questions," Wheatley said.

"You can see for yourself she's in no state to answer any questions."

"Maybe we should come back later."

"Maybe you should, but she still won't be able to answer," the stick man said, enjoying Wheatley's confusion.

"We should go," said Houdini, offering him a way out.

"But we need to talk to her, Harry. We can't just report back to Monk that the hair is real."

"I really like you, Dennis, you're a decent, trusting chap, but I'm beginning to worry that you're a bit of an idiot."

"That's uncalled for—"

"Is it? Can't you see what's right in front of your eyes? Look at *her*. Tell me exactly what you see." Houdini placed a friendly hand on his arm to stop him from clambering into the cage despite the fact that the toothless stick man seemed only too happy to open the cage for him.

The woman opened a blood shot eye.

"Well, hello there," Wheatley said, stepping forward with a smile on his face. The woman groaned like she really didn't want to come around and would much rather sleep her hangover off. He took another step, but Houdini tightened his grip and pulled him back just as the woman leapt to her feet and let out a roar so powerful he could feel the sheer force of her fetid breath on his face from where he stood.

He staggered back and almost lost his balance, glad to see the cage door slam shut as the strange woman charged at the bars.

"That's no woman!" he gasped, almost before he'd managed to gather his wits.

"Of course not! It's a bear," said Houdini. This time his laughter was loud and long.

"A bear?"

"You know, a grizzly." Houdini did a passable impression of the Bearded Lady's roar. "They shave them everywhere apart from around the mouth, and from a distance you can be fooled into thinking that it's a woman. An ugly woman, for sure, but a woman none the less."

"But…but… How do they get close enough to the bear to shave it? Doesn't it, you know…?" He slashed with his hands, pretending they were bear claws.

"That's the genius of it. They get them drunk!" Houdini said with a grin. He crossed the Bearded Lady off the list.

"That's insane."

"That's theater, my friend. Nothing is what it seems. Including our bearded lady here."

The second name on the list was the half-boy half-beast Wheatley had caught a glimpse of the day before. It sounded like a terrifying proposition, half man, half animal, but to see him the poor soul was no more shocking than any of the other freaks that had gathered to stare from a distance at the dead woman's trailer. He had no intention of making a fool of himself a second time, though, so decided to let Houdini take the lead. The escapologist clearly had a much better idea of what he was looking for with his search, whereas Wheatley had never encountered a show like this back in England. He was struggling to come to terms with some of the claims painted on the sides of the caravans and barked out by the carnival workers trying to drum up trade. But it was quite one thing to say something and another for it to be the truth. If that weren't the case, then Aleister Crowley would be the most dangerous man alive, not some pathetic little faker banished by Mussolini from his own Abbey of Thelema with his demonic tail between his legs.

Houdini dismissed the boy as a fraud in less than ten seconds. He'd only needed to look into the boy's mouth to know he was a ringer. "The teeth have been filed to points, Dennis, and if you look closely at the supposed claws on his fingertips you'll see they are in actual fact talons from a bird of prey that have been glued on." He shrugged like he couldn't understand how everyone couldn't see straight through this particular ruse. "The same goes for the fur on his body—in fact I suspect that was taken from the Bearded Lady. Looking at some bruising around his ribs and general symptoms of malnourishment, I suspect the boy is being mistreated here, but I have little faith in the authorities. They have a habit of turning a blind eye in cases like this."

Wheatley was appalled at the thought. If he understood the lines Houdini was deliberately leaving vague for him to read between he seemed to be saying the boy might be a captive of the carnival, held against his will, while being mistreated for the benefit of the gawkers who needed to see such things. It didn't sit right with him. It didn't sit right at all. He wanted to do something, but short of sheering the boy's chains and dragging him away, he wasn't sure what he could do. It was hard to know what was considered acceptable in this foreign land, but at home in England he would have had no hesitation in taking matters into his own hands. Houdini, though, seemed to accept this as the way things were and so he said nothing.

"I'm beginning to believe we're wasting our time here, Dennis," Houdini said. "It's painfully obvious that most of these exhibits are manufactured. A few like the dwarves and the skeleton man, the fat woman and the strong man are real enough, but they are a dime a dozen and none of them are on the list. They might fool people who are kept at a distance, with the aid of controlled lighting and clever suggestion, but they don't stand up to anything approaching inspection."

Wheatley had already come to the same conclusion. And if he was honest with himself for a minute, he was more interested with the murder than he was with the freaks. And he was well aware that there was no guarantee that there was any connection between the two. In fact the more he thought about it, the more it seemed likely that Collette Verney's husband was tangled up in it all in some way. If he was jealous enough to hire a private detective to watch her, then who knew what else he might be capable of? Confronting her even if his suspicions couldn't be proved didn't seem far-fetched. Losing control? Striking out? Regretting it all afterwards? None of it sounded unreasonable. In fact it sounded all too plausible. Sometimes love made monsters out of good men.

"Perhaps we should look at the husband," he suggested over a lunch of biscuits and gravy. He mopped his plate clean while Houdini chewed thoughtfully on his. It wasn't exactly what Wheatley would have called a delicacy; in fact it reminded him of dumplings, but it filled a hole.

"I can understand your frustrations and to an extent your suspicions about the husband, but—and don't dismiss my question without thinking about it long and hard—close your eyes, open yourself up to this place, the world around you... can't you feel it?"

"Feel what?" Wheatley asked, feeling stupid as he wiped gravy from his chin.

"There are forces at work here, Dennis."

"Forces?"

"The outré. The unexplained. Can't you feel it in the air? It's almost tangible."

If it was only *almost* tangible, Wheatley wondered quite how it was he was supposed to feel it, but didn't say anything as he didn't want to come across as a smart arse. *Ass*, he corrected himself again.

"But, I'm not sure we'll find the source of it amongst these people. Look at them, they are tricksters and charlatans, and while that doesn't make them above murder, it does mean that they are natural. We are looking for something else. Something *other*."

"So you think that excludes the husband?"

Houdini nodded. "Besides, we would need to locate him first."

"Not difficult, surely. What about Diamond, the PI? He'd have his details."

"He would. But before we go ask him, ask yourself this: wouldn't a stranger be more noticeable in a place like this?" Wheatley nodded. It was hard to argue the point. "I'd go so far as to wager that everyone who saw you yesterday would be able to say exactly when and where they saw you." Again, that sounded reasonable. "And ask yourself one last question: could the same be said for one of the carpenters working on the set?"

The answer was, of course, no.

"There are too many strange things going on around here for this to be anything as mundane as a domestic murder, my fine young friend. Open your mind to the possibility of the *other*. I am convinced there is something else at play here. Some force. But, as my good friend Arthur is wont to say, until we can eliminate all rational explanations, then they must be concentrated on first."

He couldn't tell if Houdini was testing him. The man was infamous for busting charlatans, disproving the presence of the magical and otherworldly over and over again...and here he was suggesting some kind of supernatural explanation for the actress's death?

It seemed...as unnatural as the stuff he was suggesting.

Wheatley had done his share of reading about unusual things, but it was hard to imagine encountering any set of circumstances where it might be considered a genuine alternative to the rational every day nature of crime. Contrary to Shakespeare's wisdom, in his experience there weren't more things in heaven and earth than were dreamed of in his philosophy. And, if he was being honest with himself, he knew

Houdini had a penchant for mischief when he was bored. How could a sleepy little village like Dunwich—no matter how big of a freak show the movie people brought into town with them—ever be enough to amuse the Great Houdini?

Chapter Ten

The door of the dead woman's trailer was open as the two men approached it.

They were on their way to check in on Monk, apprise him of their findings to date, and make sure the circumstances around their interviews with the erstwhile freaks hadn't changed again. Wheatley was almost at the door before he felt Houdini catch his sleeve. The escapologist pressed a finger to his lips, and then tapped his ear. He could hear voices inside.

"So, Mr. Collins, are you trying to tell us that you have never set foot on the set before?"

"Never," Collins asserted. He sounded tired to Wheatley. Like he was fed up with having to go over the same details again and again and not being believed. "We kept the marriage secret so that it wouldn't affect her career. She didn't even change her maiden name. Well she did, she just didn't tell people. Collette was always so sure that the studios wouldn't offer her a contract to make her a Buster Keaton girl or a Chaplin girl or a Grand girl, or Universal or whoever. She thought big studios were obsessed with building a star the world could covet, believing that but for the grace of God, she could be theirs...they didn't fantasize about happily married girls from Des Moines. She wanted to be a star, but only because she wanted them to look at her and love her. If I'd tried to see her at work people would have started asking questions, so I did what any man who loved his wife would do. I supported her."

"You sound like a saint, if you don't mind me saying," a second voice said. "But, forgive my natural skepticism, weren't you the least bit curious what she got up to when she spent all those days away from home?" The inference was: when she spent all those nights away from the marriage bed. Wheatley caught it, and so did Collette Verney's husband.

"What are you driving at, Detective? I'm not sure I like what you are inferring."

"Not inferring. Not driving. I'm just trying to understand how a man—a recently married man—with a beautiful young wife felt about her spending so many nights away from home. It must have preyed on your mind... What she could be getting up to... Those handsome leading men... The temptation? I know it would get to me. I'm only human. So are you, after all. It's nothing to be ashamed of. I'm not accusing you of anything, nor her for that matter. Just trying to understand. That's a big part of my job, if I can understand things, often I can find the answers I'm looking for."

Then came the sounds of agitation, a chair being scraped back, then toppling. Voices spiraling, a threatening shout that cut across the other voice. That was all that it took to send Houdini pushing past him and into the room.

"Ah, Mr. Houdini," said one of the three men inside the trailer. "So good of you to join us. We were rather wondering whether the esteemed magician would put in an appearance."

"Illusionist, escapologist, stunt performer, actor, historian, film producer, pilot, spiritualist debunker, and though I am a man of many talents, the last time I looked I was not capable of *actual* magic," Houdini said as Wheatley followed him into the interview room.

"Quite. My apologies. It is an honor."

"Of course it is. And you would be?"

"Chief Constable Martin and this is my constable, Ropes."

"Ropes? Excellent name. Couldn't do my job without them."

Martin looked at Wheatley. "I take it this is your English friend." He double-checked the name in the notebook he took from his pocket, but Wheatley was in no doubt he knew exactly what his name was and that this was just another piece of the theater the Americans were so enamored of. "A Mr. Dennis Wheatley? We'll be wanting a chat with both of you at some time, of course, but as you can see we are a little tied up at the moment. If you would excuse us?"

A young man in a pale suit was brushing back his hair with the palm of his hand. Wheatley thought it was particularly cruel and unusual to bring him to this of all places, where the signs of his wife's murder were still splattered across the wall for the man to see. A piece of canvas thrown over the worst of it hardly helped. His imagination would paint in the worst of it.

It was hardly surprising the man was agitated.

Unfortunately the difference between agitation and nerves was slight at best, so his distress was only serving to convince the detectives he had something to hide.

He looked at the policemen; words came to mind: prosaic, banal, mundane, ordinary... How could men like these stand a chance against whatever they were dealing with if Houdini was right? They couldn't, of course. Who could?

They obviously had no idea the man had hired a private detective and he had no intention of doing their jobs for them.

"I presume this is the unfortunate Miss Verney's missing husband?" Houdini said smoothly. He was talking to the policemen, completely ignoring the young man's presence. "Look at the man. You can't honestly believe that he had anything to do with the murder of the woman he loved, can you?"

Neither of the policeman spoke, but Houdini had the young man's full attention, and that, of course, was the whole point.

"You think I did this?" He turned and turned again, shaking his head, trying to take it all in. He waved a hand vaguely in the direction of the bloodstains which were still visible beneath the plastic sheeting. "That's why you wanted me to come here? You wanted to rub my face in it?" He clutched his head in his hands. "You think I came here and killed her? Why would I do that? Why? WHY? I *loved* her!"

"Of course you did, sir," said Martin. "That's not in question. No one would doubt your devotion. *But* we all know how arguments can start and, unfortunately, how they can spiral out of hand."

"There was no argument." He shook his head vehemently. "I've never been here before. And you," he pointed at Martin, "are a sick and twisted man!"

"I'm sure he's telling the truth, Chief Constable. He doesn't strike me as the violent type," Houdini interjected smoothly. Wheatley saw him place a hand down on the arm of a chair and pick something up while everyone had their attention focused on the accused husband. Misdirection again.

"I really must ask you to leave," Ropes said, putting himself in between Houdini and the husband and ushering him back out of the door. "We'll let you know when we want to speak to *you*. I'm sure you understand. It's a crime scene; we're trying to conduct an investigation."

"You may be a celebrity, Mr. Houdini," Martin said from behind his constable, "but that doesn't give you the right to interfere in an active investigation. If I have to tell you again, it won't be a friendly suggestion. I'll be putting your legendary skills to the test with a pair of regulation police cuffs, so I strongly suggest you leave the investigating to us."

The policeman escorted them to the door and waited in the doorway, watching until they had both moved away from the steps and onto the grass. He said nothing. They turned their back on the trailer and started to walk away. They had gone no more than five paces when they heard the click of the door closing behind them.

"Well, it seems as though the police aren't so keen on our help after all," Wheatley said.

It was all about Houdini's reputation—that was what was at risk here. If the police decided to play dirty, it would only take the slightest hint of impropriety, even the vaguest suggestion that the Great Houdini was somehow involved in the murder and his name could be tarnished forever, even if the real killer was found. As far as the world was concerned there was no smoke without fire and they loved to see their heroes humbled. Behind their hands they would whisper, "*Oh,*

I don't know... There was always something about him, the way he could get into a locked room, nowhere was safe... The way he could escape any prison...it's not natural..."

They would have to tread carefully.

But that didn't mean that they should give up at the first hurdle.

Someone had to speak for the dead.

Chapter Eleven

"Well, well, well," Houdini mused as they walked away. "It looks like they have got their sights rather firmly set on that unfortunate young man. To lose your wife must be an unimaginable pain. To be accused of her murder?" He shook his head.

Whatever it was the escapologist had palmed when they were inside the trailer had been slipped into his pocket now. Wheatley didn't draw attention to the fact he'd noticed it, after all, it could be something or just as likely nothing. He tried to remember their first visit. Was it possible they'd inadvertently left something behind? No, that was unlikely. Much more likely was the fact that Houdini had just removed evidence from the crime scene. That piqued his curiosity.

"And you're *sure* that it's not him?"

"No question. The man's only crime is being insecure. This killing was always about the film, not someone who just happens to be married to one of the people appearing in it."

"How on earth can you be so sure, Harry?"

"Because, my young friend, she was the *second* choice, remember. The second choice, but not the first tragedy to befall an actress cast in the role. The first went missing. There's a connection, Dennis. There's a connection. There *has* to be. We need to talk to Ulysses. He's the only one who can see the full picture. First, we need to know where he found all these freaks, not just the ones in Darke's Carnival, but the rest of them. My greatest fear is that in his quest for authenticity he might have invited death into our midst."

"Then let's tell him about the fakes and see how he wants us to carry on," Wheatley suggested.

"Solid thinking. Hopefully he will be through the manic phase of creativity."

"And not fast asleep," Wheatley added.

"Then we'll just have to wake him up, won't we?"

They walked through the alleyway of caravans and across the set. The ground underfoot was damp. The fog showed no signs of receding. It was unseasonably cold. Wheatley wished he'd thought to pack a thicker coat—a sheepskin top coat, something like that. It didn't have to be dapper. Fashion hadn't reached this godforsaken shore.

They crossed the soundstage area, ducking under overhanging wires to get to the offices.

Monk was in no fit state to tell them anything.

He was still sitting in the chair they had left him in, but his eyes weren't pennies in wishing wells now; they were glazed and incapable of focusing on anything. There was an open film canister at his feet and he clutched a reel of film to his chest like it was the most precious thing in the entire world. His whole body trembled violently, gripped by tremors that verged on seizures, and his mouth opened and closed again and again though he seemed to have little control over it or the word that he kept repeating over and over and over again. Just one word. It took Wheatley a moment to distinguish the syllables and differentiate the word from the rolling *clack clack clack* of sound: *Glaaki Glaaki Glaaki.*

Clack clack clack…

Like mandibles…clacking…

He had heard that sound—that word—before. Realization sent a cold shiver down the ladder of his spine one bone at a time.

"Glaaki," he repeated, "What does that mean? Is it some sort of Indian word?" he asked. Houdini had no answer for him. He gripped the filmmaker by the shoulders and was trying to physically shake some sense into him. "I heard it last night, in my room, I think… It's hard to recall, but I think it woke me up. It sounds like crab claws clicking, doesn't it? That's what I dreamed…or maybe heard."

"I have no idea," Houdini said sharply. "But this man needs help. This isn't some creative fugue state. His mind has gone. Look into his eyes. They're empty. He isn't in there. His personality has retreated."

"What do we do?"

"I don't know. I'm not a physician. There's an asylum in Arkham—that's not far from here. There are doctors there trained in the mind."

"We can't take him to one of those places!" Wheatley objected. "They're barbaric! I have seen the inside of one of them. One of the worst. Bedlam. It was a hellhole. We cannot do that to the man. I wouldn't wish the sights of Bedlam on a man. Not even as a visitor."

"It is his only hope, Dennis," Houdini said evenly. "If we can get him there before the police find him, it will save him from any unpleasant—and erroneous—conclusions they will be so eager to jump to."

"What kind of conclusions?" Wheatley asked, but he knew. He knew all too well.

"Where we see a broken mind they will see a guilty mind driven to the point of breaking, don't you see? If they can't pin the murder on the jealous husband, the madman becomes the perfect scapegoat. Filmmaker Ulysses Monk, who plumbed the very darkness of human kind in his motion pictures, finally stared too long into the darkness and was consumed by the freaks he sought there. Driven mad, he turned on the very woman who trusted him most, his leading lady. The headlines write themselves. And as long as Uly is incapable of defending himself, it falls on us to help him. Let's get into my car and away from here before anyone comes looking."

"What happened to him? What made him this way? Do you think—?"

"I have no idea," Houdini cut him short. "But like the jealous husband, he is no murderer. All I know is that he needs our help. Being locked up in a police cell isn't going to help him recover his faculties."

"Is a cell in a madhouse better?" Wheatley argued. "We should give him time before taking a step like that. There's no going back. You don't simply walk out when you think you're feeling better. If there's an alternative, we should explore it first. Take him home, get someone to watch over him, make sure he is okay while he just rests."

Houdini thought about it for a moment before nodding. "I have a mild sedative in my things. If we can help him to sleep, then God willing, some of the waking nightmare might leave him."

"It has to be worth a shot."

Monk offered little resistance as they hauled him to his feet, but no matter how forcefully they tried to pry the film from his fingers, he refused to release it. They had to support him. Wheatley could feel the man's trembling pass into him. It was like an electric shock. There was a palpable sense of relief when he was able to break contact with the man and slam the door of Houdini's car on him.

And not once for all that time, not even for a second, did Monk stop chanting that damned word: *Glaaki*.

Chapter Twelve

Mercifully, Monk drifted into something approaching a peaceful sleep once the sedative took hold. It relaxed his muscles to the point that the constant twitching had subsided, but his lips continued to move well into whatever passed for his drugged dreams, though the chant itself had long since fallen silent. They settled him into the bed that Houdini had been using rather than putting him on the couch. With luck—and a little quiet—he would sleep most of the day away and a goodly part of the night, as well.

"Could it be stress? Could that have such a pronounced effect on a man, do you think?" Wheatley asked. "By his own admission, he worked through the night, and you smelled coffee, alcohol, and cigarettes on his breath. Could this just be his soul burning out?"

"What a horrible thought," Houdini said. "It doesn't bear thinking about. It also doesn't explain this."

He pulled something from the sleeping man's hair and held it up to the light. It was unmistakable. Another strand of the green pondweed, just like the stuff they had found close to the murdered actress.

"And you know what our friendly neighborhood police officers will think if they see this and him in this state, don't you?"

Wheatley nodded. He didn't need it spelled out for him: this single piece of evidence would be damning enough to convince them they had the killer. His mind had been broken by the realization of what he had done, and he couldn't function any longer. Case closed. Houdini was right. He could almost hear them saying it. They would see him as the killer instead of another victim, which Houdini believed was precisely what he was.

"Do you think he'll be okay if we leave him alone?"

"That stuff would knock a horse out for twelve hours straight. He ought to be under for a while. I don't think that *whatever* attacked him at the studio will come this close to town." Wheatley caught the emphasis. *What*ever, not *who*ever.

"How can you be so sure?"

"I can't be certain, but the one thing that links these two incidents is this." He held up the pondweed. "And as far as I know there's only one place close to the set where this could have come from. We need to go back to the set. There's something niggling away at the back of my mind about his office and I can't for the life of me think what it is. I want to find out if Ulysses went anywhere after we left him, or if he remained at his desk."

"Because that would mean the killer came to him?"

Houdini said nothing.

As they drove through the streets of Dunwich, the fog felt a little thinner than it had been as recently as an hour before. They saw strange shapes within it, vague outlines that seemed almost, but not *quite*, human.

It was only as they made this journey they realized just how many of the malformed and misshapen had converged on the town.

Wheatley had assumed the folk of Darke's Carnival would keep themselves to themselves, preserving their mystique, but now it was almost as though the strange and bizarre were everywhere he turned.

The police had already left by the time they arrived back at the lot.

No one seemed to be in the mood for work; without Monk, the set was like a ship without its captain. Not even the set builders or painters seemed to know if they should carry on or stand down now that there was no leading lady. They had already been told that there would be major changes, but in what was becoming his familiar enigmatic style, Monk hadn't shared so much as a clue with them as to what they might be. So they sat around drinking coffee and chewing tobacco and the fat with anyone who passed their way.

Only Monk's assistant seemed to be doing any work, though that was more focused on filing and settling invoices than anything creative.

She hadn't been around when they'd spirited Monk away. Actually, come to think of it, Wheatley realized, she hadn't been around when they'd done the tour of the set yesterday, either.

"Mr. Houdini," she said as they entered the office. "Mr. Monk isn't here, I'm afraid. He *was* here a while ago, but he seems to have left. He didn't say where."

"Quite all right, Tanith, my dear. Was he in the office all morning, do you know? We saw him first thing and it looked like he had been here all night."

"He was a bit of a mess, wasn't he?" she agreed, pulling a face. "He was working on some paperwork, I think, but something about the script was bothering him so he threw himself into it. I didn't talk to him after that, apart from to say 'hello' when he stuck his head around the door before he went out for a walk earlier. I assume it was to either clear his head or to puzzle through the problem."

"A morning constitutional, to the lake, perhaps?" Houdini asked.

Wheatley caught a flicker of something in the woman's face. Surprise? She agreed with him. "How ever did you know?"

"Lucky guess. You didn't go with him?"

"No, and our paths haven't cross again today as he wasn't back when I went for my lunch."

"Do you know if he had anything planned for this afternoon?"

She moved a number of coffee cups from Monk's desk. They were filled with the dregs of cold coffee and cigarette butts. She pulled out the filmmaker's diary from beneath a sheaf of papers and opened it in front of them, running a thin finger down over the dates and times until her cherry red fingernail stopped above the letters L.B.

"That's right. He has a meeting scheduled for this afternoon. A possible new leading lady," she said.

"So soon? Surely that's…bad taste?" Wheatley couldn't stop himself.

"As I said, he was in the grip of a revelation. He said he knew how to save the film. He made a few phone calls." She considered it for a moment. "Perhaps there is some sort of facial similarity? Mr. Monk might intend to use her to stand in for some scenes and keep the footage of poor Collette that he already has."

She busied herself with tidying the papers. They were a jumble of different shapes and sizes, no doubt letters and invoices that needed attention, and as the sleeve of her blouse rose up Wheatley caught sight of a small tattoo on the inside of her wrist. At first he thought it was just a smudge of ink, but it had clearly defined lines. She pulled her cuff back down quickly as if conscious that he might have seen it. *Well, that's interesting*, he thought, but said nothing of it.

She turned her back on the pair of them and slipped the pile of papers into a drawer.

"If there's nothing else, gentlemen, I'm going to head home. There's nothing for me to do here."

This was clearly the signal to make themselves scare. They made their farewells, offered thanks, and left her to lock up the office behind them.

Houdini made a show of looking over his shoulder and offering a flirtatious wave as they left. Wheatley knew it would be wise to do the same, because obviously Houdini wanted to *see* something. There was nothing the man did that wasn't calculated to the nth degree. Unfortunately he had no idea of what he should be looking for, so couldn't be sure if he saw it or not.

So he watched her walk away in her sensible shoes and skirt that fell closer to her ankles than her knees. She wasn't unattractive, if a little too prim for his tastes, but he didn't think that she was Monk's type, given the temptations on offer to a filmmaker like him. He wondered if the same thoughts were going through Houdini's mind. Of course if they were, the escapologist was far too much of a gentleman to make mention of it.

"Did you notice anything odd about the room?" Houdini asked. It was a rhetorical question. He didn't wait for Wheatley to answer. "No script. It was missing. All that paper and no script."

"Maybe she tidied it away," Wheatley suggested.

"You think? And leave the rest of the mess until later? That seems unlikely. It was there when we left and now it is not. That leads to one inescapable conclusion: someone has taken it. I would like to know who."

Chapter Thirteen

Houdini had already decided against sleep—again. There was no time to lose. His discipline over his body was legendary, but at some point, he knew, it would fail him. For now, though, he would drive himself on, will over sheer exhaustion. He could sleep when he was dead.

He had come back to Monk's house after dropping Wheatley off at the boarding house. His young English friend had looked so utterly exhausted, keeping him awake had just seemed cruel. He needed him to be on his game in the morning. Things were accelerating. And Houdini was still three steps behind, playing catch up. He didn't like that. He was used to being the cleverest person in a room.

The filmmaker was still sleeping. He couldn't tell if it was peaceful or not. It didn't particularly matter; he needed to rest either way. Hopefully when he awoke he would be his old self.

It was late in the evening. The fog turned the days into near-perpetual night. It was disorientating. Lack of sleep didn't help matters.

He wanted to talk to some of the crew, but it would have to wait until the morning; perhaps Monk had given one of them some kind of indication of his changes. It was a slim hope. No doubt Monk guarded his secrets as closely as any Masonic initiate. It was a reasonable assumption given that he had only ever seen the pages directly relating to his own input, not the whole script. Monk didn't seem like a man prone to sharing his secrets. But perhaps it was different with the crew as they needed to build things to fit his mad vision and that took time?

He was also fairly certain Monk hadn't come back to the house between setting out for his lakeside walk and losing his mind, so where was the manuscript? Even so, Houdini scoured the place when he returned, hoping to find at least a working copy of an earlier iteration, but nothing. He wasn't exactly sure how finding an old copy would help, given Monk would only have marked up his changes and corrections on copy he'd had with him in his office.

But even pre-fevered revelation there had to be a link between the story then and the story now—and why Monk had been so obsessed with amassing an army of freaks for his film.

He could try to recover all of the pages from the actors of course, and piece it together, but even then there was no guarantee that it would be *complete*. Could the missing manuscript have anything to do with Verney's murder, or was that a stretch too far? Sometimes the shadows weren't worth jumping at and the clues weren't clues at all. There *were* peculiar goings on around the film...but did that mean there was a connection between them all?

He was back behind the wheel of his car before he really knew where he was going, his subconscious one step ahead of his mind, so only two steps behind the racing sequence of events, which was actually an improvement on the last few days.

He had an idea.

There was little point in going back to the film lot; the place would be abandoned save for the caravans from Darke's Carnival. He was already starting to think of them as entertainers rather than freaks, but that didn't mean there were no genuinely strange people amongst them. If you saw past the fact that as a whole they were trying to shock, it was all about misdirection, like so much of his life. He needed to hold a mirror up to it. To see if the creature cast a reflection, metaphorically speaking.

Curiously, he found himself reluctant to return there at night, especially alone. That one fact was enough to make him do just that. He always was a contrary soul.

He made a deal with himself: just drive in, stick to the open public places, see if he could find any signs of life, if not, drive out again. Halfway there he realized his stomach was growling. He could never think clearly on an empty stomach.

As luck would have it, he found all of his needs met in one place.

The lights of Rosie's Diner cut through the fog far more effectively than the headlights of his car. They were like a beacon in the darkness calling out to the starving. He parked across the street, realizing once he was halfway across the foggy road that he wouldn't be able to see the vehicle from inside. So be it. Of all the things worth worrying about, having his car stolen was not one of them.

He pushed the door open. A small bell rang, causing a few heads to turn. Walking inside he was hit by a wall of warmth. He must have driven past this place a couple of dozen times without thinking to sample its delights. Now he wished he'd visited sooner.

All of the stools at the counter were taken.

A couple of the occupants turned, taking a quick glance in his direction. Most smiled. He nodded in return. He hadn't seen any of them around, or so he thought, but it was safe to assume that at least one of them recognized him. But, there was a feel about this place—they weren't about to hop down from their stools and come bounding over to shake hands and ask for an autograph. They were there to eat, which in their heads meant he was there to eat, and it was just a happy coincidence that they were going to satisfy that need side-by-side. For an hour at least they were equals. Just hungry people. His smile broadened.

"Hey there, honey," a woman behind the counter beamed at him. "Why don't you grab yourself a booth and I'll be right over?"

Houdini saw a man slip from one of the booths and head for the door. His arms and legs were a little too long for his body, awkward and ungainly, and he held his head at a strange angle, as if his neck couldn't extend fully. It left him perpetually looking down. The man made no effort to look up as he made his way past Houdini and out into the fog.

He slid into the booth the man had just vacated and pushed a still half full coffee cup toward the edge of the table, splashing a little of the liquid onto the tabletop. He started to wipe the surface with a napkin lying beside the saucer before he realized there was a drawing on it. He stopped before the liquid seeped up into it and ruined the image. He was certain it was the same design that he had caught a glimpse of on Tanith's wrist before Monk's assistant had covered it. He'd noticed Wheatley's slight double-take and followed his gaze. It was an unguarded moment. He had no idea what the image signified, but here, again, was another coincidence. They were beginning to add up. He slipped the napkin into his pocket as the woman—he assumed was the eponymous Rosie—approached bearing a fresh cup and a jug of steaming coffee with a broad smile.

She placed the cup down, wiped the surface, filled the cup and slid it in front of him in a single fluid motion. "First cup of my famous coffee on the house," she winked.

"Well, thank you, Rosie. Much appreciated," he replied as she removed the cup and saucer discarded by the booth's previous occupant.

"My pleasure, honey. So, you hungry? Everything's good."

He reached for the menu.

"The special's a nice roast turkey dinner," she suggested.

He put the menu back in its holder without reading another word.

"Sounds good."

"Taste's better. Back in a few," she said. "Just shout if you need anything else."

"Will do."

She was right, the coffee tasted good. He sipped at it steadily, despite it being hot enough to burn the roof of his mouth, while he waited for his food. He took the opportunity to look around, checking out the other customers. A few of them left while he sat in silence, going about their life. None of them stood out as particularly suspicious.

In a booth across on the other side of the diner he spotted a couple of familiar faces.

One of them was the narcissistic Taylor Andrews.

Houdini had the man figured out: he was capable of turning on the charm and the smiles when the camera was rolling, or when there was an adoring fan to be charmed back to his trailer, but equally quick to let the mask slip when the moment had passed.

Tonight he was all smiles and, surprisingly, at least from here, they seemed genuine. Houdini had to crane his neck a little to see the reason. He realized then that in Andrews's place he suspected he would have been smiling too. Sitting opposite Monk's leading man was a girl who looked every bit as radiant as the dead girl. In fact, looking at her, the similarities between her and Collette Verney were astonishing.

And troubling.

"Here you go, honey," Rosie said, putting the plate in front of him. He hadn't even realized that she had returned. He'd been so enthralled by the sight of Verney's doppelgänger.

"Pretty young thing, ain't she?" Rosie said, smiling down at him now that she had his attention.

"Sorry?" Houdini said, only half catching what she was saying.

"The young lady. She's quite the looker."

Houdini began to deny it, but smiled instead, caught bang to rights. "She certainly is," he said. Then in a vain attempt to defend himself added, "She reminds me of someone."

"Oh, I know... When she walked in, thought I'd seen a ghost. She's the spitting image of that actress who got herself killed yesterday." Rosie shook her head like she still couldn't quite believe it.

Houdini had no idea if the newspapers had gotten hold of the story yet, but wasn't really surprised that it was already a topic of conversation among the locals. Death—especially a violent death—had a way of doing that.

"You knew her?" he asked, fishing.

"She came in a couple of times, usually with that guy over there...the *actor*." The way she said it made it obvious she wasn't impressed with Taylor Andrews. She confirmed it with her next breath. "Seems to think he deserves special treatment. Like we should all scurry around to his beck and call." She shook her head. Houdini found himself liking the down-to-earth woman. "Some of the other guys who work up there come in regularly—after all, they all know good food, even these Hollywood types. This one, though, well he doesn't let the grass grow under his feet, does he?"

"You think there was something going on between them?" He knew without a doubt there hadn't been, but it was always good to gauge other people's perceptions…especially when it involved murder.

"Ah, honey, in his head *maybe*, but not hers." Rosie laughed, loud enough for a couple of her customers to turn their heads toward her, including Andrews and his new leading lady. She had an easy laugh. It wasn't hard to see why the place was so popular. Who wouldn't fall in love with a laugh like that and a full stomach? Rosie's was the kind of establishment where you could come in alone and never feel lonely. He liked that.

"I guess not, then," he said with a raffish grin.

"Anyway, enjoy your meal, Mr. Houdini," Rosie said, revealing that she did indeed know who he was, and left him to clear another table.

Houdini couldn't remember when he had last enjoyed a good meal. Not since he'd left home for this latest stint on the road, for sure.

The work on the film hadn't been particularly arduous, and for the main had meant him hanging around for hours on end, unable to leave in case he was called upon to observe a scene and offer an opinion. And, of course, that didn't happen too often. But it was good to be away from the hustle and bustle of the act, the need to perform. He did, however, miss it. Live long enough in the spotlight and, rather like cocaine, it became addictive. And, of course, when he was doing his own shows there was always someone there to make sure that he ate properly and took care of himself.

And with that thought he gave the meal the attention it deserved.

"Mr. Houdini," a voice cut in even before he'd managed two mouthfuls. He looked up to see that the actress had slid into the booth to sit opposite him.

"That's right," he said. He pretended like he had not already worked out who she was. He waited for her to tell him.

"Louise," she said. "Louise Brooks." She held out a hand and he took it in a soft handshake.

"Pleased to meet you," he said, delighted that his suspicions had proven correct. Louise Brooks. This was clearly the L.B. that Monk had arranged to meet. He wondered how long it would take the industrious constabulary to discover the diary and add her to their list of suspects.

She obviously wanted to talk and he was more than happy to let her.

"I'm a big fan," she said. "I saw one of your shows once when I was a little girl. You won't remember me after all this time, obviously, but you signed my best handkerchief for me at the stage door. It was all I had with me you could write on."

That was not a great compliment, reminding him of how much older he was than the young and very beautiful woman, but despite bruising his ego, it actually made him smile. It was just part of living and something he was going to have to get used to. Fans came in all shapes and sizes, but if he was honest, few came as easy on the eye as this particularly lovely one with her heart-stopping eyes, and perfect cheekbones like geometry.

"So are you here to work on the film?"

A flush rose in her cheeks and she looked a little flustered. "I was hoping to. I auditioned for the part before but didn't get it." He had to wonder how such a heavenly creature could be passed over. Verney had been beautiful, no doubt about it, but in less than a minute in her aura Houdini was sure that Louise Brooks was the single most divine woman he had ever encountered. The policeman had called him a magician when they'd been introduced. There was no magic in the world capable of recreating the effect this woman had on a man in her presence. He inclined his head slightly, fascinated by her natural allure. That she had been passed over once was a crime, but twice…? "The girl who got the part let Mr. Monk down. And now the girl who took her place has, well, you know… It's horrible…but part of me thinks, third time's the charm," she said self-deprecatingly. "Is that wrong of me? Of course it is.

No one wants to trade on someone else's tragedy. What must you think of me?"

A thought flitted across his mind, bright enough to stir his curiosity. Could it be relevant? Louise and Collette shared an uncanny resemblance, but what if the first actress, the one who had disappeared, shared the same basic bone structure and coloration? It was a classic look, certainly, one that many would consider true God-given beauty.

"Taylor keeps trying to tell me that I shouldn't worry about stepping into a dead woman's shoes, but it's just so morbid, isn't it? Did you know her?"

"Not well."

"It must have been such a shock."

Again he nodded. This wasn't why she'd come over to talk to him. He let her work her way up to it.

"I keep trying to tell myself to be professional. This is it, the chance I've been praying for. My shot. I know it could be my big break. I know I may never get a chance like this again. But it just feels…wrong."

"It's possible," he agreed. "This could be your chance, but what's the alternative? It could be the thing that destroys your career, couldn't it? It's already ended two vivacious, talented women's lives—" And as he said it he knew he was right. That first actress Monk had cast, the one who had disappeared en route: she was dead. There was something tainted about this film. "Don't let him tell you what you should do." He had meant Andrews when he said it, but he realized he meant Monk, too. Both men had power over her, and he knew enough of them to know they'd have no compunction if it ever came to exerting it. "My advice, for what it's worth: make up your own mind. That way, whether it turns out to be the right thing or the wrong, you will only have yourself to blame. You won't look in the mirror and think, I hate him for what he did to me. Own the choice. We learn by our own mistakes, not by those that others make on our behalf."

"The wisdom of the world's greatest magician?"

"Or a life lesson learned by a guy who's made a few mistakes along the way and wishes he'd known then what he knows now."

She smiled.

It was a nervous little smile.

It only made her prettier.

She had every right to feel nervous. Houdini was struck by the sudden image of opening a door and finding her body sprawled out across the floor in a grisly pose like Collette Verney. He couldn't shake it. He forced a smile.

"So when did Monk call?"

She shook her head. "He didn't, actually. Out of the blue Taylor gave my agent a call yesterday afternoon to tip him off that the part had become available. I haven't spoken to Mr. Monk yet. I was supposed to meet him here this afternoon, but he didn't show. Guess I was stood up."

"Ah, possibly not. Ulysses was taken ill earlier today."

"Is he all right?" He could see she feared the worst. He'd already hinted his own suspicions that the film was cursed. It sounded so dramatic, but that didn't necessarily mean hoodoo, juju, or any other superstitious mumbo jumbo. Sometimes it was just a coming together of negatives. Not even forces. Just negatives. The world, he truly believed, was one of balance. The positive and the negative keeping each other in check. For every lucky man there was an equally unlucky soul walking around wondering why it was always him. For every guy who found a lucky buck on the pavement there was a Shoeless Joe who reached into his pocket wondering where his last buck had gone. Who was to say that there wasn't a locus of negatives all converging on Dunwich, and on Monk's film in particular?

"I think the murder hit him hard," Houdini said. He wasn't lying. Whatever final tipping point had caused Monk's mind to snap, he was convinced it originated with the murder. Perhaps he had witnessed it? Visual stimuli were, in his experience, often the root cause of trauma. Had someone or something visited his office? Had he been subjected to threats? Promised he was next? He'd seen no hint of the pernicious presence of men in dark suits leaning on the director, but that didn't mean that Mafia money wasn't wrapped up in the picture, did it?

He looked around the diner, but couldn't see any obvious wise guys, but that didn't mean there weren't any in town.

"Hope he's feeling better soon," she said, though it was clear that the words were just to fill an empty space. There was no real concern for his welfare, but neither could he sense the self-serving aftertaste of someone whose future depended on the man's rapid recovery and return to work. He promised to pass on her regards.

What was confusing, though, was why Andrews would go out of his way to make sure she was aware of the sudden availability of the role—and that he hadn't called the woman, trying to lure her into his bed in return for the role, but had called her agent, doing it all properly and aboveboard. What did he stand to gain, then? Because make no odds about it, Taylor Andrews wasn't the kind of man to do things out of the goodness of his soul.

Rosie refilled his coffee cup. He smiled his thanks. She put another in front of the actress, but it was cold by the time she raised it to her lips. Half an hour passed without him noticing. He barely spoke a word. He listened as she told him about the small town she came from and how her mom still kept chickens, about the two brothers who were back home rooting for her and about her father who had died before he had the chance to see his little girl up on the screen. She told him her life story without artifice. There was a little dampness in the corner of her eye when she spoke about her father, but no actual tears. She only spoke of good times, and he knew the unshed tears were for the days they would never have together, rather than the bitterness of him being taken away. She really was a captivating woman, and in so many more ways than looks alone.

The police would no doubt single her out as a suspect; it was their usual banal line of thinking. Had she murdered her rival to get the part? Couple that to the disappearance of the first leading lady and two and two started making seven. She was no killer. What she was, though, was the kind of woman that men would kill for. And that was a different matter.

CHAPTER FOURTEEN

Sleep came with considerable difficulty again that night.

Dennis Wheatley didn't know whether to put it down to the unfamiliar surroundings, the uncomfortable bed, or the million things running around inside his head refusing to let him just surrender to sleep. It was almost certainly a mix of the three.

He had left his window open a crack to let some fresh air in, but his room seemed to attract the fog. Tendrils of the stuff crept in through the crack, bringing with them the cold and damp.

He lay in his bed staring at the ceiling and wondering just how many more nights like this he would have to endure.

So much for the grand adventure.

He was already beginning to think that he would trade the company of Houdini and the beautiful people of the motion picture world for the comfort of his own bed and a day at his desk. Perhaps he would start that novel he had been thinking about when he returned home? It was ironic, part of the reason for coming here had been to try to break the monotony of day-to-day life, to experience something wonderful, but that had been replaced by something that was essentially the same but different, and certainly not better. Admittedly there was a certain adrenaline rush, but hand-on-heart, he couldn't say that he was enjoying his first visit to the Americas.

He heard a sound in the street.

He ignored it at first, but when it didn't go away he got out of bed to investigate. He knew, logically, that it was most likely a cat rifling through a trash can, but hoped the distraction might offer something else for him to think about instead of the dead woman and her myriad of possible killers. The fog made it difficult to see all the way down into the street below with any sort of clarity, but there were no animal sounds: no cats fighting in the alleyway, no dogs snarling as they roamed the streets in search of food.

He was tired.

Too tired.

That made it difficult to sleep.

At home he would have made himself a beaker of hot milk and added a slug of brandy, but somehow he didn't imagine Ma Mocata would be too happy to have him knocking at her door asking for alcohol, given the Temperance Union sign hanging over the door downstairs, but perhaps he could take a wander with Harry tomorrow and see if they could find one of the country's legendary speakeasies.

Something moved in the grey of the street; something darker than fog, its edges undefined.

He stared at it, trying to see what it was—and then when he saw it, trying to *understand* what it was.

It moved toward the boarding house. *Fast.* At first he thought it had an impossible number of limbs. His heart tripped. He rubbed his eyes. He couldn't trust them. They must be playing tricks on him. Anything else was inconceivable.

Someone opened the door below.

Light flooded out into the street.

And with it he saw that the shape wasn't a single beast moving through the fog at all but a tight huddle of people walking in silence.

A huddle of strange, misshapen people shuffling awkwardly from side to side.

Everything about their movement was unnatural.

Instead of distracting him, the sight of the curious group set his mind spinning into turmoil once more.

The town had become a magnet for these people, and now, it seemed, the strongest point of that magnet, the pole, was this place.

They were an unearthly congregation.

He recalled the filmmaker's words about the freaks being the children of the gods, like Hercules.

Looking at them down in the street they looked more like children of the damned than any deity he'd ever considered.

He watched them make their way inside.

The last of the group looked up at him.

Even through the fog he could see who it was.

She was unmistakable with her white hair floating and mixing with the mist and the bell jar still clutched to her breast. The Whateley woman.

Long after the street had fallen silent he still stood at the window.

Arms wrapped around him, he shivered with a mixture of cold and unease. He couldn't begin to explain where the fear was coming from. Couldn't rationalize it. They were people just like him. They had been born differently, that was all. He had seen people damaged by war, good men who had lost limbs in battle, had been scarred and badly burned, and when he looked at them he didn't see them being different—they were still his brothers-in-arms. Damaged, but not different. But not the freaks out there.

And how he hated that word: *freaks*.

Eventually, he crawled back into bed.

When sleep came he was tormented by the sounds of battle once more, by glimpses of half-remembered death and destruction, and in the yellow fog of violence he heard voices crying out to him. Sometimes they called out in pain, sometimes they shouted for help, sometimes they simply sobbed for their loved ones they had left behind as the reaper came for them. And of course there was Eric. Dear, mad, wonderful, larger-than-life Eric Tombe. Dear, mad, wonderful, larger-than-life, dead Eric Tombe. In the midst of it all there was another sound calling to him across the battlefield, a sound that was so eerily familiar, like the clack of mandibles, like the clack of claws, or his tongue on the roof of his dry mouth, but he couldn't be sure...he couldn't quite hear it...he couldn't make out the word...the single word...being repeated over and over again. It had no meaning to him.

Glaaki, Glaaki, Glaaki.

The moment that his brain registered what the word was his eyes snapped open.

He sat bolt upright in bed, rudely awakened.

It took a moment—the long hitch of a breath—for him to realize he could still hear voices chanting the word.

Reality had crept into his dream and drawn him back from that horror that still haunted him even this far from the battlefields. No young man should have to go through what he had. He held his breath while he listened, hoping that somehow it would start to make sense, that he'd grasp the true meaning of that guttural word, as the last remnants of sleep drifted away. But it was hopeless. All he could do was try to isolate the source and hope that offered up answers.

He concentrated on the voices. He was sure the noise was coming from the other side of his bedroom wall—even though there was no other door on the corridor. He slid out of bed as quietly as he could, wincing as the bedsprings of the brass bedstead creaked and ground loudly enough, surely, to wake the dead. He stood motionless, listening. Waiting for a cry. Nothing. He stood beside the bed in silence and took the glass tumbler from the nightstand. He placed it carefully against the wall, holding it in place before pressing his ear to it. The glass amplified the sounds on the other side.

The words held a steady rhythm. He could hear that word amongst the rhythm. It was repeated again and again in different sequences. Different rhythms. *Glaaki. Glaaki. Glaaaaaakikikiki.*

It was clearly an important word, the way they used it perhaps even a name.

Wheatley froze, the filmmaker's words about the freaks being the children of gods back in his mind. What if it was true? Or rather, what if that was what they believed? That Glaaki was some kind of god or demon and they were trying to summon it? It was not always about truth and fact, sometimes it was simply about what people believed.

His own notebooks held a vast and cramped scrawl of notes on the weird and wonderful, not specifically the occult. He was no believer in *that*. Sacrifice and devil worship, yes, that was human wickedness. He could understand that. Was that what they were doing on the other side of the wall? The thought sent a cold shaft of dread all the way down into his core. Were they trying to summon up some kind of demon? Making a sacrifice? Was that why Ma Mocata's Boarding House was a beacon for the freaks?

He felt sweat start to flow from every pore and dribble slowly down his brow, down his back to cradle in the hollows there, despite the coolness of the night.

All he could think was, *Walk away. Leave now. Go.* But some primal part of him, something that existed beneath the fear, said the opposite. This was a challenge. An experience. Something that could shape him. Something that could be the making of him. And that part of him wanted to dive into the mystery, not hide away from it.

He would speak to Houdini in the morning. They needed to devise a strategy. In the meantime he determined to transcribe the chant. It *must* mean something to someone. And deep down he was coming to believe that this had to be connected with the bizarre events at the film set.

First Intermission

The voice calls to me. Chooses me. I am the special one. I will do its bidding. I belong to it. To HIM. I belong to him. His voice is my life. There was a time…before…when something like this would have been unimaginable. I am special. I am important. I am doing the Great One's bidding. The Great One. Praise be his name.

I walk through the fog that is His breath.

I know that it will shield and sustain me.

The mortals ignore me. They are lost in their make-believe world. They cannot see me while I do the Great One's bidding. They are blind to my presence.

They stood on the banks and watched when my name was called. They watched as I set foot into the water. They watched as I walked in deeper until the water closed over my head. They watched. And they heard his name.

I see things shift and swirl in the murky depths. Shapes and sounds shift inside my head.

I cannot remember who gave me the knife. I have no recollection of taking it. But the moment my hand closes around it I know it is right. I grip it tightly. Its bone handle is a perfect fit for my hand. The razor sharp flint blade gives it the perfect balance.

Even as it touches my skin I know that this knife has been used many times, but it has only ever had one purpose.

Sacrifice.

The blade sings with history.

The blade speaks with the tongues of the dead.

I can hear every one of them.

I can feel that moment of sweet pain as the knife plunges in deep.

I can taste that exquisite fear.

As my lungs fill with water.

I can taste pondweed in my mouth as I emerge. I am still me. I still own my mind. But He is with me, even if He has relinquished control of my body. He is in me.

The Great One.

I willingly sacrifice my body in service to my god.

It is His to do with as He wishes.

I have no way of knowing if He would return to me.

I no longer care.

I am more than the worshippers in their white robes could ever imagine. I can feel the envy in their eyes. It stings them that they were not chosen. They cannot believe they are not as important. But I am part of Him and He is part of me.

Through my eyes He catches sight of faces beneath the hoods. Their masks are allowed to slip in the knowledge that they are safe. These are more than just freaks. These are more than sideshow exhibits for the curious. Like me they are all children of a god, though none have been favored as I have.

The mist is inside and outside of me as I make my way toward my victim. Let them lose themselves in their pointless pursuits. Their film is about nothing of consequence. They are of no matter. I am there to do His bidding. Nothing else.

The door is open.

The mist led me here. I will find her. Her blood calls to me. She barely raises an eye to look at me as she applies her makeup. She takes no notice as I step behind her. She matches my smile in the mirror. I see the milk white skin of her throat inviting me. She is the sacrifice He demands.

She does not scream as I place my hand over her mouth. She makes no sound as I draw the knife across her throat. The sharp edge of flint slices deep into her flesh.

It is done.
The red mist rises as blood fills the air.
The fog descends swiftly, choking the town.

Feature Presentation

Reel Two

Chapter Fifteen

The sun was fighting a losing battle against the fog as it rose. Its rays wouldn't warm the ground, and its pale light barely cast a dull glow into Wheatley's room.

He was lost in a dream. He had no body. His consciousness floated in a great cosmic emptiness. He was nothing in the vast barrenness of space. It had no beginning and no end. There was a desperate need to fill this void, a hunger that he knew he would never be able to sate. And then he began to see something in the distance; something so far away that it would always remain out of reach.

But there was something else.

Somewhere in the void there was a sound—a steady insistent pounding that demanded his attention.

He opened his eyes and discovered the sound wasn't inside his head at all. It came from outside his bedroom door.

He struggled to gather his thoughts.

He could hear the voice, but it was difficult to make out what it was saying through the door. He felt odd, unbalanced, as if part of him had been left behind in that monstrous dream place.

His eyes adjusted to the half-light.

He pushed himself up in bed. Stretched. Every muscle ached. It hadn't been a restful sleep. He couldn't recall the last time he had simply slept without being plagued by bad dreams, without being hounded by the guilt of what had happened back to the murder in April '22 . He couldn't even bring himself to think of his friend's name. He shook his head and in doing so caught sight of something written on the wall above the headboard.

It hadn't been there when he had gone to sleep. The thought sent a cold shiver of dread sliding deep into his heart. There were letters daubed in red, a scrawled hand that spelled out a single word. A name. *Glaaki!*

The pounding on the door continued. Wheatley couldn't move. He couldn't get out of bed and walk across to it. They had been in his room while he slept. They had scrawled that damned word in blood on the wall above his head.

He was afraid.

Genuinely afraid.

He stared at the word, at the blood, as it dripped down his wall, and realized there was even a dash of it in his hair.

He wanted to be violently sick.

He pushed away from the wall, scrabbling across the bed, making enough noise for the man on the other side to hear.

"Rise and shine, Dennis!" Houdini called, banging on the door again.

"Harry! Just a minute," he said, stumbling from his bed. He pulled on his suit pants and tucked in his starched white shirt, adjusting the collar before unlocking the door.

"Ulysses has come around," the escapologist said instead of hello. "Sort of. The poor bastard woke up screaming *Glaaki* over and over again—" Houdini stopped dead, staring at the word written on the wall. He breathed in deeply, nostrils flaring, and looked from the bloody message to Wheatley and back again. "Is there something you want to tell me?"

"It wasn't there last night," Wheatley said as if he needed to explain himself. "Obviously." The two of them stared at the word for a moment. Houdini gave his full attention to the physical evidence while he waited for Wheatley to finish dressing. He hopped up onto the bed and bounced closer to the wall.

"You locked your room last night?"
"Of course."
"And it was clearly still locked this morning," he said. It was a statement, not a question. Wheatley had needed to unlock the door to let Houdini in.
He washed and finished getting dressed while Houdini examined the daubs with his face only an inch away from the wall.
"It really is a mystery isn't it?" he mused, seeming to enjoy it a little too much for Wheatley's liking. "Someone manages to get into a locked room, paint this on the wall in blood..."
"Is it human?"
"Almost certainly," Houdini said. "If this were a message, say from a Mob wise guy, it would be rat. But," he touched the blood with his fingertip and touched it to his tongue, "this isn't rat."
Dennis stood slack-jawed. Human blood? On his wall?
It felt as though everything was building, pushing at him, bullying him one step at a time toward the edge and sooner or later he would be tipped over and falling into nothing. Was that what had happened to Ulysses Monk? The urge to flee this place, to return home, washed over him but he fought against it. He would not return home. Not while the finger of blame was so eager to turn to him. It felt as though death was determined to dog his footsteps. And again it wasn't just happening around him. As with Eric Tombe's murder, it was happening *to* him. He had become enmeshed in the web of mystery. Who, if they knew his past, could ever believe that he was innocent?
"They did this while you were sleeping, shocking yes, but more interestingly, I think, is that they managed to break *out* again and lock the door behind them while in the process leaving the key on the inside of the door. That is no mean feat."
"What are you suggesting?"
"Nothing at the moment, my friend. It's a classic locked room mystery. I love a good mystery."
Wheatley looked from the writing to the door and then back again, still unable to grasp how it had been possible.

How could they have broken in without waking him? And how then could they have stood over his bed—over his head—and painted the wall in blood without waking him? He shuddered at the thought. It was as though they had simply walked through the walls.

He turned to the window, double-checking that he hadn't left it unlocked. It rattled in the frame, but was still secure and any attempt to open it would have been loud.

"A conundrum, for sure. Unfortunately, we don't have time waste on it at the moment. I had to leave Ulysses alone while I came to fetch you. I almost brought him with me, but all things considered, it's rather fortunate that I didn't." He motioned toward the writing. "But rest assured, there is an answer, and we will find it before you close your eyes and rest your weary head, Dennis. You have my word."

Unsurprisingly, that didn't put his mind at ease.

He said nothing as they left Ma Mocata's Boarding House. He said nothing as they crossed the street and clambered into the car. He said nothing as they drove away. It wasn't until they were ten minutes from the boarding house that Houdini reached into his jacket pocket and handed something over to him that they finally started talking again. "I picked this up at a diner last night."

Wheatley unfolded the napkin carefully and even before it was filly open he could see the partial symbol that had been drawn on it. "I've seen this before."

"Of course you have. It was on the wrist of Monk's ever-efficient assistant. Open it again."

Wheatley did as he was told, opening another fold and knowing what he was going to see even before it revealed the word written beneath the design. Six letters. They were ingrained on his brain. Six letters he would never be rid of. *Glaaki.*

"I think we are going to have to find out a little more about this Glaaki, but it isn't as though we can just start asking around, is it? Not here at least. I can't imagine people in the town who actually know what it means are likely to be forthcoming."

"It's all connected, isn't it? The murder, this missing actress,

Monk's madness, breaking into my room, the voices I've been hearing, this. It's all connected."

"It most certainly is. And let's not forget young Tanith. There's definitely more to her than meets the eye."

When they reached the director's rented house they found a calmer Monk, but there were still obvious signs of anxiety.

He was sitting up on the edge of the bed, his hands constantly clawing at the bedspread, broken fingernails catching in the threads as they dragged across the linen. But—and it was only a small mercy—he had stopped saying that damned word.

Houdini sat on the bed beside him.

He spoke softly, his tone reassuring.

Monk was clearly glad that he was there.

Wheatley was about to head for the kitchen to make coffee when he heard the heavy *clump, clump, clump* of shoes on the stairs.

Houdini pressed a finger to his lips and was up and moving silently toward the door. The man's control of his body was phenomenal; the sheer grace of his movement almost preternatural.

The door swung open to reveal Monk's secretary with a small bottle in her hand. She did not seem unduly surprised to see them there. Ignoring the escapologist, she stepped around him into the room and took his place on the edge of the bed beside the filmmaker. She unstopped the bottle and was about to put it to Monk's face when Houdini grabbed her arm and stopped her.

"What the hell are you doing?" he demanded, prying the bottle from her hand and lifting it to his own nose. He could smell the unmistakable odor of ammonia.

"Spirit of Hartshorn," she said, snatching the bottle back from him. She wafted it close to Monk. Even the briefest exposure to the astringent fumes was enough to bring him out of his stupor.

"Smelling salts," Houdini said for Wheatley's benefit. He wondered why she had used some ancient-sounding name instead of calling a spade a spade or in this case *sal volatile.* Wheatley had encountered it on the battlefield of Passchendaele where it was a staple of the medic's kit.

He was as keen as Houdini to find out what had happened to Monk back at the studio, but there was no way they could while she was there. Monk's assistant may have been as pure as the driven snow, but the symbol on her wrist suggested otherwise.

Chapter Sixteen

They had to be quite blunt about their need for privacy before Monk's assistant would leave. On the surface it seemed like diligence, wanting to stay with her employer and make sure his every need was catered for, but Wheatley was unconvinced. And the longer she stayed the harder it was for them to ask Monk what had happened.

The only good thing about her presence was that it gave Wheatley the time to become familiar with her voice, and the more he listened to it the more certain he became that she wasn't one of the people he'd heard chanting through his bedroom wall. But that didn't mean she wasn't in cahoots with them.

And while he couldn't prevent her from reporting back, he was damned if he was going to give her everything on a plate. So until she was gone he did nothing to raise her suspicions.

Houdini was obviously thinking along the same lines.

"We don't all need to be here," he said, smoothly, and with no intention of leaving. Wheatley saw the woman begin to nod, agreeing, but before she could offer to look after him Houdini said, "We can hold the fort here. The police are going to need access to Ulysses's office though. They'll want to look at his appointments diary to piece things together. If the door's locked…" He shrugged, leaving the inference hanging, hoping the woman wouldn't want to risk their breaking in. It was a gamble, but if she had anything to hide there was a good chance she'd keep it close at hand. He was right.

"They wouldn't dare," she said, but clearly she thought they would. Even as she spoke she was slipping into her coat. "Tell Mr. Monk not to worry, I will keep everything ticking over. If there are any problems that I think he should know about I'll send word. Not that I anticipate there being any, but if the police want to speak with him, what should I say?"

"Make an excuse. Tell them you don't know where he is or when he will be in."

"But I do know where he is," she objected, flustered. This was unexpected. The idea that telling a lie for her boss could be an issue seemed painfully at odds with her being involved in a murderous conspiracy. Perhaps he'd misjudged her?

"That's true, but not necessarily correct. You know where he is right now—but he might not be here by the time you get back. We may indeed go out for a walk, a constitutional down by the water. The air will do him good. Equally we might visit Rosie's for a bite to eat and a cup of her glorious coffee. There are any number of distractions we might choose to keep him occupied. It's a world of possibilities out there. But, if you feel compelled to tell them that we are here, then please pick up the telephone and let us know that they are on the way so we can make ourselves scarce."

"I'm not sure…"

"He really isn't up to being interrogated is he?"

She shook her head and smiled. "No. No he isn't." For a moment Wheatley thought she was about to give her employer a kiss before she left. She seemed caught in indecision. So was that why she was overly protective of him? Were they lovers? She left with the briefest of goodbyes.

Wheatley waited until she had closed the door behind her and watched her start off down the road from the window.

"She walked all the way from town?" Wheatley said, watching her disappear into the fog.

"I didn't see a car," Houdini agreed. "But the set isn't so far from here, and there's a path that cuts off a huge chunk of the road. In this weather I'm sure it could be quicker and safer than driving."

"How long do you think it will take her to get to the studio?"

"On a day like today, anybody's guess. Twenty minutes? An hour?"

"That gives us some time then."

Houdini nodded. "Best not waste it."

Monk had maneuvered himself back onto the bed, sitting up against the headboard. There was still something off about his eyes. He obviously wasn't fully recovered, but he was lucid.

"Do you know what the word Glaaki means?" Wheatley asked.

A look of terror returned to the director's face as he struggled to control his emotions. Monk shook his head. Words refused to come out of his mouth. It was a full minute before he was able to speak.

"I…I… Once. Only once. But it is better if you hear it for yourself." He tried to get himself out of bed but Houdini stopped him.

"You're in no fit state to go anywhere. Sit. Tell us what to do."

"There's a reel of film," the filmmaker started.

"This?" Wheatley asked, recovering it from the top of the chest of drawers where he had put it after wresting it from Monk when the sedatives kicked in. "You didn't want to let go of it."

This time Monk was insistent that he was getting out of the bed. "We only need to go into the other bedroom. There is a projector setup." Houdini handed him a bathrobe and the three of them crossed the landing to the smaller bedroom.

It was filled with equipment. Wheatley couldn't begin to name even a tenth of it. There were blackout sheets over the windows. So this was why Monk, and now Houdini, had been sleeping on the sofa? There was only the one bed in the house.

Together Houdini and Wheatley cleared various devices out of the way until they had made enough space to reach a viewer at the far end of the room. Monk shuffled through, breaking open the canister. He held a couple frames up to the light to check, then expertly fitted the reel into the projector and ran the tape through the wheels.

They watched for a moment as the image moved on the flickering screen before Monk wound it back. "Sit. Please."

Wheatley watched as a blonde woman appeared—a beautiful blonde woman. She was made up to the nines. A femme fatale ready to snare any red-blooded male foolish enough to look in her direction. She looked uncertainly at the camera, cocking her head slightly as though listening to a voice they couldn't hear. She nodded, composing herself. She straightened her dress and her mouth began to move. The sound quality was so poor they could barely hear her. Wheatley had assumed it was silent at first, but then he heard her scratchy voice. It was like listening to a ghost trying to make contact from the other side. Monk apologized. "The machine's in desperate need of being serviced. I had told her to look scared," Monk said and they watched as the girl gave full vent to her emotions, screaming the same word over and over again. They all knew what the word was, even though the sound was poor. *Glaaki.*

Monk had turned his head so that he did not have to watch the woman, but Houdini was absolutely captivated by her. And with good reason. She was *beautiful.*

"Is this the actress who was killed?" Wheatley asked.

Monk shook his head. "No, this is the screen test for Catherine Beddows."

"Catherine Beddows?"

"The actress originally cast in the role?" Houdini guessed.

The filmmaker nodded. "She didn't turn up when we were due to start filming. No explanation, nothing. It was very disappointing. We were lucky to get Collette..." His voice trailed away.

He wasn't telling them anything they didn't already know, but there was something strange about seeing her face on the screen. The similarity to her dead replacement was uncanny.

"Do you still have her contact details?" Houdini asked.

"Only for her agent. He spoke to her the morning before she set off."

"But she never arrived," Houdini finished.

Monk shook his head. "No. I just assumed... This business...it's all about money. I thought someone must have made her a better offer. I rang her agent to check, but he hadn't heard from her and denied knowing anything about her getting another job. He was more concerned about the possibility of her cutting him out of a deal than the fact neither of us had any idea where she was."

"Caring soul," Houdini said. He looked at the girl on the screen. There was no such thing as coincidence, meaningful or otherwise. "You won't want to hear this, my friend, but I suspect there's only one reason why she never reached you and that doesn't involve money or better offers."

"I don't understand. Why else would she not arrive?"

"I think you know, even if you haven't been able to voice your suspicions. I believe that there has been foul play."

"You can't be suggesting she was murdered, surely? Not two people playing the same part...that's..." It was obvious he wanted to say impossible, but it was anything but. Wheatley was a decent judge of liars, being accomplished in the art himself. Monk's register, the shock in his eyes, it was almost certain he had not even considered the possibility.

Why would he? Until Collette Verney's murder there was nothing to suggest foul play. Theatrical types were flakes. They blew about with the wind. He'd just assumed she would turn up somewhere, eventually.

"Okay, so we've heard it for ourselves," Wheatley said, gesturing toward the reel. "But what the hell does it mean? Why was she saying it over and over again? Why were you saying it over and over again?" *Why were the chants repeated in exactly the same manner*, he thought but didn't say. "It sounds European, Eastern, maybe? Perhaps even Russian?"

"You have a better ear for languages than I do. I've no idea," said Monk, still keeping his back to the viewing machine. He shook his head. "Here's the stupid thing...I don't even *remember* her saying the word at the screen test. It was just there on the film when I went back through it the other day. I scoured everything I had on film, even the screen tests, to try and see what I could salvage after Collette—," he broke off, remembering something. "I saw a face at the window."

"A face?"

He nodded. "The next thing I remember is waking up here this morning."

"Did you recognize the face?"

"No. Not really. It was peculiar. Gaunt. Haunting. I'd have remembered it, I'm sure."

"Can you describe it?"

"Long, thin, no trace of color. Not a single hair on his head."

"Could it have been this Glaaki?" Wheatley mused, wondering if they may have stumbled onto something finally. They were due a little luck.

Monk shrugged. "Who knows? One minute he was there, the next he was gone." He looked like he wanted to say more.

"But?"

"I don't know. Maybe it was just my eyes playing tricks on me, maybe it was just the reflection of the moon on the glass, and he wasn't there at all."

Thinking like that, covering their eyes from the miraculous or horrific or outré or whatever it was wouldn't get them anywhere. Even if there was nothing supernatural going on that didn't mean there wasn't a gaunt, pale-faced killer on the film set... And if there was, surely someone else would have seen him? Wheatley had the distinct impression they were clutching at straws. A pale gaunt face did not a killer make. He thought of the name again: *Glaaki*. Why did it appear on this strange piece of film? What did it really mean? Had it affected Monk? And if it had, why hadn't it affected him or Houdini?

"What happened to the manuscript?" Houdini asked, breaking his train of thought.

"The script?"

"The last time we saw you before..." Houdini seemed reticent to say, "lost your mind," and struggled to find another word to describe what had happened to Monk. Clearly none would suffice. "When we saw you in the morning you were working feverishly on rewriting the film script."

"Ah, yes, yes, of course. That was why I was looking through the rushes, you see, to see what could be salvaged and reworked."

"What happened to the pages?"

He looked puzzled, as if the question was meaningless. "On my desk," he said, and then the puzzlement was replaced by concern, then near panic. "Tell me that they are still there."

Houdini shook his head. "No sign."

The filmmaker was visibly shaken, imagining the sheer amount of work that had gone to waste if the pages were lost. And even if he could remember exactly how he'd intended to rebuild his film whatever he managed now would not be the same.

"My work...gone? Everything? Stolen? But why? Who would do such a thing? I don't understand... What have I done to deserve this? To be singled out like this?"

A telephone rang downstairs. It stopped him from sinking all the way down into the depths of despair.

Wheatley and Houdini remained in the room while Monk stumbled down the stairs to answer the call. Wheatley stared at the woman on the screen. Her face seemed to be calling to him. The frame was frozen in place, but her lips twitched as though she were still trying to say *Glaaki*.

"I wonder where she is?" Wheatley asked.

"Beside some railway line between her home and here, most likely, assuming she was thrown from the train. Scavengers will no doubt strip the bones so there's nothing left to discover."

It was an awful thought.

Thinking it didn't make Wheatley feel any better.

The idea that another woman could have been murdered was bad enough, but the idea that a body was out there somewhere rotting away to nothing was just tragic. To die alone was one thing, but to be left unmourned, stripped to bones by hungry coyotes? He shuddered at the thought. It seemed so...primitive.

"We can't keep operating in the dark," Houdini said. "We have to find someone who can shed some light onto the nature of this *Glaaki*, whatever it may be. And if they *don't* know, well let's pray they can point us in the direction of someone who does. There's only one person I can think of who might know, or be nosy enough to find out: our friendly neighborhood private investigator, Diamond."

It was logical. Diamond knew the case, or at least an aspect of it. He was clued in to the place and used to operating down amongst the detritus of humanity. He had connections. If anyone could find the source of the word, be it a gangster from the East, a new gang in town, some creditors chasing Monk, or any variant thereof, Diamond had the best chance of sourcing it.

It was that, or more banging their heads against a brick wall.

"Harry? Can you come down here?" Monk called from the bottom of the stairs.

Wheatley stood on the top of the stairs.

Monk looked up at him. He was shaking visibly. His skin had taken on a waxy white sheen. He held the telephone receiver down by his side. Houdini rushed down and took the receiver from him. He listened for a moment before putting it back on the cradle. Wheatley knew what he was going to say before he said it.

"There has been another murder."

"Who?" His first thought was the new actress—L.B.—that Monk was supposed to meet yesterday. If it was, then the finger of suspicion was leveling coldly on him. And even if it wasn't the mysterious L.B., anyone connected in any way with the film and the police would move Monk up their list of suspects.

"Edward, one of the technicians." Houdini licked his lips. "He did the underwater stuff with me." It was almost as if the very spark of life had been extinguished in a single moment. Before them stood a normal man, Harry Houdini, not some giant caricature of a man with endless reserves of energy and boundless good humor. He was every bit as fallible and breakable as the rest of them. "We should get over there," he said at last, still obviously struggling to comprehend what had happened and how it changed things. Three deaths around the film meant it had to be about the film. There was nothing else it could be about. Someone was deliberately targeting people involved with it. Why? Why go from the on-screen talent, two near identical actresses, to the man responsible for the underwater footage?

It didn't make sense.

Chapter Seventeen

"Well now, isn't this interesting?"

"Isn't what interesting, sir?"

"I've just had a nice long chat with our friends at Scotland Yard, Ropes."

"Illuminating?"

"Very. It seems death's just wild about our friend Wheatley. Follows him everywhere he goes."

"Interesting."

"Most certainly. The unfortunate Mr. Tombe—a con artist and petty criminal with close ties to various among the criminal fraternity including indulgences such as sadistic orgies and every form of excess imaginable, according to the good officer—was brutally beaten for his sins, and by that I mean to the point of death. They finished the job with a bullet to the back of his head. Tombe's body was found down in a cesspool that had been filled in with waste and concrete."

"Unsavory."

"Not pleasant, I agree. But it gets particularly interesting post mortem. Every last dime—well Franc in this case—was drawn out of his accounts in Paris. Following the money, it had been transferred from his London bank to a Parisian within a few days of his death, and drawn out over the counter by a man."

"Wheatley?"

"We don't have his description from the French, but it is unlikely. Scotland Yard's prime suspect is one Ernest Dyer, who was essentially Tombe's thug. And just so happened to meet an untimely end, himself."

"So where does Wheatley come into this, sir?"

"Apart from being Tombe's best friend, Ropes? He provided Dyer's alibi, so I'd say he's right in the thick of it, wouldn't you? Flees London after alibiing a murderer, the man believed to be guilty of said murder himself turns up dead, while a second murder-cum-disappearance occurs on the ship he's traveling here on, and on his first day here a young woman becomes victim number three…or four depending upon how you count."

"Racking up quite a score isn't he?"

"That he is, Ropes, that he is," Chief Constable Martin agreed. "But I think we've got his number now."

Chapter Eighteen

The fog thickened to the point of impenetrability.

The pair crawled along. It would have been quicker to walk. Wheatley wondered how Monk's girl Friday could have made the journey across country to the film set when they could barely see the road beneath them never mind the twists and turns up ahead. The thought of being out there in this peasouper made him shiver.

Houdini had given Monk a sleeping tablet rather than run the risk of him wandering out, or worse still, opening the door to the police. Perhaps the rest would allow his mind to recover.

They reached the fork in the road. Left or right? Town or set?

They took the turn toward the town.

Houdini was eager to find Diamond and start digging into the mystery of Glaaki. Wheatley was secretly pleased. He had no interest in seeing another body so soon. And keeping away from the set meant keeping away from the local flatfoots. He didn't like the way they looked at him. He couldn't say why, but there was just something about the way they eyed him up. He'd seen that look before, back with Swann, a copper from the Yard who was sure he was mixed up in poor old Eric's murder. It was a look Swann reserved for suspects.

It wasn't difficult to track down the only private investigator listed in Dunwich. Wheatley couldn't help but smile as a stray thought entered his head: *even that half-wit detective who couldn't tell his spinach from pondweed would have been able to find him.*

The office was a seedy little one-room above a feed store. The smell of dried cattle feed permeated up through the floorboards. Even the reek of Diamond's forty-a-day habit couldn't mask it. He had a bottle of bourbon for company.

"A bit early in the day isn't it?" Houdini asked.

"I like to think of it as a liquid lunch." Diamond reached into his desk drawer and lifted out two more mismatched tumblers and put them on the battered work surface. Wheatley took a slug, knocking it back in one and gasping his satisfaction. Houdini politely declined. "Ask me no questions and I'll tell you no lies," he said, nodding toward the bottle. "Have another, by the looks of it it's going to be a long day."

Wheatley put his hand over the top of the tumbler. "I'm good, thanks. Better keep a clear head."

"Smart thinking, that man," the private dick agreed, pouring himself another three fingers of bourbon.

"How's business?" Houdini asked, pulling up a seat.

The detective smiled and tipped back his chair, planting his heels on the corner of the desk. Just like everything else about Diamond, the soles of his shoes had seen better days. There was something reassuring about a down-at-heel dick. You didn't want a man wading through the scum of the earth in pristine two-tone spats. You wanted beaten up old boots and ragged bootlaces; the kind of thing you could use to strangle a man if the worst came to the worst. Diamond fit the bill. "There's never a shortage of missing cats. Unfortunately, the fog makes them a bitch to find. Luckily there's always enough husbands following their little heads instead of using their big ones, and they can't exactly hide up a tree, so I get by."

Wheatley smiled.

There was something about the man that he liked.

No airs or graces. He wasn't trying to be smart with them, he just had a way of talking that avoided putting too much flesh on the bone.

"Strange question for you."

"My favorite sort, Mr. Houdini."

"Does the word Glaaki mean anything to you?"

Diamond took a mouthful of his drink, reducing it to one finger in a single swig. The bourbon obviously helped him to think. "What's it in connection with? Our dead actress friend?"

"Could be," said Houdini.

"Sorry. Can't say it rings any bells. Gimme some context: Is it the name of a person? A thing? Is it even English?" He swung his feet down from the desk, which Wheatley took to be him showing interest.

"Your guess is as good as ours, but it keeps turning up." Houdini was obviously unsure about how much they should tell the man at this stage, but there was no point keeping secrets or playing those metaphorical cards too close to the chest. "Monk saw a strange fellow lurking outside his house: gaunt, pale, bald as a coot. You seen him?"

"This your Glaaki guy?"

"We don't know."

"Well, boys, there are so many strangers in town one more would have made no difference. I mean, the guy sounds like a freak, and we've got a dozen a day turning up right now. They're taking over the place."

"Darke's Carnival set up camp a while back though, right?"

"Ain't talking about Mr. Darke's mob. They come and go, but after a few years you start to recognize the faces. Same folk working the rides. Same freaks behind the glass and in the cages. Sure he'll pick a new one up every now and again and add to his collection, but with most of them it's—what do you magicians call it? Smoke and mirrors?"

"That's right," Houdini said.

"They just ain't what they seem."

Wheatley asked, "Is that how you see them? A collection?"

"What else would you call them? You have a better collective noun? A gathering of freaks? How about a nightmare of freaks? That works for me. You guys don't know what it's like. You don't live among them. When this is all over you will be up and gone back to where it is you live, but I'll still be here. And so will most of them. Sure, you learn to live with having them around, but that doesn't mean you ever get comfortable with it." And then something seemed to occur to him. "Have you tried asking some of them what this Glaaki means?"

"We wanted to start with someone we trusted."

He laughed. Wheatley was no expert, but he liked to think he could read people, and laughter was hard to fake convincingly. Diamond seemed genuinely amused by the notion of being trusted—and given how they'd first met, that was hardly surprising. "Flattery will get you absolutely everywhere, gents. If you want me to check my extensive catalogue of knowledge amassed from countless hair-raising adventures where I've put my life on the line for truth, justice, and the American way, all you have to do is ask."

"How much?" Wheatley asked.

"It's a favor, right? So I'll take a favor in return. I figure being owed one by the Great Houdini has to be worth something," he said with a wicked grin. He placed his glass down on the desk and pushed himself up to his feet. Diamond wasn't a large man but he was powerfully built—not exactly a prizefighter's physique, but big powerful arms and a bull's neck, so Wheatley was sure he'd hold his own in a fight. No doubt Houdini could testify to just how well given the ease with which the private dick had bundled him into that alley.

One entire side of the office was lined with filing cabinets full of index cards. Diamond pulled one drawer out and Wheatley could see just how many cards were in there: thousands. That wall was a lifetime's work.

"People get this job all wrong. They think it's all legwork," Diamond said as he worked his way meticulously into the cards. "But the thing is it's all about a system. I've got a system. It's taken me years to perfect it, but what it comes down to is this: information is key. The more you know about any given subject the easier any job will be. I was lucky. I had a partner who had started this long before I even cracked my first case, and God willing, I'll be able to pass it on to whoever takes over fro me when the time comes. Sure, you've got encyclopedias full of stuff, but this stuff here, this is life. Our life here in Dunwich and round about. Everything that's ever happened to anyone in this place—including the rumors—is recorded in here. Some of it is who had an affair with whom, who harbored grudges in the past, squabbles, fights, robberies, you name it, but that's just the mundane stuff. Some mighty strange stuff has happened in these here parts over the years, believe me. Stuff that's impossible to explain."

"I'm beginning to think there's a lot of inexplicable stuff goes on around here," Houdini said.

"More than you could ever know." Diamond plucked a card from the drawer, making sure to leave the one directly behind it protruding like a tongue so it would be easy to slot it back in the right place. "Hmm, well, there's good news and there's bad news. The good, your word 'Glaaki' is in the system. The bad news, there's only one word on the card, 'arcana' with a question mark after it. Not sure that helps any."

He handed the card to Houdini who gave it little more than a cursory glance before passing it on to Wheatley. "Arcana is basically my old boss's shorthand for shit we shouldn't be meddling with."

"I'm afraid it's too late for that," said Houdini wryly.

"The minute I heard you were sniffing around the dead girl I figured that out. That's why they pay me the big bucks. Here's the thing, though, I deal in truth. I don't add this kind of stuff to the archive. That was Charlie's thing. He was into superstition. But the thing is, sometimes it *has* helped me find connections between seemingly unconnected things. Sometimes. Other times it is just mumbo jumbo and it stays that way. But if it's not a fact then, well, that doesn't mean there aren't people who know about it. Whenever I see the word arcana turn up on one of Charlie's cards there's only one place I trust." He paused, obviously uncomfortable with the direction the conversation was taking. He took the last slug of bourbon from the glass. "There's a book. It might be able to help you. It's rare. There are only a handful of copies in existence. There's one in the library of the Miskatonic University over in Arkham. It's called the *Necronomicon*—the book of the dead. I've got a guy there, might be able to help. I can't guarantee that he'll let you read the book, hell I don't even know if he'll let you *look* at the damned thing, that's just how precious it is. But he's your man. Talk to him, say I sent you."

He handed a piece of paper to Houdini. Wheatley craned his neck to see the single name written on there. *Professor Armitage.*

Now they were getting somewhere.

"Be careful out there."

Houdini was the first to rise. He put a couple of bills on the table.

"Get yourself another bottle. It will help to keep out the cold and damp."

"I still want my favor," Diamond said, palming the cash.

"Of course you do," Houdini said, opening the door.

The two of them headed back out into the fog.

It was starting to feel like a shroud.

Chapter Nineteen

Less than a mile outside the town limits the fog started to lift. Wheatley was left with the distinct and uncomfortable impression that it blanketed the town and nowhere else. His first thought was: *Is it keeping something in...or out?*

The university was signposted from the Arkham city limits.

It was a quaint town—very much what Wheatley expected when he imagined an American town with a mix of clapboard houses with picket fences and more colonial-style houses on the outskirts of town moving in toward a stone-built center that wouldn't have been out of place in one of the old university cities back home. Wheatley found himself looking at the windows and wondering at the stories of the lives that went on behind them. How different were they from the lives in Cambridge, in Oxford, Durham, Canterbury?

Before long Houdini was pulling up in the campus's car lot.

Finding the library was a little more difficult, as there was no obvious choice. The university appeared to be a model of impenetrability designed to test students' initiative. If they couldn't find the lecture halls or the library building, they obviously weren't worthy of the wisdom the place promised to impart. Eventually, though, they stepped through the great oak doors and into the hallowed halls of learning. The reception was an impressive book-lined room with the leather spines of gathered knowledge stretching from floor to ceiling. They smelled old and musty and leathery, just like a library ought to smell in Wheatley's opinion.

It was already late afternoon, and most of the desks were occupied with scholars poring over open books. Dust hung heavy in the air, motes moving sluggishly through the beams of sunlight that speared in through the high windows.

A short, fat, grey-haired man behind a counter gave a well-rehearsed and extremely polite cough to attract their attention.

Houdini nodded toward him in acknowledgement and they walked toward him. Some people had a natural affinity for their surroundings. The librarian was one of them. He seemed to have grown organically out of the polished mahogany desk, swelling to fill the tiny space available to him.

"We are here to see Professor Armitage," Houdini said, his voice pitched a little too loudly for the eerie quiet of the reading room. It caused a few heads to turn and eyebrows to be raised. Wheatley couldn't help but smile when someone actually shushed the Great Houdini.

"And you have an appointment?" the man replied, pitching his voice in a perfect whisper Wheatley had to strain to hear.

"No, I'm sorry, we don't. Is that a problem?"

"Well, the professor has classes, and obviously tutorials. He's a very busy man. It's always wise to make an appointment." He turned away from them, intimating the conversation was over.

Houdini reached into his top pocket and gave a little cough, just like the librarian's; quiet enough not to disturb any of the readers but loud enough to attract the man's attention.

"Is there something *else* I can help you with?" From his tone it was obvious he didn't believe there was.

For a moment Wheatley thought Houdini was about to grease the wheels with a bribe, and was both thrilled and mortified by the notion, but then he saw that the escapologist was handing over one of his business cards with a flourish. The librarian took it, read the details, saw the black ink silhouette of the world's premier prestidigitator, and looked back at Houdini, clearly mortified.

"Mr. Houdini, I do beg your pardon, I didn't recognize you," he stumbled, the words struggling to get out of his mouth without tripping over his tongue. "Without the handcuffs." It was a poor attempt at a recovery, and he ended up speaking a little louder than he had no doubt intended, drawing a few unwanted eyes. Even the unflappable souls of academia were, it seemed, flappable in the presence of Houdini. There was another round of shushing until one of the readers said, "Holy smokes, is that Houdini?" and the girl beside him looked up and nodded. Suddenly everyone was staring intently at their books, not daring to complain. Though, of course, the girl came over and asked, "Would it be possible… Would you mind… If it wasn't too much of an imposition… but could I have an autograph?"

"But of course, my dear," Houdini indulged her happily, uncapping a pen and signing the memento she had brought over to him, and as she went back to her reading desk he turned back to the librarian who was looking a little more collected.

"The professor?"

"Of course, of course, I am sure Professor Armitage will be delighted to receive you. Let me go and find him for you."

"There's a good man," Houdini said, and turned back to Wheatley. "Sometimes fame has its advantages," he whispered as the librarian waddled with deceptive speed between the rows of reading tables and study booths to the far end of the room where he disappeared into the stacks. When he emerged a moment later he was waving frantically for them to join him and beaming proudly like he'd discovered the secret entrance to the Seven Cities of Gold.

They made their way to the doorway.

"This really is a very exciting day for us, Mr. Houdini. We seldom entertain such vaunted guests. We are just a little university library; it's rare that the great and the good have cause to visit, and we keep ourselves very much to ourselves, as I'm sure you can appreciate. But this is really quite wonderful. A treat."

"The pleasure is all mine, I assure you," Houdini said smoothly. "Our minds are the keys that set us free, after all. You are doing the world a great service, curating the secrets of this great nation of ours."

"You honor us, sir. May I ask as to why you wish to see Professor Armitage? I don't mean to pry, but does it involve your stage show? The professor is the preeminent scholar of the arcane. I can quite imagine him consulting on Egyptology, symbolism to add authentic ancient mysticism to the act—it is all so wonderfully theatrical—oh, do listen to me prattling on…"

Houdini said nothing, matching the librarian stride for stride. The corridor was narrow. Wheatley could smell beeswax and furniture polish deeply ingrained in the wooden paneling that lined the walls. The Miskatonic was a quintessentially English establishment. He half-expected to see gentlemen sitting in one of the side rooms they passed, smoking and sipping at expensive brandies in their wing-backed chesterfields. The fat librarian just carried on walking and talking, every now and then craning his head back over his shoulder to talk to them.

"I'm sure you understand, but I can't really say," Houdini said finally.

"Oh, no, of course not. Must be circumspect at all times." The librarian tapped the side of his nose. "Trade secrets. Don't want others learning your hard-won knowledge and turning them into something as prosaic as mere tricks."

"Exactly that," Houdini said as the librarian stopped in front of a door with Armitage's name on a little brass plaque. He rapped on it once, sharply, nodding to them, and opened it with a little flourish, like the dénouement of a particularly unimpressive trick. Wheatley smiled, imagining he'd just pulled a rabbit out of his hat. Though any rabbits that hopped into the librarian's vicinity would no doubt wind up in a stew long before they ever reached the gilded stage.

The librarian stepped aside to let them through.

"They are not tricks," said Houdini, pausing for a moment in the doorway. He stepped inside. His face didn't betray a single emotion, but Wheatley knew he was fuming.

He followed quickly after him and closed the door behind them, leaving the fat librarian in the corridor wondering if he'd just put his size tens well and truly in his mouth.

"Mr. Houdini." The matchstick man behind the desk unfolded as he rose, hand out to grasp the escapologist's outstretched hand. The contrast between him and the librarian could not have been more pronounced. No doubt the librarian was scoffing all of the good professor's rations and telling him they were down to the bare essentials. "I'm sure Thomas said, but this is something of an honor. I've been an ardent admirer of your exploits for many years. Of course, I don't actually understand what could possibly have brought you to my door, but I'm not about to look a gift horse in the mouth. Please, sit, take a load off. Something to whet your thirst? We have a wonderful supply of whiskies here, despite the best efforts of Miss Nation and her Temperance Movement. A man needs to whet his whistle every now and then, wouldn't you agree?"

"Not for me," Houdini said. In all the time they'd spent together, Wheatley had never seen so much as a drop of alcohol pass his lips but he offered the offer himself. "And to answer your question, a mutual friend suggested you might be able to help me, Professor."

"Well, now I am intrigued." He opened the northern hemisphere of a rather impressive globe to reveal an even more impressive array of crystal decanters and tumblers. "Who might that mutual friend be, I wonder?" He poured very generous measures for each of them and shared the tumblers around. "This taking of alcohol is in itself a curious ritual," he went on before Houdini could tell him about Joe Diamond's recommendation. "Back in the time of the Vikings they would fill a horn with mead and pass the horn around the fire, each man taking a swallow. They wouldn't refill the horn, so each of them would have to drink just the right amount to make sure none of the assembled warriors was insulted by being offered an empty horn—"

"Nothing worse than an empty horn," Wheatley said, before he could stop himself.

"Quite. Only when everyone had drunk from the horn

would the summit begin, so, *skol*, my new friends," Armitage said, downing the amber liquid in one bitter swallow. Wheatley did likewise, putting his empty glass on the desk in front of them. "It's the origin of a Swedish word, *Lagom*," Armitage continued, getting into his stride now, "which means just exactly the right amount of something. Not too much, not too little, but exactly perfect to go around. It's a curious concept; Swedes will even use it to measure things like happiness. They can claim to be 'lagom happy.' Imagine being just the right amount of happy." He smiled at that. "There's no equivalent word in the English language. So, now we've got the formalities over, let's get down to business shall we?"

"This is Dennis Wheatley, he's English, so everything he says sounds a good fifteen percent more intelligent than anything that comes out of my mouth, but he's a good man." Houdini quite deliberately avoided telling Professor Armitage who had given them his name. "As I said, we were led to believe you might have the expertise to cast a little light on a word—or perhaps a name—that we believe may have some sort of arcane if not merely archaic origin."

"Of course, of course." Armitage tapped his temple. "Our mutual friend was quite right to send you to me. If it's archaic, esoteric, odd, or just plain old peculiar, chances are I'll have stumbled across it and filed it away up here. So, let's hear what it is we're dealing with, shall we?"

"Have you ever come across the word *Glaaki*?" Houdini handed the professor the napkin with the name and symbol written on it. "I suspect it could be a name, perhaps?"

"Well, well, well, would you look at this… Quite wonderful…and unexpected…" There was a look of surprise but also delight in his eyes as he picked it up.

"You recognize it?"

"Indeed I do, Mr. Houdini. Indeed I do. I think we certainly need to talk. All of a sudden I have a lot of questions for you."

"We'll start with one of ours, first. Our friend suggested there might be mention of the name in a book? I believe he called it the *Necronomicon*?"

"Ah, the mad Arab's masterpiece. Well, you really are a

delightful surprise, Mr. Houdini. You are correct, *Glaaki* is indeed mention in that particular volume, but there is another book devoted to this particular god."

"God?" Wheatley asked, dubiously.

"Oh yes, absolutely. Not a god in the sense of heaven and let there be light—don't confine yourself with any Catholic interpretation of the word. *Glaaki* was one of the Old Gods who came to this Earth millennia ago."

"Like pagan gods? Roman gods? Like Jupiter and Mars?"

"More like leach out your mind and leave you a quivering wreck unable to grasp the sheer vast infinity of their evil gods, if you want to put a label on it," Armitage said, and Wheatley really couldn't tell if the man was joking or not. "We have a copy of *The Revelations of Glaaki* here in the university library, actually. It is a very rare book indeed; almost as rare as the *Necronomicon* itself. Where on earth did you come across his name? It's rarely mentioned, as far as I can tell, other than by his servants and those few of us devoted to the study of hidden knowledge. This symbol," he tapped one finger on the napkin, "Is the symbol borne by the Servants of Glaaki. You will often find it tattooed on their—"

"Wrist," Wheatley interrupted.

"I see what you mean about your English friend," Armitage said, turning to face Wheatley. "Full of surprises. I'm going to make the logical deduction that while you don't know the name you have seen his symbol inked on someone's wrist. That means that you have met one of the Servants of Glaaki."

"It doesn't sound very good when you say that…'Servants of Glaaki'…makes them sound like a fraternity of assassins… a cult."

"Oh, true worshippers are definitely cultists. Tell me, was it a man or a woman? Alive or dead?" He drew in a deep breath. "This really is very fascinating you know. Of course it could just be a fantasist, it doesn't necessarily have to mean you have stumbled upon an actual cult. There are plenty of people who like to dabble in the arcane without a clue as to what they are actually meddling with. I'm sure you of all people understand that, Mr. Houdini."

"Of course, but for argument's sake, let's just assume we

really are dealing with the existence of a modern cult worshipping this ancient god, what then?"

"If it were possible to research their present activities, to understand their rites and rituals, that would be splendid. So much knowledge is lost, and the actual practice of worship mutates over time. What was true of the Servants of Glaaki two hundred years ago might not be true of them today."

"So we're groping around in the dark?"

"Hardly. There's one thing we know for sure about the servants."

"And that is?"

"They are very dangerous people."

"Wonderful," Wheatley said. "Why is it never—oh, they're the salt of the earth?"

Houdini laughed at that.

"Is there any chance we might see either of these books?" Houdini asked. "It could be interesting to see what has actually been written about this god." *If god is really the correct word*, Wheatley thought, still struggling to grasp the idea of ancient deities lurking out there in the cosmos. People all around the world worshiped any manner of things as a god, but that didn't actually make them gods. It just meant gullible people praying to them in the hope somehow it would cheat whatever odds it was they were facing in their lives. It was all about the upper hand. If some god could help protect thieves breaking into houses, then thieves breaking into houses would offer a quick silent prayer in the hopes that they'd get in and out smoothly and away with the swag long before the law turned up. Just because they did get away didn't, however, necessitate the existence of a god of thieves. It just meant they were good at what they did, or lucky. And sometimes lucky was better than good.

"We don't *normally* allow visitors to examine some of the more precious books in our care, but I am sure that an exception can be made in this case, given that it is you, Mr. Houdini. But, I regret to say that you will be unable to *touch* them yourselves; you understand, some of these books are upwards of a thousand years old, there are chemicals secreted by the fingertips that could cause untold damage, so care must be taken. I will of course locate the relevant passages. If you'd be so kind, it should only take a few moments to locate the text."

He left them alone.

"So what do you think?" Wheatley asked. "Barking mad?"

"Too many years with only books for company," Houdini agreed. "Old gods, ancient rituals? It'd be enough to drive anyone crazy. Frankly, if I'm being honest, I'm impressed he's even heard of me. He lives in another world. But I guess my fame is interstellar now."

"Well, perhaps our friendly neighborhood librarian tipped him off?" Before Houdini could say anything they heard footsteps in the hallway and the door opened again.

The professor carried a simple cardboard box file. He placed it reverentially on the desk. "I'm afraid this is a real mystery, gentlemen," he said, shaking his head. "*The Revelations of Glaaki* is not where it should be. There is no record of it having been signed out, but I have asked Henry to make sure that no one is currently using it for their research. We are fastidious when it comes to loans and paperwork. This is highly irregular."

"Not to mention an unlikely coincidence," Houdini said.

"Quite. I thought perhaps we might have loaned it to another university, but there's no record of that, either. So I've asked a couple of students to search the stacks. It must have been put back in the wrong place."

"Or stolen," Houdini said.

"I fervently hope not, as something like that…it's irreplaceable. The loss of the knowledge contained therein, it doesn't bear thinking about." He shook his head and turned his attention to the box on the table. "There is little in the *Necronomicon* concerning *Glaaki* but it will be relatively straight forward to find the passage that refers to him so that you can see for yourself. The book was written by the Arab Abdul Alhazred; fortunately we have an English translation here which was written shortly after his original composition." He opened the box file to reveal the volume that nestled snugly inside.

Although the book was clearly cared for with absolute reverence, it was showing signs of significant age; the leather binding was cracked in places where the inner boards had warped after being allowed to exist in damp conditions at some time during its long history.

The professor slipped his hands into cotton gloves before lifting it out of the box, awe plain on his face, almost as if this was part of *his* religion; not the words written on the dry and dusty pages inside, but the book as a physical object. This was a man who seemed to worship books in themselves even above the written word. A genuine bibliophile.

He sat down behind his desk without opening the book and reached into a desk drawer for a notebook. He turned backwards and forward in the notebook, running a finger down each page until he found what he was looking for. He let out a sound that might have been delight, then moved to the ancient tome, slowly opening the heavy boards of the cover, and turning each page carefully until he found the one he was looking for.

"I have been working on an index for this book for many years," he said, pointing to the notebook on the blotter beside the *Necronomicon*. "I sincerely hope it will be of the greatest value to scholars in future years. It is my contribution to the world."

He beckoned for the two of them to join him on the other side of the desk and pointed out the lines that referred to *Glaaki*. Wheatley was disappointed with how little was written there. Four lines:

Great Glaaki stirs in still water deep
Where long dark silence ensures his sleep
There he waits for the calling from the East
And mortal man may prepare for the feast

"That's it? That's all that is written about this...*Glaaki*?" Wheatley said.

"I am afraid so," Armitage confessed. "Though, as I intimated, there is the other book which tells us much more about him. I am sure that once we recover it, it will satisfy all of your questions." The man was obviously in denial. *The Revelations of Glaaki* had been stolen from the Miskatonic library, not waylaid. And Wheatley was in no doubt that the thief was wrapped up in the murders back in Dunwich. Houdini was right, there really was no such thing as coincidence, not when it came to this case. "Perhaps you could let me know how we might be able to contact you?"

"It might be easier if we contacted you, Professor. We don't really know where we'll be from one hour to the next at the moment. Perhaps we could give you a call tomorrow?"

"Of course. Of course. It is some time since I took a look at the book myself, but I seem to recall that some of the writings about *Glaaki* are contradictory. From memory, the consensus is that he lives in the depths of a vast lake having arrived on a twin-tailed comet. The precise location of the body of the water, though, like so much else, is open to debate. There is no such thing as the absolute truth when it comes to these Old Ones, you see."

Wheatley was not sure how to take the man; Houdini was right, it was almost as though he was from another world, not just another country. In England he would have been laughed at for talking of things like this, not given an office in the hallowed halls of academia. He genuinely seemed to believe it was all *real*, which was preposterous. It was nothing but a good story. Wheatley was prepared to accept that there were foolish and unenlightened people who might believe such absolute and utter rot, but this was an educated man, a man of learning. He couldn't imagine an Oxford don holding the same conversation unless it was about the deities of the Ancient Greeks and the peculiar rituals of their adherents.

"These Servants of Glaaki," Wheatley said, knowing that when it was all reduced to the very basics, the people in the here and now were far more important than any concept of god because they were the ones capable of causing harm. Religious zealots, no matter what their faith, were some of the most dangerous men and women in the world. "Can you tell us anything about them?"

"Very little, I am afraid. The activities of cults are always shrouded in much mystery. There are always punishments for revealing the secrets, and those punishments go far beyond anything any devotee would risk. We are talking about subversive movements, deeply buried, that make your Freemasons seem like a gregarious bunch. That mystery alone is what makes them so utterly fascinating, of course."

"Do you think they would be capable of committing murder?" Wheatley asked, not sure what sort of answer he was hoping to provoke.

A smile was the last thing he expected.

"Murder? But of course. Without question. Sacrifice is at the heart of so many cults that still worship these old gods." He spoke as if he was talking to children even younger than the students he addressed in the university; as if they should have been aware that sacrifice was integral to these beliefs.

Sacrifice.

They hadn't thought of it like that, but once the word was out there, a genuine possibility, that changed things. Things began to fit. His suspicion that the chanting behind his wall was in some way connected to the death of the actress was well-placed.

"These people are obsessed," Armitage went on. "They search for hidden meanings in *everything*; the shapes of clouds, the flights of birds, even the cracks in the sidewalk. Make no mistake, these people are deranged, and once they get an idea into their heads they will not veer from their aim. That makes them incredibly dangerous to normal people like you or I. They belong in Arkham Asylum, sedated and in a room with padded walls and no windows. My advice, forget you ever heard the name Glaaki. Give his servants a wide berth. These are people not to be messed with."

Chapter Twenty

The sun was already low in the sky by the time they stepped out into the fresh air again.

Fresh. That was a joke. There was nothing fresh about it. It tasted toxic in Wheatley's lungs, like a forty-a-day man's catarrh-fugged breath. Even so, after the stale and dusty air inside the Miskatonic library, it was a blessed relief. Wheatley breathed in deeply.

"Not to be messed with," Wheatley repeated. It was the first words he had spoken since they had left the professor's office.

"Collette and Edward's fate already convinced us of that, wouldn't you say?" Houdini agreed. "The problem is that we can't exactly keep out of their way when they are the ones who keep finding their way into ours."

Something moved in the bushes causing a faint rustle. Wheatley wouldn't have noticed it if he wasn't already on edge. They neared the parked car. "Did you see that?"

Houdini's brow furrowed. "See what?"

"There's someone watching us, I'm sure of it."

"Jumping at shadows?"

Wheatley shook his head, sharply, once. "Someone's in the bushes over there."

They stood beside the car, making a show of talking, taking in the air. "You have a smoke?" Houdini asked, encouraging Wheatley to light up a cigarette. They waited for a moment, Wheatley drawing deeply on the cigarette and affecting a pose against the roof of the car while Houdini angled himself better to catch sight of whoever—*whatever*—it was lurking back there.

Eventually he caught the briefest glimpse of a man dressed in black with a skull that was bone white in sharp contrast to his clothes. Wheatley wasn't even sure he could trust his eyes. The man's ears appeared to be too long for his incredibly long and cadaverously thin face, and there wasn't a single hair anywhere on the wax-paper skin. Realizing he'd been seen, the man disappeared into the undergrowth, bolting. The very sight of his bizarre features shook Wheatley to the core. All the talk of rituals, mad Arabs, and dead gods only served to amplify the horror, but in truth the watcher was no more hideous or freakish than any of Darke's crew. Even so, he had seemed different somehow, more menacing.

"What the hell was that?" he whispered.

"The man that Ulysses saw at his window," Houdini said. "The last thing he saw before being driven out of his mind by that piece of film." He mulled something over in that steel-trap of a mind of his. "And while he was certainly a peculiar individual, did he strike you as dangerous, Dennis?"

"Dangerous? He followed us here!"

"Did he? Who says? Don't leap to conclusions. It is quite possible we were just going to the same place, isn't it? Aside from the logical problem of how, exactly, he would have been able to follow us through the fog, it's far more likely that we have arrived at the same place at the same time, and if he is involved in the mysterious cult of Glaaki, it is much more plausible that we just saw the man behind the theft of Armitage's book, wouldn't you say?"

Wheatley had almost managed to forget about the fog—it had been an ever-present since long before his liner docked. It just seemed to be a fundamental part of American life, like the fabled apple pie.

Houdini started to walk across the road, angling toward

the bushes. "Come on, Dennis, we don't want him getting away, do we?"

Wheatley wanted to argue that they didn't actually know the professor's assumptions were wrong—the book could have simply been misshelved—because the thought of that man, that *creature*, stealing it would have meant him actually moving through the library, a place where his very weirdness would have been even more conspicuous. He would have been seen, remembered, remarked upon. What he did know, and all that he did know, was that there was some kind of connection between him and the film set.

Houdini moved quickly and quietly, trying to flush his quarry out of his hiding place, but before he was even half way across the road, the cadaverous stranger bolted, bursting from the undergrowth. His arms and legs were as long and spindly as the spider man they'd seen amongst the freaks, but his coordination and speed was almost unearthly. He strode toward the university buildings without looking back and without breaking into a run. But even running, they struggled to keep up with him because his long legs ate up the ground so much faster than theirs.

For a moment Wheatley lost sight of him in the shadows as he skirted close to an ivy-covered building, but he spotted him again as he slipped into a narrow alleyway across the way. He struggled to keep up with Houdini, who was hard on the man's heels. In turn, Houdini struggled to keep up with the man. Wheatley's chest felt like it was going to burst inside his ribs. He felt intense, searing pain of exhaustion in his lungs that brought barely suppressed memories of the battlefield flooding back. Running for his life. Running from the whistling shells. Slipping and stumbling in the mud and the blood. He stumbled and fell to his knees, gasping for air, knowing that he couldn't carry on. Not another step. Not even if his life depended upon it. The world swam threateningly in and out of focus.

The next thing he could remember was sitting with his back to a cold stone wall, feverish sweat trickling down his face and back, his arms hugging his knees up close to his chest, and stinging tears running down his cheeks.

He fought the memories off and choked back the taste of gas. It wasn't real, he knew that, but that didn't stop the pain.

"Are you all right?" Houdini asked, crouching beside him. The concern was obvious on his face.

Wheatley couldn't answer him for a moment.

He just stared into the middle distance, willing death and all of his friends to leave him, to just go, let him live a normal life.

"A minute. Just give me a minute. I'll be fine," he said finally, though a minute was nowhere near long enough. He doubted if he would ever be fine again. He was just going to have to learn to live with feeling this way, to adapt, build mental walls around the memories of the Great War, because no matter how hard he tried, he just couldn't push the memories out of his mind and trust they would stay gone.

Houdini sat on the floor beside him, leaning up against the wall so that they weren't looking at each other, and said, "He got away, I'm afraid. This place is a maze."

"The whole puzzle feels like a maze," Wheatley said, finally putting what he was feeling into words. "Everywhere we go, we just seem to end up right where we started, facing a dead end."

"That's not quite true, Dennis. It might feel like that, but it's more a case of two steps forward, one step back, but we *are* learning. For a start, in the last hour we've learned that Glaaki isn't a word, or indeed a person. We've discounted the possibility that it might be the man at Monk's window. We know that the people who woke you with their chants on the other side of your bedroom walls are almost certainly members of this cult, the Servants of Glaaki, and we know that they are dangerous. And, thanks to Armitage, we can be reasonably sure that the murders committed by, or on behalf of this cult, are most likely sacrifices. I'd call that progress wouldn't you?"

"But we are no closer to knowing *who* these cultists are."

"Again, not true, my friend," said Houdini, hauling himself back to his feet. He offered Dennis a hand. "As you are aware, there's no other doors on your landing that could lead into a room behind yours, which means for them to be able to get into that space behind your bedroom wall, Ma Mocata must either be part of it, or at least know one person who is."

"One other person," Wheatley said, thinking of Tanith, Monk's assistant, and her devilish tattoo.

"That's using your head," Houdini said approvingly. "And going back to Ulysses's list, we've still got a couple of freaks who listed Ma Mocata's Boarding House as their address. It's not much, but it's more than just a start, I'd say."

He couldn't really argue with that.

Chapter Twenty-One

The fog still held the town of Dunwich in its stifling grip. Night was falling.

The strands of mist reached for them with wispy grey tentacles as they approached the town limits, trying to draw them in.

A feeling of dread seemed to fill the car but both of the men knew that they could not just walk away from this mystery any longer. It was far too late for that.

They'd talked during the drive, but after a while it was obvious they were just covering the same ground over and over again, always coming back to the same points and the same possibilities. One such point they kept touching on was the fact that these people were dangerous, but as Houdini pointed out with a perverse sort of glee, "They'll still be dangerous whether we try to do anything about them or not."

Wheatley couldn't argue with that assertion. The fact that they'd left pretty stark and incontrovertible evidence of their presence inside his room while he slept could only mean one of two things: either they'd left their mark purely to scare him off, or they'd turned him into a marked man. And one of those options was far more appealing than the other; especially if the one choice meant they'd singled him out as a future sacrifice.

"We need to be on our guard," Wheatley said.

"Actually, I think we'll need to be on guard, period," Houdini countered. He was beginning to think this could be their opportunity to flush the cultists out from their hiding place behind the walls. "Take turns on watch, two hours on, two hours off, through the night. Better that we get some rest rather than none at all."

Lights were already burning in most of the rooms in the boarding house when Houdini parked opposite the building. He took the list from his pocket and unfolded it with the solemnity of a ritual in and of itself. The first on the list was one Daniel Mason who, it seemed, had traveled all the way from New York City. The only description Monk gave was "severe deformity," which could have meant anything.

"Do you recall seeing him on set at all?" Wheatley asked as they climbed the stairs to the man's room. He was on the floor below Wheatley's, closer to the staircase.

The escapologist shook his head. "Not at all. Word was sent to Ulysses that he had arrived in town and that he should be sent for when his presence was required on set, but not before. Most irregular, but Ulysses seemed content to play by his rules. And far as I know he has not been seen since the moment he arrived." He double-checked the room number against the list before rapping hard on the door twice. "Well, here goes nothing."

Wheatley could hear a sudden flurry of movement inside the room before the rap of his knuckles had ended. A moment later he heard a strange gurgling sound not unlike water going down a drain.

He cocked a curious eyebrow at that.

There was a shuffle of movement coming from behind the door, and eventually a key turned in the lock inside. The door failed to open. Wheatley looked at Houdini, unsure what had just happened. Had the door just been locked to keep them out? It certainly seemed that way.

The shuffling receded.

A few moments later, a chair creaked as the room's inhabitant sank down into it. "Come in," called a strained voice after a moment. Wheatley steeled himself, not sure what to expect, and opened the door.

The man faced them, half in shadow, as the fog and the curtains kept out most of the failing light. There was only a single candle burning on the dresser. And no mirrors. The shadows couldn't disguise the man's deformity. His limbs were curiously twisted, his joints protruding at angles that were unnatural and most definitely wrong. Even sitting, it was obvious one shoulder was considerably higher than the other, and his head was held gingerly on one side, his pockmarked cheek almost resting on the higher shoulder. He wore a hat tilted forward to obscure his features.

"Mr. Mason?" Houdini asked. "Daniel Mason?"

The man moved. It wasn't really a nod, but Wheatley took it as one. "Have you come from the film company?" he asked. Speaking was clearly difficult for him. His voice had a peculiar liquid quality to it, like his lungs were full of water. Despite the obvious discomfort he gave no sign that he did not want to talk. It was almost a matter of pride that he could.

"That's right," said Houdini. "Mr. Monk has asked us to meet with a few of the people who have put themselves forward for roles. As I'm sure you can appreciate, he has been inundated with representations from people claiming to have the kinds of physique he is looking for only for it to turn out they're trying to fool him."

"So he's sent a master of lies and illusions to see what is real and what is fake?" The man laughed and almost choked on the buildup of phlegm in his windpipe as he did so. He took a glass of water from the table beside him with hands bent and twisted with arthritis, and struggling to maintain his grip, needed both hands to hold it steady as he supped. "I should be flattered."

Houdini hadn't introduced himself but the man clearly knew who he was, and unlike a few who could be mentioned, was not the least bit star-struck. It was quite refreshing. Wheatley closed the door behind them, then moved to help him put the glass down as he splashed water on the table, but Mason waved him away.

"I may have difficulty in maintaining my independence, but I refuse to relinquish even that little of it while I am still able. Spilled water isn't the end of the world." He paused for a moment, but did not seem to expect a response. "You haven't come for idle chit chat, or to nurse a cripple, as you say, you've come to see if I am fake or not. So, take a good look, and then tell me, in your expert opinions, do I appear to be a fraud to you? Have I feigned my grotesqueries simply for a moment on the big screen?"

Wheatley began to apologize, feeling more than a little uncomfortable that they had intruded on the man's privacy, and that he quite obviously was not faking his deformities, but Mason cut him short not with words, but with a simple action. He removed his hat, and with it banished any lingering doubts as to the hell the man's life must have been. His head was lumpen and misshapen in the extreme. The sight of it, made worse surely by the chiaroscuro of shadows, made him draw a sharp intake of breath.

All of the air seemed to be sucked from the room in an instant. Wheatley had seen deformity like this only once before in his life, and dearly hoped that he would never see it again.

He had seen Joseph Merrick's body at the Royal London Hospital where it had been on display for anyone with curiosity morbid enough to want to see it. Joseph Merrick, the Elephant Man. What they were doing there was no better than Darke's Carnival; the hospital only pretended at civility and didn't charge people for the privilege. The affliction that this poor man was suffering from was clearly the same; though Wheatley couldn't recall the medical name, he could only too easily imagine the daily hellish life of Daniel Mason. Even something simple like rising from bed and getting dressed in the morning, would have been a feat fit for Hercules. Wheatley felt ashamed and embarrassed and wanted them to get out of there as quickly as they could. They had done everything they had been asked, and could let Monk know with confidence that the man was no fraud.

Houdini clearly had no intention of leaving quickly, though.

He moved closer to the man to get a better view of his oversized head and misshapen features. His questions seemed grossly insensitive to Wheatley, but Mason fielded them with good grace and seemed happy to discuss his condition. Perhaps it was better to be asked straightforward questions rather than being started at, point at, mocked, but not spoken to? Perhaps there was no perhaps about it?

Still, it was like some huge oppressive weight was lifted from Wheatley's shoulders as they finally closed the door behind them.

"Fascinating man. Such strength. You have to admire him," said Houdini.

"Pity more like."

"Oh no, not pity, that's a weak man's emotion. Mason is not a weak man and doesn't deserve to be viewed as one. Every single day of his life he conquers insurmountable odds. Every single day. In his place, could you do that?"

Wheatley shook his head.

"Me neither. There are days..." Houdini looked down at his own hands, as though he expected them to somehow betray him, turned them over, palms up and shook his head. "There are days when I wonder how much longer I'll go on. How much longer I can keep subjecting my body to the physical demands of this job. And then I look at Mason and think how can I ever stop?"

"Well, then the answer's obvious, don't," Wheatley said, clearly uncomfortable with the existential direction the escapologist's musings had taken. "So, who's next?"

"It would appear that our bell jar-clutching Mrs. Whateley is along this corridor, though why she should be lodged here is beyond me, as she owns property not far from town. Why would she choose to pay to stay here when she could remain at home?"

"Perhaps she feels it is more convenient to be here with the others?"

"Or, and here's a stretch, perhaps there is someone at home who would not approve of her taking part in the film?" Houdini suggested. Given the nature of the motion picture, it was not difficult to imagine a husband not wanting his wife to be associated with such a damnable piece of filth.

They stood outside her door for a moment before knocking. Again Houdini went through the ritual of checking the number against his list. There was no answer, though there was a pale light seeping through from beneath her door suggesting she was home.

Houdini tried again, this time a little louder—*knock knock knock*, miss a beat *knock knock knock*—and finally they heard movement inside.

"Who is it?" A woman's voice called through the closed door.

"It's Mr. Houdini, Harry Houdini. Mr. Monk has asked me to speak to you about the film."

"Oh," she said, then fell silent for a moment. "She's not here. You'll need to come back later."

"Mrs. Whateley?"

The door opened a fraction and a single washed-out pink eye of the albino woman with the wild white hair appeared in the crack. "My daughter's not here. She's the one who is supposed to be in the film."

"When would be a good time?"

"Don't know." The reply was sharp and accompanied by a fractional closing of the door. She would have closed it completely, but Houdini placed a hand against it. He made no move to push it open, even so it would have taken all of the weight of her body to close it. She was a slight, frail old woman.

"We'll call back again later," he said, removing his hand. The door closed without another word. They heard the key turn in the lock.

"Friendly soul."

"Daughter?"

"Hard to imagine, I know, but so it seems."

It was only when, a few moment later, they were standing at another door, waiting to see someone else on the list that Wheatley realized Mrs. Whateley was staying in the room directly beneath his. He wished that he'd paid more attention to the corridor. Perhaps it would have shed some light on the space that clearly must exist on the other side of the wall beyond the head of his bed.

The door was opened almost immediately and they were welcomed by a genial man who was only too happy to let them examine his hand, which bore an additional finger. He grinned as he flexed them all, each phalanx moving quite independently, showing that each was capable of making a pincer grip with his thumb. As freaks went, this was hardly the most bizarre Wheatley had seen, and unlikely to merit inclusion in Monk's mad vision. Certainly it was unlikely to impact on the fellow's daily life other than when it came to buying gloves, but there was little doubt that he was genuine. And that, after all, was their only concern.

The fourth door they knocked on brought no response. They knocked again, the same *knock knock knock*, miss a beat, *knock knock knock* pattern, still nothing. The absence of light beneath the door led them to believe that the occupant was elsewhere. Day had dragged into night and Wheatley was all for calling it quits. There was a bottle of whisky in his room he'd brought with him all the way from home, and he was about to offer Houdini a snifter, when he remembered the corridor outside Whateley's room.

"Do you mind if we check something out?" he asked, leading the way without waiting for a response from Houdini.

The light was still glowing from beneath Mrs. Whateley's door. Wheatley tried to tread as softly as he could as he walked past, knowing the old boards creaked and groaned at the slightest weight. He didn't want to alert anyone to their presence in the hallway. He did it in such an exaggerated manner that he hoped it would be obvious to Houdini what he was trying to do.

Houdini waited by Mrs. Whateley's door, listening intently for movement inside.

Wheatley had half-expected to find another door beyond Mrs. Whateley's in the hall; another room occupying the space that *had* to exist beyond his room. There was nothing. No door. He wasn't sure what that meant. A void beyond each of the last rooms on this side of the building? Architecturally speaking, that made no sense.

The only way they could confirm or deny his theory was to take a look outside in case there was another explanation—low sloping shingles, something he hadn't considered. Another building encroaching on this one? Wheatley couldn't remember if there was another building attached to this one, perhaps interlocked, meaning that the empty space could, of course, belong to that building. It would have made sense but for the fact that he remembered finding

Houdini and Diamond in the alleyway that ran between this building and the next.

He took the few strides back toward Houdini none the wiser, and as he did, Houdini knocked on the door again.

"Just in case her so-called 'daughter' has returned."

"You don't think there is one?"

"I don't think anything, my friend. I just want the facts, plain and simple. What we know and what we don't. No more second-guessing. Just the facts."

There was no answer to the first knock, or the second, and there was no sign of movement inside.

Houdini placed a hand on the doorknob and twisted it slowly.

Although Wheatley desperately wanted to see the inside of the room—a lot more so than he actually wanted to meet the woman—he was uneasy about breaking and entering, despite his accomplice's obvious skills in that department.

He suspected that locking the door was to keep the world away from her rather than protect her possessions.

The door offered no resistance.

It swung inwards soundlessly.

The room was empty. Silent. A single oil lamp was burning. It looked as if Mrs. Whateley had slipped out for a moment, obviously intending to return at any moment.

They wouldn't have long.

A quick glance around the room revealed that this one was much larger than his own, with a door at the end that he suspected led to a walk-in closet of some description. That at least confirmed that a discrepancy in space existed and wasn't just some anomaly caused by the shape of the building.

Houdini was looking for something else, though: proof of what he believed about the thing in the jar. What was the point in taking the risk of breaking in if they ignored the opportunity to kill at least one other metaphorical bird?

On a small table beside the lamp a piece of cheesecloth covered a familiar shape. It took Wheatley a moment to realize what it was: the jar Mrs. Whateley always clutched so close to her breast.

He was surprised she had left it, and knew he wouldn't get another opportunity to look at its contents, but rather than pick it up, he crouched down beside it and carefully removed the cloth.

Houdini's hand reached out and plucked something from the table. "Look," he whispered, holding it out for Wheatley to see. A piece of paper. Like the napkin from the diner it carried the same symbol and the same single word. *Glaaki*.

Houdini replaced it on the table and Wheatley turned his attention back to the bell jar. It appeared to contain some kind of dark liquid.

He touched a finger to the glass without causing so much as a ripple, but something moved inside.

Something darted toward his finger.

He caught a glimpse of that *something* in the inky darkness.

"What the hell do you think you are doing in here?" a voice demanded behind them.

Chapter Twenty-Two

They turned their heads in unison to see the albino woman standing in the doorway, a towel draped over her arm, clearly fresh from the bathroom along the landing. She barged into the room angrily, pushing between them. She snatched the cloth out of Wheatley's hands and laid it carefully back over the jar of dark liquid.

"We're terribly sorry to have intruded," said Houdini. There was no charming smile this time. He appeared genuinely apologetic. "We had hoped to find your daughter returned."

"Well, that don't give you no right to come sneaking into our room like thieves, does it?"

"No, of course."

"Right, well, I'd like you to take your thieving hands and get out of my room now, if you don't mind."

"I really am sorry, Mrs. Whateley, sincerely. It was my idea, not my friend's. I rather bullied him into assisting."

"More fool him then."

"I can only beg your forgiveness. I'm sure you'll understand, what with everything that's happened, Mr. Monk has been pushing me to finish my inspection, vet the hopefuls and provide a definitive list for him to cast off as soon as humanly possible. Really, if you think about it, I was only trying to help your daughter."

It was a stretch of logic, and the woman wasn't having any of it.

"Well you can stuff your job, 'cause she ain't interested in taking part no more. Go ahead and cross her off your list and forget all about us. We'll be out of here before you know it, and then you can forget you ever clapped eyes on us."

She ushered them out of the room, ignoring yet more embarrassed apologies.

She slammed the door on them, then very slowly and very deliberately turned the heavy key in the lock.

"Well that went well, didn't it?" said Houdini, still looking at the closed door.

"In as much as getting a door slammed in your face can go well," Wheatley said wryly. He wasn't thinking about the white-haired woman, but rather the jar, or more specifically, what he had seen inside it.

Or thought he had seen.

He wanted to talk to Houdini about it, but how could he possibly explain what he'd seen floating in the inky blackness? It had only been a fleeting glimpse, but he could have sworn it looked like…like…a tiny, perfectly formed *child.*

Instinctively, he'd turned that glimpse into a rationalized reality, a porcelain doll floating in the inky solution, until it blinked at him.

But how could he say that without sounding like a hysterical old woman?

"Oh, I think we learned quite a lot, or we could learn quite a lot, if we chose to open our eyes and think about what we saw, so let's start by taking another look at your room, shall we?" Houdini was away from the door and striding toward the stairs, suddenly full of energy. He called back over his shoulder, "Come on, Wheatley!" And was gone.

"What are we looking for?" Wheatley called, chasing after him.

"We'll know it if we see it," Houdini said, throwing open the door and stepping inside.

There was no indication of intruders, in fact there was no

sign that anyone had been in there since they had left it earlier in the day, including the maid; the word *Glaaki* was still written on the wall, but now it was taking on a new significance. All Wheatley could think, looking at it afresh, was that it marked him out as a future victim—a sacrifice to this cult's god. If it had been a warning, surely it would have said *Go!* or *Run!* or *Get out!* or even *Die!*, not the name of an obscure deity no one had heard of—that only encouraged curiosity, it didn't engender fear.

Houdini moved close to the wall, placing his hands either side of the bloody word, and leaned in, sniffing it, pulling a face, looking at it from the side, below and above, while Wheatley poured two tumblers of whisky.

At that moment he felt like he needed it, and was thankful that Prohibition Agents hadn't searched his luggage as he'd disembarked *The Dunwich Ghost*. Life without alcohol was no life at all, but he would think that, being a vintner's son.

The first taste burned the back of his throat, but the second eased the pain and some of the stress drifted away.

He offered the second glass to Houdini and sat down on the edge of the bed

The escapologist waved it away, turning his head aside so that not even the fumes reached his nose. Houdini reached inside his pocket and produced a card.

"I found this in the trailer where Collette Verney was found, not when we went there the first time, but when we went back and the police were interviewing her husband. While I can't be certain, I don't *think* it was there the first time we were there."

"Which means that someone dropped it *after* the murder?"

"Or planted it there deliberately, knowing it would be found."

Wheatley took the card from him and read the name on it: Catherine Beddows was printed in gold italics, beneath was a telephone number in a simpler font. The name was familiar but he could not recall where he had heard it before. He flipped the card over. There, in handwriting that was barely legible, was an address: *The Lake House, Dunwich*, and beneath that a date and a time. He handed it back to Houdini.

"I don't understand. What's the significance?"

"Catherine Beddows is the name of the actress originally cast in the film."

"The one who disappeared? But why…?"

Houdini held a hand up, deferring more questions. He had more to say and was clearly intent on getting it out without being sidetracked.

"The date, you'll note, is the day that she boarded the train to come here. The date she disappeared, in other words. I will place a sizable wager that this is her handwriting. No doubt given the address for the rendezvous, she scribbled the details down on the one piece of paper she had to hand. What this confirms beyond any shadow of a doubt, my young friend, is that she didn't head off for another job. She *was* here."

Houdini looked decidedly smug, and with good reason. He'd managed to deduce all of that from a single piece of paper—and it made perfect sense. More importantly, the police had missed it, which put them more than one step ahead of the police in the investigation. Looking at the escapologist, Wheatley could tell there was more to come, but Houdini was waiting for him to make the next leap of logic for himself. He tried to puzzle it through. If he were plotting this, how would he tie it all together?

"Okay," he said slowly, thinking on his feet. "So if this card belonged to Catherine Beddows, how on earth did it get into Collette Verney's trailer? If you're right and it wasn't there the first time we visited, who could have been in there between then and when we returned?" Wheatley could see Houdini's smile begin to spread. He had already covered this ground, reaching a conclusion he was absolutely sure of. "The police, we know for sure, and then Collette's husband. It's unlikely in the extreme that the police would have planted or misplaced evidence, meaning the most likely alternative is that the husband dropped it, no?"

It was falling into place like the last few pieces of a jigsaw.

"So Catherine Beddows was lured to this Lake House address by Verney and her husband, engineering an opportunity to remove her from the movie. It starts out non-threatening, they offer to pay her off, to buy Verney her big break, if that doesn't work maybe they kill her, but whatever they do, the motivation is the same: they're making it possible for Verney to step into Beddows's shoes. So we were right from the beginning?"

"It does make a very specific kind of sense, doesn't it?" agreed Houdini. "Means, motive, opportunity. Now if we could link the husband to this cult of Armitage's, the Servants of Glaaki, it would all tie neatly together. We could even put a ribbon on it before handing it over to the bumbling detectives."

Wheatley nodded. It did make sense, and as Harry had said, means, motive, and opportunity were the fundamentals of any investigation, but there was something about the whole thing that didn't quite ring true. Unfortunately, he couldn't put a finger on what.

Before he had the chance to air his doubts, Houdini put his glass down and was on his feet again, pressing his ear to the wall. Instead of listening, though, he placed two fingers against it and used his free hand to start tapping in different spots, listening to the sound it made.

"Harry!" Wheatley rasped. "They'll *hear* you!"

Houdini shook his head. "There's no one in there." He tapped again. "This wall is thin, no more than a partition." Houdini clambered past Wheatley and went to the window. He opened the sash as far as he could, and pushed his head outside into the fog, leaning as far forward as possible, obviously trying to see around to the side of the building, then was back inside and closing it again. Even that brief time had caused the temperature inside the room to drop considerably. Wheatley took another sip of his whisky, warming himself.

He didn't try to stop Houdini as the escapologist bounced back up onto the bed and began checking the wall again. Houdini shook his head, obviously confused by what he heard. He hopped down again and rushed over to the door, flung it open, and stepped out into the hallway. Wheatley heard him grunt, then *harrumph*, then poke his head back inside the room. He stood there in the doorway, one hand on the doorknob.

"One of us needs to go outside to take a look at the building, to see if there is anything strange in the dimensions."

"I'll go," Wheatley said, taking his cue.

He had reached the top of the first flight of stairs when he heard the loud click of the key turning in the lock.

He took the stairs quickly, pausing when he reached the first landing to listen for footsteps, but the boarding house was silent save for the sound of a radio coming from one of the rooms.

Chapter Twenty-Three

Houdini stood by the window and waited.

He had locked the door behind Wheatley and left the key in the door. When he'd thrust his head through the window to look outside, he had been unable to see beyond a protruding support pillar that stood between the window and the end of the building. It obscured a good portion of the façade. What he wanted to know was if there was another window beyond the pillar, as that would be all the confirmation he needed of the secret room he was sure the wall hid. Not that the existence of a window would shed any light on how to get in and out of that space, but he was already beginning to develop a theory about that. Mechanisms were his stock-in-trade, but this, if it was a mechanism, was seamlessly constructed.

He picked up his whisky glass and waited by the window for Wheatley to appear in the street down below.

Just the mere sight of the fog sent a chilling shiver down his spine. There was something utterly *wrong* about it.

The street was deserted.

There were plenty of shadows and shadowy places in the mist.

He caught himself wondering what it was hiding.

In the silence of solitude he listened to the creaks and groans of the old house as people moved about above and below him; one man's ceiling was another man's floor. In the glass of the window he glimpsed movement, and instinctively tried to fathom what was moving in the fog.

Those wasted seconds cost him dearly.

The movement, and the face that formed in the glass wasn't outside at all; it was the reflection of someone behind him.

His heart started to race, but he mastered the urge to spin around and confront his would-be attacker. Instead, he remained motionless, letting them think he was drawn toward something in the fog and using the extra moments to prepare for the fight, but he misjudged it by just a fraction of a second, and a hand holding a chloroform-soaked cloth snaked around his head and clamped over his mouth.

He struggled against it, dropping his whisky glass in the process. It smashed as it caught the windowsill.

He grasped the hand, trying hard not to breathe to buy himself extra seconds to fight before he was overcome by the fumes, but it was one thing to hold your breath for a water escape and quite another to try and do that when you weren't ready.

It didn't help matters that his attacker was wiry and incredibly strong.

The face reflected in the window twisted and shifted.

Pale flesh seemed to fall away to reveal something far more terrifying beneath, as though his attacker were revealing their true self.

Houdini closed his eyes against the caustic sting of the chloroform and kicked out, tipping over the table and sending Wheatley's imported whisky bottle and glass crashing to the floor. He couldn't call out, and even if he could, no one would come running. His only hope of help was outside in the street looking up at the window, oblivious to the fact that Houdini was fighting for his life.

The man—if man he even was—who'd taken hold of him, dragged Houdini away from the window while he kicked out frantically with his feet in a vain attempt to find purchase. He tried to think. If he could balance himself long enough to push back *hard*, he might be able to take his attacker down.

If they hit the floor, that moment of impact would surely buy him a second to break free of his vice-like grasp.

If.

But as the man lifted and twisted him in a backbreaking bear hug, he knew that any hope of escape had slipped away.

Houdini heard a mumble of voices and that damned word, *Glaaki, Glaaki, Glaaki*, over and over. He opened his eyes to see others beginning to slip into the room through a crack in the wall that had opened up. He took no great satisfaction in knowing that he'd been right all along because the sight of their faces made him want to scream; these were the stuff of nightmares given grotesque flesh.

That single glimpse stole his breath away, and no matter how desperately he tried to scream, he couldn't draw the air into his lungs to make a sound. His mind swam. Color spots blurred his vision. He clawed at the hand around his throat, and slipped into chemical blackness.

Chapter Twenty-Four

The street was deserted.

The feeble gaslights along the street did little to relieve the oppressive weight of the fog. It was impenetrable. Suffocating and claustrophobic. It reminded Wheatley of the worst of the London fogs of his childhood, but even London was cleaning up now. He couldn't shake the feeling that there was someone out there, out of sight, watching him. But that was logically impossible—if he couldn't see more than a few feet through the fog, the mysterious watchers couldn't see more than a few feet through the fog either.

He craned his neck to look back up at the boarding house.

Most of the rooms had lights on, increasing his field of vision. He couldn't see Houdini through the gloom, despite the light in his room. Every window on his floor had a lamp of some description burning. He couldn't be sure it wasn't his imagination, but the light from the last window—his window—seemed to flicker a lot more than the others, as if it was different somehow. Had it been candlelight, he supposed, that might have accounted for it; but the only light burning in his room was the oil lamp on the dresser.

He caught a flicker of movement at the next window along,

and for a moment saw Houdini's silhouette, confirming what he'd thought all along, his *wasn't* the last room on the landing. Houdini stepped quickly away from the window.

There *was* another room.

And there was a light burning in it…

He caught another flicker of movement—a change in the shadows thrown across the gable.

There was someone in there.

The creeping sense of dread mounted. There *was* someone else in the street with him. A trashcan clattered as it was overturned. The squall of two cats fighting in the alley almost had his bones jumping out through his skin. He laughed at himself, but that did nothing to banish the sense of anxiety that gripped him. The fog made everything so much more sinister. "Is there anyone there?" he called out, feeling foolish. The sooner he was back inside, the safer he would feel. No one answered him. It was almost funny to think that returning to the room where cultists had quite possibly marked him for death could ever be considered safer than an empty street, but Houdini was up there. There was strength in numbers. Alone he was weak.

Wheatley studied the building's façade again, wondering how he could have missed the presence of that extra room beyond his. He'd walked from the car to the porch a dozen times already. Even if the drainage pipe and guttering did obscure its presence from his window, that was no excuse. It was about being aware of your environment, observant. He couldn't imagine Houdini having missed the obvious if their roles had been reversed. Very little got past the escapologist. He had a way of deconstructing the world that was quite unique, and in this case exceptionally useful. Thinking about Houdini, he waited for the man to reappear in the window and give him the signal to return.

He saw his shadow cast against the window, but Houdini didn't return to the window. It was only when the lamp went out and there was still no sign of the escapologist that he truly began to worry.

Wheatley glanced around nervously. He couldn't see the far side of the road, but he could see a black blur of shapes that appeared to be moving through the fog. He shivered. "Who's there?" he called out again, willing whoever it was to announce their presence, and dreading the thought that they would. The blurs were twisted and lumped—like the freaks that had been haunting his dreams.

Something shot out from the alleyway in a skitter of sound and flurry of movement. And even though he should have known that it was just one of the mewling cats, it set his heart racing.

He didn't laugh this time.

The creature ran close to his legs, brushing up against him as it flew down the street. Instinctively, Wheatley recoiled, and stepped back into the arms of one of the freaks. He recoiled, lurching away as the freak opened his mouth in a smile that was far too wide. Wheatley pushed himself free only to find another freak emerge from the fog, too close to him for comfort, and another, tongue lolling in his twisted mouth, a low ululating mewling sound gurgling in his throat that was far more feline than anything the fighting cats had managed; and another and another, the blurs taking on substance until he was surrounded by a crowd of freaks. He had never seen any of them before. In a town full of freaks these were the most afflicted, the most twisted and aberrant. They shuffled and dragged heavy limbs, circling him.

Wheatley panicked and pushed his way forward, shoving an emaciated woman—who appeared to have a fully grown child emerging from her stomach—out of the way, to open a break in the circle. He didn't look back. He ran blindly toward the steps and the boarding house's porch, and inside, looking for sanctuary with no hope of finding it anywhere in this godforsaken town.

He slammed the door behind him.

Breathing hard, he bounded up the stairs, taking them two and three at a time. He stumbled once, catching his shins on the riser, and winced at the sudden flare of pain, but didn't slow down and didn't look back.

The ground floor was still silent.

The only sound he could hear was the radio that was still

playing in one of the guest rooms, and his own heartbeat pounding wildly in his ears.

He made it to his room, yanking on the handle. The door was still locked.

"Let me in!" Wheatley shouted, rattling the handle.

There was no reply.

He risked a swift glance back down the hallway; if the freaks found their way into the boarding house he didn't want to be out in the hallway. But of course they knew what room he was in—they'd daubed the word Glaaki across his wall while he slept, hadn't they? It had to be them. Who else could it have been? The Servants of Glaaki? Maybe that was what they were, freakish servants of some old god? He shuddered and hammered on the door again, willing Houdini to open it. There was no reply.

"Harry! Damn it, Harry! Open the door!" Still nothing.

And now panic and frustration turned to concern. Why hadn't Houdini come back to the window? What were those shadows he'd seen, if not Harry's? He knew that he had to be inside, and short of being a narcoleptic, there was no way he could have fallen asleep in such a short time, no matter how exhausted he might be. Which meant something was wrong. Coupled with the freaks in the street, Wheatley began to panic. "Harry!" he shouted, hammering on the door. "Come on!"

No answer.

He pressed a shoulder against the door, leaning his weight against it to test the lock's resistance. The door was thick and heavy, and, unfortunately, the lock secure. He crouched down, peering through the keyhole. The key was still in place. He stood again, rocking back on his heels and bumping the door, but it showed no sign of giving. He stepped away from the door, threw his entire weight behind the shoulder barge, and at the third attempt hurt his shoulder. The door held firm.

Houdini was in there, and he was in trouble. There was no other explanation for the locked door and the silence.

Wheatley had to find another key to get in there, and quickly.

There were no freaks waiting as he ran down the stairs.

There was a difference between being afraid for your own safety and knowing that a friend was in trouble. You could run away if you were the one in danger, but abandoning a friend meant never being able to look in the mirror again. Wheatley had seen people on the battlefield who were so buttock-clenchingly terrified of going over the top and facing enemy fire they couldn't move, but did not so much as hesitate when a friend was hit and dying, no matter how much peril it put themselves in.

"Ma Mocata? Ma Mocata?" He hammered on her door. Even when she responded and he heard her moving he kept knocking, trying to hurry her up. "Ma Mocata!"

Her door was uncomfortably close to the front door, and through the glass panel he could see blurred figures standing in the fog out there; watching and waiting. He didn't know what they were waiting for—what they could be waiting for, apart from him?

"What's all this ruckus?" the old lady demanded, opening her door an inch. "Oh, it's *you*," she said with such an obvious air of disappointment, Wheatley wondered why she was so unhappy to see him. A paranoid little voice at the back of his brain whispered: *because she knows what's going on. She's part of it.*

"I need a key to my room, please," he begged.

"Now don't go telling me that you've gone and lost it. I don't want to have to be changing the locks, expensive things, lots of work, you know."

"No, no, nothing like that. My friend's inside. He's locked the door and I think he must have hurt himself; he's not answering. I'm worried about him."

It was a lie and it wasn't, but Ma Mocata didn't care, she just seemed even more annoyed than she would have been if he'd lost the key. "That's a single room occupancy—no guests."

"Oh, don't worry Ma Mocata." He tried to laugh but found it hard. "It's nothing like that." She'd quizzed him rather aggressively on his first night, demanding to know why an Englishman had come over to do a job when there must have been hundreds of men born and raised American who were more than capable of doing anything he could do. When he had said that he was over at the behest of a friend, and that friend was Harry Houdini, yes *the* Harry Houdini, her tone had changed. Suddenly she couldn't do enough to help make his stay comfortable.

"Is it Mr. Houdini?" she asked.

He was reluctant to confirm that it was in case she decided she had to be the one to run up and save the day, exposing Harry to his overzealous and self-proclaimed number one fan. But it would be the quickest way to get the key.

"Yes."

Like all of those battlefield heroes, she didn't hesitate. Ma Mocata disappeared for a moment, returning with a key clutched in her pudgy hand. She'd forced her feet into a pair of shoes instead of the slippers she had been wearing when she'd answered the door, and pulled on a housecoat.

"I don't really think he's up to visitors at the moment Ma Mocata. Perhaps I could get him to pop in when he leaves, if it's not too late? Maybe have a cup of tea with you?"

"Would he really? Do you think? With me? That would be wonderful. I've never met anyone famous before, you know. But if he's not feeling well, perhaps he should call tomorrow? I could bake a cake. Perhaps that's best? Do you think?"

"I think that sounds perfect. And I'll make sure that he brings a signed photograph for you, for all your help." He reached out for the key.

She took the hint and handed it to him, then clapped her hands in delight like a giddy schoolgirl. "Be sure not to lose it," she said. "That's the only copy I have. I really need to have it back."

"Of course. I'll bring it straight back down, you have my word." But she had already turned her back and headed back into her apartment, no doubt to prepare the list of the ingredients she would need.

The moment she closed he door, Wheatley gripped the key tightly in his fist and charged back up the stairs to his room.

"I'm back, Harry!" he shouted at the door, hoping Houdini was alert enough on the other side of the door to realize help was at hand.

The key would not fit into the lock.

He jammed it into the keyhole, but it wouldn't slide into place.

His first though was that Ma Mocata had given him the wrong key, but of course, his own key was still in the lock.

Cursing himself for an idiot, Wheatley managed to use the spare key to push the other key out of the mechanism with a few careful jiggles, so he could finally unlock the door.

Wheatley swung the door open. "Harry?"

The room was empty.

Chapter Twenty-Five

The police were not interested in anything he had to say. Wheatley had interrupted Ma Mocata's cake preparations to use her telephone. She fussed and bothered around him, but her concern wasn't for Houdini's safety, but the fact that she might be cheated out of meeting the great man.

The police claimed to have enough on their plates with the two murders without worrying about a grown man going missing, especially when he had only been gone for a few minutes. "What do you think we are? Nurse maids?" the voice on the other end of the line muttered, then the line went dead. He had almost forgotten about the second murder in the madness of their own enquiries over in Arkham. Were the two deaths connected to Harry's disappearance? They had to be, but aside from an overturned table and a broken glass—indicating a struggle had taken place—there was no evidence to connect the disparate events.

He had tried to impress upon the detective the nature of Houdini's disappearance, only to be told that they weren't about to waste time or fall for one of the man's great illusions like a bunch of country rubes. Wheatley had heard laughter in the background.

So that was that—no official help. No body, no crime. And no interest from the police.

Wheatley's only hope—and it was thin at best—was that Houdini had discovered something in the moments he was gone, and somehow found a way out of the room without needing to use the door. If there was a way in that the cultists had used to paint their threat on his wall while he slept, there had to be a way out Harry could have used, solving the riddle of the locked room mystery.

But he was damned if he could find it.

He went over every inch of the room, trying to locate a draught, a change in structural integrity of the walls, a floorboard the shifted differently under his weight, anything.

Nothing.

It was fruitless and frustrating.

By the time he finally gave up the search it was too late to go anywhere else. The prospect of sleeping in the room didn't appeal to him, but he didn't exactly have a choice in the matter, unless he wanted to brave the freaks in the fog and try to get to Houdini's car.

The fog had thinned little.

He could see as far as the opposite side of the road.

The car waited. And would carry on waiting. He wouldn't discover the secrets of the room by driving somewhere else. He would have to sit it out, wait, listen, and hope that the proverbial lightning would strike twice. He sank down into the chair and stared at the damned name still daubed on his wall.

Glaaki.

He'd cleaned up the broken glass, but the room still stank of whisky. The fumes hung heavy in the air. Such a waste of good whisky. He wished that he had another glass to help steady his nerves, but short of getting down on his hands and knees and sucking at the carpet, that wasn't going to happen.

For an hour he didn't leave the chair.

For the hour after that he paced the room trying to find any kind of clue as to how Houdini could have left the room.

He considered the possibility that it had not been a struggle at all, but rather Houdini had stood on the table to reach something, some trigger mechanism that would spring open some hidden door, and it had toppled over.

He clambered up onto the table, balance precarious at best, but still couldn't see anything that might so much as hint as to how anyone could get in and out of the room other than through the door.

He didn't dare get into the bed.

He was dead on his feet, which meant deep sleep would inevitably follow, and deep sleep meant leaving himself vulnerable to the cultists behind the walls and the freaks of Dunwich. Instead he settled back down into the chair with the oil lamp turned down so low it managed only the dimmest of lights. The chair was uncomfortable enough that he couldn't sleep.

He had a lot of thinking to do, and the last place he had seen Houdini was as good a place as any to do it.

Wheatley's thoughts made little sense.

No matter how eagerly he chased the threads of mystery around in his head, pulling at them every way imaginable, he could find no solution.

The door couldn't have been locked from the outside with his key still in the lock—he had already proved to himself, discounting that possibility. That could only mean that there was some secret way in and out of his room that eluded discovery. He'd checked every inch, opened every cupboard and door, lifted the rugs in search of a loose floorboard, pushed and prodded in search of a trigger, moved ornamentation, adjusted those creepy oil paintings on the walls, anything and everything, but there was nothing.

The faces of the freaks he had seen in the street replaced the puzzle, one fusing into another until they were all the same to him.

They circled him while he stood in the middle, turning the opposite way, always the opposite way, turning, turning. They chanted that word over and over and over again: *Glaaki, Glaaki, Glaaki*. The chant grew faster and faster, becoming ever more urgent until it became a constant stream of sound.

As he turned he became part of the circle, his mouth opening and closing over and over until his voice joined the song.

He was becoming one of them.

There was nothing he could do about it.

He couldn't fight it.

But in the next instant he was more than that. So much more than that.

He flew through the skies with only stars for company.

No longer a man, but more than a man. Everywhere, all around him, within and without, he could here that name, *Glaaki, Glaaki, Glaaki*. His name. They were calling to him.

He was all, he was everything.

He was an eater of worlds and he was hungry.

The taste of expectation was ash in his mouth.

Then the blackness was liquid.

He gasped and choked for breath but no matter how desperately he tried there was no air…but he wasn't drowning… He could breath underwater, but this was not his body, this was a young naked girl at home in the dark water. He tried to swim, but hit a solid surface. He could go no further, despite the siren song of a light on the other side beckoning him.

He pressed himself up against the surface and saw a face on the other side. The face of a giant looking in at him. He recoiled, slipping back into the inky blackness. Even as he did, he realized that it had been his own face looming close… but that was impossible. This was his home. Here in the inky darkness. He was the thing that lived in the glass jar.

There was no telling the edges between what was real and what was dream, what was memory and what was his mind still trying to draw the threads of mystery together even as he slept fitfully.

The voices existed both in sleep and wakefulness.

They spoke in unison. *Glaaki, Glaaki, Glaaki.*

He opened his eyes. The oil lamp had burned out.

Something moved within the darkness of his room.

Chapter Twenty-Six

Dawn brought with it the same all-pervading greyness. The slight thinning of the fog last night was a temporary thing. Once again it was as dense as it had been at any time since Dennis Wheatley had debarked from *The Dunwich Ghost*. He felt awful; like spikes had been hammered into his eyes by perverse elves who snuck in in the middle of the night intent not on cobbling shoes but tap, tap, tapping six inch nails into his brain. He'd succumbed to sleep, eventually, but not rest. He woke groggily, searching the room still half-asleep. As far as he could tell there was nothing to suggest that anyone had been in the room, but that part of the dream had been so *real*. It was hard to know where the dream ended and waking began. Harder still to know what he could trust in this crazy town.

But he had exhausted everything he could learn from the room.

He knew that there was a room of some description on the other side of the wall, but no possible means of access.

In the madness of his fitful sleep he'd even considered clambering along gutters and drainpipes like Harold Lloyd to work his way around the side of the building, just to see if he could reach the window. He'd dismissed the idea in the fuggy light of day when a quick look outside confirmed there were no handholds. The one man who could have made the traverse was of course the one man who wasn't there to make it, Houdini.

Still he couldn't shake the feeling that there had been someone in the darkness of the room with him.

He could not afford to spend another day in the room just waiting.

He had to do something.

Wheatley made a decision. The best thing he could do was leave a note in case Houdini should return, telling him to stay put as he would return later in the day, then left his key with Ma Mocata along with strict instructions to let him have the key to his room if his friend returned. Of course, she'd been delighted to oblige, insisting that she would make sure to save him a slice of her cake.

Wheatley didn't envy Houdini—in fact he began to wonder if, just maybe, he'd be better off if he'd been spirited away. He certainly didn't trust Ma Mocata. There was something not quite right about her and her building. She couldn't curate the place and remain oblivious to what happened within its four walls, even if she was not part of it.

He took Houdini's car. It was larger than anything he had driven before but that was nothing compared to getting his brain accustomed to driving on the right, or rather the wrong, side of the road.

The town wasn't so large that he couldn't find his way to Monk's house, and the film set was impossible to miss, though he wasn't sure if he was ready to head back there yet. The idea of willingly heading back toward the freaks made his flesh creep. Each time he came into contact with one of them he felt more uncomfortable. So, Monk's house it was.

He doubted very much that Monk was even aware that Houdini was missing. He really didn't like to be the bearer of bad news, but Monk needed to know. It was just courtesy. But part of Wheatley hoped Houdini might have contacted the filmmaker. It was his only other point of contact for him in Dunwich. And even if he hadn't heard from Houdini, that didn't mean others hadn't made their presence known, including their cadaverous white-faced stalker from Arkham.

Sane or not, Monk was an ally. He had precious few of those.

He knocked on the door of the small house, then stepped back from it for a moment, looking up at the upstairs windows in case Monk was in the bedroom. He'd spent enough time around Monk to know he was more than a little paranoid. He expected to see him peering out from behind a twitching curtain. But, equally wouldn't have been surprised if Monk just covered his head with blankets at the sound of his knock and pretended the rest of the world didn't exist.

"Ulysses!" he called. No response. He rapped on the door again, this time harder. Still nothing.

The curtains in the downstairs window were open, but there was no sign of any life inside that he could see when he pressed his face up against the glass. He tried tapping on the glass, too.

Eventually he heard the sound of footsteps on the stairs.

He returned to the front door and waited for it to open.

A dark shadow appeared at the front room window and then was gone. He only caught a glimpse of it in his peripheral vision. A moment later the door opened a fraction of an inch. Rather than finding Monk on the other side, it was his assistant—he'd forgotten her name—who had responded to the knocking. She'd obviously moved in in Houdini's absence.

"Yes?" she said, like he was something the cat had dragged in. "What do you want?"

"I was hoping to talk to Ulysses, to Mr. Monk."

"I know who he is. And you can't. He's sleeping. You upset him last time you were here, you and Mr. Houdini."

"I need to talk to him. There have been developments. I've got news for him about Mr. Houdini. He needs to know."

"Then tell me and I'll make sure that he gets the message."

Wheatley shook his head. He'd been about to tell her, then noticed her tug at her sleeve cuff, hiding that tattoo, and realized that she, out of all the people in and around the film, was one he could not trust. "I need to tell him myself."

She started to try and close the door, but he forced his foot into the opening.

Above him he heard the sound of a window sliding open.

Wheatley stepped back, sacrificing his hold on the door for the opportunity to talk directly to Monk, who stood at the window. The man was a wreck. He looked wretched, washed out, his skin waxen and drawn back too tightly against his face and cheekbones, and his eyes had sunk deep into his head. He looked like death warmed over.

"Leave me alone," Monk called down. "Just go. I don't want you here."

"I need to talk to you about Harry," Wheatley said. "Please. Let me in."

"No keep away. Go. I don't want to talk to you. I don't want to talk to anyone. Leave me alone. GO!" He covered his ears with his hands like a stubborn child. He backed away from the window, moving out of sight.

Wheatley kept calling his name, but knew it was a pointless exercise. The filmmaker wasn't going to return to the window.

"What have you done to him?" he demanded, rounding on the woman who still stood in the doorway.

"Me? How dare you. This is all *your* doing," she said, turning it back on him. "Until your meddling yesterday he was starting to feel better, but then you did this to him. It's all your fault!" Her voice had spiraled to a near-scream by the time she slammed the door.

It all added to the confusion that was raging inside Wheatley's head. He had no more idea if this woman was with them or against them. She seemed to care about Monk's wellbeing, but *why*? What was her motivation? She had the sign of Glaaki on her wrist, marking her out as one of them, a Servant of Glaaki. Or more correctly one of *his*, she belonged to the crazy dead god that they worshiped. What did Glaaki want with Monk?

He backed away from the door, feeling more alone than ever.

What to do?

Who to trust?

Where to go?

Home?

It really was tempting.

Dejected and beaten, he walked back to Houdini's car.

He missed the man. Badly. He was frightened for him, too. More than he cared to admit.

He headed back into Dunwich.

Driving was a constant battle with the fog. It seemed to take on a writhing, creeping, insidious life of its own, moving the world around behind its shroud so that it never felt as though he was moving forward. More than once he could have sworn he saw landmarks he had already driven by. But eventually he reached the town limits, the now familiar skyline slowly beginning to emerge from the fog. He had no idea what he should do—even could do—but he knew where he was going: Diamond's.

Which was all well and good in theory, except for the fact that Joe Diamond's office above the feed store was locked. There was no sign of life. Stymied, Wheatley scribbled a note on a page from his pocket notebook and slid it under the door. The message was simple: *I need to talk to you, I'm staying at Ma Mocata's Boarding House. Urgent. Dennis Wheatley.*

He saw a spotty-faced youth shifting sacks in the feed store, but when questioned, the boy claimed not to have seen or heard Diamond that morning. "Sure," he said. "That's not unusual, though, Joe's a late riser. Keeps antisocial hours. Comes and goes as he pretty much pleases when he's on a case. Some days he doesn't even come in to the office."

"Do you have an address for him?"

"Nah, sorry. No idea where he lives. Out of town somewhere, I think. The boss'd probably know, given that he rents Joe the office, but before you ask, the boss ain't in either."

"Not my lucky day, is it?"

Some days were like that—he was Sisyphus rolling that bloody boulder up the hill. Today was one of those days. He knew he could spend the rest of the day driving around chasing Diamond's shadow and getting nowhere fast. He tried to think like Houdini, make a puzzle of it to be solved. He assumed this was pretty much par for the course with Diamond's job. Lots of waiting, no real progress, and nothing to show for days on end wasted staking out errant husbands who refused to stray at the convenient moment, or business partners who were just as uncooperative and refused to hit their cohorts over the back of the head with a statue and make off with the loot when he was looking. But Diamond had his ways, surely? Experience? He knew how people ticked—or at least he knew the darkness in their souls, didn't he? When you were rooting around in the trash of humanity you needed a man like that on your team. So he had to find Diamond. It was as simple as that.

He checked in with Ma Mocata, but her main complaint was that Houdini hadn't arrived yet and her cake was going to spoil if he didn't turn up soon. That was the least of Wheatley's worries, though.

He reached the only conclusion that made any reasonable sense; Houdini was being held somewhere. And that meant Wheatley was going to have to rescue him. He wasn't a hero. The idea of riding to anyone's rescue was almost comic, and certainly fanciful, but it appealed to his vanity.

And it was better than the alternative; that Houdini was already dead.

Thinking about that something else began to prey on his mind. He'd stubbornly tried to ignore it, but ever since the notion had first wormed its way into his brain it had refused to go away. Had Houdini been taken in his place? Had the cultists grabbed him thinking they were taking Wheatley? After all, they'd snatched him from his room, and he was the one who had been marked up by the sign of Glaaki above his bed… It made a sickening kind of sense. He couldn't help feel responsible—if it had been him…if they'd thought they were taking him… Houdini could be dead because of him. Save a man's life, you become responsible for his future according to some cultures, but what if you cost a man his life? What were you responsible for then? Wheatley shivered, and thought, *Someone just walked over my grave.*

He crossed himself.

He took the stairs much slower than he had the night before. He wasn't rushing to Houdini's aid this time. His friend wouldn't be there. The first landing was silent apart from the background noise from the radio playing behind one of the closed doors. But there was no sign of any of the freaks emerging from their rooms.

He paused for a moment and thought about the thing he had seen in Mrs. Whateley's room. Had his dream revealed the truth? Could the thing that floated in the water be the daughter they were looking for? Surely that was madness. Wasn't it?

He reached his own room.

He paused for a moment before putting the key into the lock, pressing an ear to the wood, praying that there wouldn't be any surprises waiting on the other side and dreading the fact that the silence could mean he would open it to see Houdini's mutilated body spread-eagled on the bed.

He was coming to think there was nothing more frightening than simply opening a door—the fact that anything imaginable could be on the other side. And in this place, anything unimaginable, too.

Gritting his teeth, he opened the door.

There was no horror waiting on the other side, but his heart beat a little too fast for comfort just the same. The room was exactly as he'd left it. Silent. No. Not exactly the same, he realized, seeing a folded piece of paper on the carpet. It had been pushed beneath his door.

He closed the door and locked it behind him before picking it up.

Locking the door was second nature now, but it didn't put his mind at rest. These people—whoever they really were—could get in and out freely regardless of whether the door was locked or not.

He unfolded the paper.

The message was handwritten, but not in a hand he recognized. Meaning not from Houdini—whose handwriting he knew almost as well as his own now after their long correspondence. The message was simple: "*Be at the old jetty on Spring Glen at midnight if you want to see your friend alive again.*"

Chapter Twenty-Seven

Houdini was still alive.

That was his first thought reading the threat.

And it was a threat, he was sure of that.

But the message was still a flicker of light in the fog.

There was a second level to it, too. It meant that he was safe for the time being, didn't it?

Not that he could say the same thing come midnight in the middle of nowhere. Out there he'd be vulnerable. Was that why they were trying to lure him out there? Even if it was, could he afford to ignore their summons?

The lack of real sleep over the last couple of nights had left him bone-tired, and with half the day still to while away he decided to give in to the call of the bed. But first he consulted the map he'd found in Houdini's car, making sure he knew the route up to the lake known locally as Spring Glen. Then he stretched out on the bed and was asleep before his head hit the pillow.

He woke refreshed to hunger gnawing in his belly and the sound of someone tapping at his door.

Tapping, not knocking.

The room was in near darkness. The chink in the curtains

seemed to emit a weird white glow from the fog, almost as if it burned a light all of its own. Wheatley clambered groggily out of bed and crossed over to the door.

The tapping came again.

He unlocked the door and opened to see Ma Mocata carrying a tray of coffee, sandwiches with the crusts cut off, and a slice of the cake she had clearly baked for Houdini.

"I thought you might be hungry," she said, offering him the tray. She made no attempt to cross the threshold, though she did try to peer beyond him, checking that he was alone. "No sign of Mr. Houdini then?" Her disappointment was palpable.

"I'm afraid not," Wheatley replied. He didn't mention the note or his midnight meeting. There was nothing to be gained by it if she was a part of the conspiracy, and no benefit in dragging the old woman into the mess if she was not.

"Well, let me know if he turns up. There's plenty of cake left." She winked, again causing him to doubt how she could be part of any grand conspiracy. She was just a friendly old woman; a grandmother for all of her transient guests.

She headed back along the hallway without looking back at him.

Wheatley watched her walk away. He noticed that once again a pair of shoes had replaced her usual slippers. She'd obviously hoped to find Houdini in the room, which, if anything, was another indicator of her innocence in all of this.

But it didn't mean she wasn't turning a blind eye to things.

The whole thing was turning him into a paranoid wreck.

He looked at the clock on the wall above the dressing table. He still had a couple of hours to kill before he set off for the lake. He scarfed down Ma Mocata's feast, then dressed warmly, with double layers to keep out the cold night.

* * *

It was barely eleven o'clock when he set off for Spring Glen, which gave him an hour to make the rendezvous.

It was the only stretch of open water between the town and

the sea. Walking along the approach road, Wheatley realized it had to be the place Houdini and the murdered technician—he couldn't recall his name, Edward? Eric?—had planned on filming the underwater scenes.

It was also the only logical source for the green pondweed they had discovered in the dead woman's trailer and in Monk's office after his episode. It occurred to him he hadn't asked *where* the film technician had been murdered. Was it out here at the lake? Scouting the location? Back in the studio? In the tank they planned to use for the controlled underwater scenes? Somewhere else entirely?

And then there was the Lake House...on the side of the water...where Catherine Beddows had likely arranged to meet someone. She had probably believed that she was meeting Monk according to the business card—not a million miles from the jetty he was heading for.

Everything screamed trap.

He'd taken Houdini's car as far as the film set, knowing that left a long walk along a bridal path Houdini had pointed out vaguely when he had first been taken to meet the filmmaker. The car would have only attracted attention; its engine wasn't silent, its lights barely cut through the fog, and he had no idea of how far along the track the car would have got him, or how easy it could be to turn it around. The only thing that prevented him from wandering off the path was the crunch of gravel underfoot. Without it he could have ended up anywhere.

He had the map in his coat pocket, not that it would help in the dark fog, but it offered some sort of comfort, like he was in control when he clearly wasn't. If he wandered off the track he wouldn't find the lake until long after midnight, if at all. This wasn't exactly God's Own Country.

Not for the first time he wished he was back in England; in a city with lights that made it possible to see your way even in the thickest fog; in a place where it was easier to know what he needed to be afraid of because life made sense and wasn't filled with the madness of old dead gods and murderous freaks.

The gravel was reassuring under his feet.

He pulled the collar of his coat up and thrust his hands deep into his pockets.

As he strode deeper and deeper into the fog the sound of the gravel crunching underfoot created an echo behind him. It was disorientating. After less than a couple of minutes of walking he began to doubt his own hearing, convinced that instead of it being an echo, someone was following him.

He stopped, listening, but every time he did, the world fell silent.

He tried to peer through the fog behind him but there was nothing to see.

There was no point in worrying about anyone following him; he had been invited, they knew he was coming, there was no way he couldn't. Not if he wanted to see Houdini alive. It didn't matter if they were following him; they were waiting for him, which amounted to the same thing.

He kept walking until at last he saw the dim glow of lights through the fog up ahead.

He had expected the fog to be much thicker out here away from the town center, but it seemed that the lake water was somehow keeping it at bay. The air was clear and the moonlight shone through like an oasis in the desert.

People were gathered at the water's edge.

He saw a series of fires burning. The flames threw fitful shadows and tongues of light across the entire scene; it wasn't as though day was transformed into night, but there was no mistaking the line of the path as it wended its way down to the water, or the people down there, including the unmistakable whiter than white skin of Mrs. Whateley.

The bridal path cut through the hillside. There were grassy banks on both sides, and a few trees lining them. They created pockets of shadow. He stepped into one of them, watching.

If Houdini was down there, he wanted to be able to do something—but he hadn't really thought it through beyond getting here. He didn't have a pistol. He didn't think they'd be frightened off by him running down the hillside brandishing a big stick over his head, either. But he couldn't leave him behind. He knew that. He'd just have to improvise. Whatever that meant.

He dropped down to a crouch, watching them as they

danced on the shale and listening to the drum beat rhythm of their chant, *Glaaki, Glaaki Glaaki*, and even if he couldn't hear the word, he could feel it in his chest; each time it sounded was like a punch in the solar plexus.

Wheatley saw the albino Mrs. Whateley clutching the damned bell jar close to her chest with one hand.

There were others around, though—freaks he didn't recognize. As far as he could see not one of them had been on Monk's list. That in itself was curious. Why would the freaks come here if not for the film?

Before he could ponder the implications of that further, the motley gathering of figures on the water's edge slowly formed a circle—just as they had in his dream, he realized, a sickening sense of dread sinking into the pit of his stomach.

They were circling around something, but he could not tell what.

He moved closer, moving from his shadowy spot to another deeper shadow beside the lightning-scarred remains of a blackened tree. He crouched low. He could see more from here, but almost wished he couldn't.

A stake had been driven into the ground and there was a figure tied to it.

Despite the hood over the man's head, it could only be Houdini. And he was at the mercy of them all.

He had no choice but to go and challenge them, to run screaming down the hillside, and hope to God some kind of plan hit him on the way down.

Wheatley rose unsteadily to his feet. He really didn't want to run. It could have been Ypres or Passchendaele or any number of battlefields, going over the top, certain death waiting down there. He breathed deeply, struggling to calm himself. He would have killed for a gun. Just for the weight of it in his hands. It wasn't as if he could shoot every last one of the revelers down there. The odds were stacked against him. If it came to violence he would lose. But what else could he do? They'd summoned him. If they wanted to string him up, they'd have a fight on their hands, but it was a fight he couldn't win. He might as well just walk down the hill, calling Harry's name. Stealth was redundant.

Before he could take a single step, a gloved hand clasped tightly over his mouth. He started to struggle but was pulled to the ground.

"Don't move," a voice rasped in his ear. "Don't scream. Don't say a single word."

Chapter Twenty-Eight

Wheatley panicked.

The smell of leather smothered his face. He couldn't breathe. He lashed out, thrashing in his assailant's iron grip. A wild swing caught the man on the side of the head, but it wasn't enough to break his grip. Wheatley bucked, kicking out, the red mist of fear clouding everything. He reached up, clawing at his attacker's face, only to realize that it was the private detective, Joe Diamond. Even so it took a moment more for Wheatley to stop struggling.

Diamond gave a soft *shhhh* and removed his hand from Wheatley's mouth.

"You followed me?" Wheatley accused, when he'd finally got his breath back. So he hadn't been hearing things out there in the mist, someone had been walking behind him?

The detective shook his head. "No," he spoke in an urgent whisper. "I was here waiting for you...or at least for someone...but I *hoped* that it'd be you or Houdini. I didn't know which of you was going to be on the stake down there." He nodded toward the water's edge where Houdini was motionless against the stake. "Then I found your note, and knew that it wasn't you that was being held in the old Lake House."

Dennis hadn't even noticed the ruins of a house nestling on the hillside. He'd been preoccupied with the stake and the fires on the waterfront and the freaks down there, but seeing it looming over the scene like some great grey shadowy ghost sent a chill through him.

"I've been doing a little digging about this *Glaaki* of yours," Diamond said. "Like I said back at the office, I deal in facts not make believe, *but* these people, his servants, they're not to be crossed. That's a fact."

"I'd noticed," Wheatley said dryly.

"I came across something else—now's probably not the time to dump it on you, but forewarned is forearmed and all that. The police have marked you as the prime suspect in their investigations, pal. Something about an associate of yours back in Blighty, Eric Tombe?"

Wheatley's heart sank. He should have known it'd follow him here. There was no escaping it, it seemed.

He nodded. "Thanks." And then after a moment he said, "Aren't you going to ask if I did it?"

Diamond shook his head. "This stuff started before you landed. I've checked you out, trust me. I want to know who I'm getting into bed with."

"Good. Well, from what I can tell, Glaaki seems to be some dead god—don't ask me, I don't claim to understand it all, but your man read something from his book of the dead and explained how some of these Old Ones like Glaaki still have fervent cult followings."

"Which is more than I got."

"There's more, but the main resource, some rare ancient book dedicated to the Servants of Glaaki, was missing."

"Stolen?" Diamond said.

Wheatley nodded.

"Well, well, well. All roads point to cultists and sacrifice, then?" Diamond's eyes darted toward the shadowy shape of Houdini in the distance as he said the word sacrifice. "One thing I've noticed is people become very tight-lipped at the mention of Glaaki's name. I know people. They're frightened. Every single person I spoke to recognized it. Every single person. But no one would say much. I don't blame them. These guys have some seriously weird ideas. From what I *could* gather, it seems that in their religion, this Glaaki is supposed to have arrived here from outer space? I mean, seriously." Diamond shook his head.

"That's what Armitage told us. That and the fact that Glaaki has made his home deep underwater."

"Oh, not just any water, pal," said Diamond pointing toward the lake without spelling it out.

Wheatley had reached the same conclusion. Even if he couldn't quite rationalize the idea that a traveler from outer space could fall to earth and live submerged in a lake, he absolutely could understand and accept the notion of belief and just how powerful a thing that could be. If people believed, truly *believed*, they were more than capable of doing extreme things in the name of a god. It didn't matter what that god was called, how many arms he or she had, or anything else, people would queue up to commit atrocities in their name.

Wheatley shuddered at the thought.

"And you know what they are planning to do to your friend?"

"Bait to draw me down here. That's why they left me a note to be here by midnight. He's not the sacrifice, I am." Wheatley couldn't believe that he had spoken those words out loud, but he'd been thinking them ever since he'd found the note. "They marked me out, daubing their god's name on the wall above my bed while I slept."

"He's the sacrifice," Diamond said.

"It has to be me. They sent me a note to be here before midnight. Why else would they do that?"

"They want you here as a witness. They think something is going to rise out of the water and drag Houdini down to join the hungry god in the watery depths."

"And you believe that?"

"Not a chance, buddy, but remember what I said about facts—they *do* believe it and that's what we have to worry about."

"But what will they do when nothing comes out of the water? Will they just let him go?"

"Wishful thinking. They'll make sure something comes

out of the water, even if it's just one of them dressed up. The Grand High Poobah has a fancy sacrificial knife fashioned from bone and flint, and knowing religious nuts intimately, they'll be itching to use it."

"Then we have to do something. We should call the police."

"Already have. They weren't interested."

"Not interested?" Wheatley couldn't believe his ears. "How can they say that?" It was one thing not being concerned when Houdini had only been missing for a few hours, but this? When the weight of evidence said his life was in danger, when the specific location was identified, surely they should have come running?

"Honestly, you. They thought it was a stunt to build interest for his new shows, seems he's due to do a few appearances in September and October and he's never been one to shy away from the spotlight to sell tickets and enhance the mystery around him. But now they've found out about your troubles back home, they think you're behind it, somehow. You ask me, that detective's not an idiot, though. He's sharp. So that makes me start thinking and asking myself questions. There are a lot of people who know about what is going on in Dunwich, but do nothing about it. They keep quiet because it's easier, because it's safer. That detective, Martin, he knows exactly what he's dealing with. Why else would he want to place the blame on outsiders so quickly?"

That seemed to make sense. They couldn't rely on the law. Wheatley would have rather believed the officers were incompetent—that fit with his impression of policemen from back home—but they weren't. Martin and Ropes might not have been Holmes and Watson, but they were a long way short of being idiots.

He looked up at the moon as though it could tell him how close to midnight it was. "Any ideas how two men can rescue someone from a horde of insane cultists?" he asked.

The private dick produced a revolver from his coat pocket. The gun gave Wheatley a feeling of reassurance as long as he didn't think about the mathematics of it. The revolver fired six shots. There were a lot more than six people down there, so even if he didn't miss, he'd run out of ammo long before he ran out of targets to shoot at. But at least he'd come prepared.

"We're going to have to play this cool. If we go wading in there—especially if they haven't performed their ritual—we're going to run afoul of the angry mob. We can't take 'em all on. Not the two of us with six bullets," Diamond said, echoing Wheatley's fears. "This thing's all about the threat. I don't shoot until someone starts shooting at me. I'm not some wise guy looking to start a small war."

Moonlight shone through the isolated patch where the fog had parted. He guessed it was approaching midnight because the intensity of the chanting down by the lakeside was growing louder.

They moved closer, scurrying along the edge of the path without leaving the safety of the shadows. Houdini didn't seem to be in immediate danger—but it was all levels of degrees. Danger had changed from some intangible threat to there was no knife pressed at his jugular just now.

The people down on the banks of the lake seemed oblivious to the two men; they were lost in the chant, cavorting around the staked man in the center of their ring.

Through the fog, Wheatley heard the dull sound of a bell tolling. He couldn't tell where it was coming from. It couldn't have been from the town, as he hadn't heard it on previous nights. The bell had to be related to the ritual. He looked up at the ruins of the Lake House to see if it had a bell tower. The tolling sent a low moaning echo across the water.

The circle stopped turning.

Diamond dug his elbow sharply into Wheatley's ribs and pointed out into the center of the lake.

Wheatley couldn't be sure…but…were those ripples?

They were.

Forming ever-increasing circles as they rippled toward the shore.

"There's something moving in there," Diamond said needlessly. He shifted his position, keeping his revolver at the ready.

The circle parted to allow a white-robed figure to shuffle forward. It was a cruelly twisted freak whose lumpen face looked almost demonic in the moonlight. He reached up with a clawed hand and pulled the sack from Houdini's head.

Even from his hiding place, Wheatley could see the bruises where the escapologist had been beaten.

The freak shed his robes, standing naked before them.

Wheatley recognized him instantly; him and his cruel affliction.

It was the elephant man-freak they'd visited in the boarding house. Wheatley hadn't suspected the man in the slightest. Worse, he'd *liked* him. He'd admired his courage in the face of such a challenging hand dealt by life. He'd pitied him because of what it meant to be him. But not once had he thought that he was part of this conspiracy of worshippers.

The man's body appeared to be almost bent double, but as the bell tolled out its second strike he began to rise, straightening and stretching out his gnarled bones. The air suddenly split with the hideous sound of skin tearing as it could stretch no more, and the thing inside it became too big for the sac that contained it.

Blood, muscle, bone, and sinew became exposed. Flesh fell away. And with each chime of the bell he *grew*.

Became a *man*.

But there was more than that.

More than just what it meant to be a human held inside a prison of flesh too small to contain it. There was something *strange* that had no business being beneath skin and bone, something that had more to do with the sea than the land.

Something truly monstrous.

Indescribable.

The overlarge skull split and fell away; it was akin to witnessing a shell being shattered and cast aside by a pearl diver.

The *thing* approached Houdini.

Houdini turned his face away, clearly unwilling to face the horror moving toward him.

Wheatley couldn't move.

He couldn't look away.

The sight of the freak's true nature was hideous and revolting. Truly grotesque in a way that defied imagining.

As the creature closed in on Houdini, Wheatley and Diamond were spared the true horror of its countenance, the creature turning its back to them. That was enough. It was a shiny black carapace that glistened beneath a mucous membrane. Wheatley felt a wave of nausea swell inside him. He looked away from the freak.

A second robed figure came up behind Houdini, freeing him from the ties that bound him to the post, though his hands were still bound behind his back.

The creature grasped him and half-lifted half-dragged him the short distance to the water's edge.

Houdini didn't seem to fight it.

Wheatley watched, horrified and helpless. "We have to do something! We have to stop that...that...*thing*!"

The bell sounded for the last time.

The water at the center of the lake stopped rippling. Bubbles began to surge and foam as the water appeared to boil.

"There's nothing we can do," Diamond said flatly. "It's too late for that. We can't help him. He's as good as dead. We couldn't even get down to the water before they fed him to that...*thing*."

"But we can't just stand here and do *nothing*!" Wheatley rasped. "Shoot it! Six shots. Shoot it."

"From here? I'd never hit it. Hell, I'd be more likely to hit Houdini from this distance. He's as good as dead. Sorry. But I don't intend to go the same way. I'm rather partial to my skin."

Wheatley slumped down against the lightning-blasted tree; this was it, defeat. He felt empty. A hollow man. He'd failed his friend more thoroughly, more completely, than he had ever failed anyone in his life.

He couldn't look as Harry Houdini disappeared beneath the surface of the lake. There was no great escape for him this time. Wheatley wanted to scream. He wanted to yell at the sky and curse the gods. All of them. The ones he'd heard of and the ones he hadn't. Diamond was saying something but he couldn't hear him. His world was reduced to two things: grief and fog.

Chapter Twenty-Nine

"I'm sorry," Wheatley said, barely loud enough for Diamond to hear. The detective probably assumed he was apologizing to Houdini, but he wasn't. "I can't just sit here. I can't let this happen."

The surface of the lake began to calm itself. In a moment it looked as though the creature had never been there, had never drawn Houdini down into the depths.

"If you're not going to come with me, then give me your gun." Wheatley held out a hand.

Diamond didn't hand it over.

"Will you be quiet!" Diamond whispered, pulling him back down to the ground. Wheatley tried to see what had got the private dick so worked up. It took him a moment: someone had burst out of the trees near the Lake House and was racing headlong toward the freaks gathered at the water's edge. Dressed all in black, the white of the man's skin seemed to glow in contrast.

"*Take me! Take me!*" the man screamed, his accent unlike anything Wheatley had heard before. He charged down the bank, and splashed into the water, fighting the freaks off as they tried to stop him. He was unmistakable: his gaunt, cadaverous features, his haunted pallor, his hairless skull. It was the man they had chased through the grounds of Miskatonic University in Arkham. The man who had lurked outside Monk's window as he lost his mind. The man they'd originally suspected of being Glaaki.

And now he was here.

"Do you know him?" Diamond asked.

Wheatley nodded. "Sort of."

"I've never seen anyone quite like him," Diamond said. "And I've lived in a town where freaks have come and gone all my life, but this guy is something else."

"That he is."

"But he doesn't seem to belong to this crowd. Look at him."

Diamond was right. As freakish as he appeared, he wasn't one of them. He wasn't twisted in the same way. His soul wasn't blackened.

These freaks had just killed Houdini. They'd have no hesitation in doing the same to him and Diamond if they found them there.

The freaks splashed into the water after the cadaverous man and clawed at him, dragging him back up to the shore even as his screams tore into the night. "We have to get out of here," Diamond insisted, pulling Wheatley toward the bridal path and the waiting car.

Leaving meant admitting he'd failed Houdini.

But leaving also meant that he could be avenged.

Chapter Thirty

It was as though Diamond could see in the dark.

His sense of direction, even in the fog, was unerring.

The private dick moved urgently along the bridal path, encouraging Wheatley to run. They didn't have time to stumble around. The freaks would be out in force looking for them. It was gone midnight and they knew he was here, even if they didn't know Diamond was out there with him.

"We should have done something," Wheatley said. He felt lost. It was overwhelming. Shock. "Anything. Instead we just sat and watched like a couple of cowards skulking in the shadows ready to get away."

"Snap out of it," Diamond said. "Unless you want me to slap you senseless?"

The detective's car was parked just off the track in the gateway to a field, closer than Houdini's car, which he'd abandoned at the film set. Wheatley had no idea how he had managed to walk so close to Diamond's car on his way down to the lake without seeing it, even with it being dark and thick with fog.

Wheatley cast one last look back toward the lake; it wasn't there for him to see, the fog had swallowed it every bit as completely as it had taken Houdini.

"Get in the goddam car," Diamond snapped. "Now!" In an instant he was behind the wheel and firing up the engine. Anyone within a few hundred yard radius would know they were out there, but the fog was their friend now. "This is real life. You want to be a hero, great. You need to stay alive to be a hero. So get in the damned car!" Wheatley clambered in beside him and slammed the door. "Look, hate me all you like, this isn't war. You aren't fighting for a cause. This is staying alive. Simple as that. Good guys don't always win. They don't even get a glorious damned death or leave a good-looking corpse. Sometimes it just flat out stinks."

Wheatley said nothing.

The car lurched forward, the sudden movement pushing Wheatley into the leather seat before jerking him forward again as Diamond grated through the gears. The tires spat mud and gravel into the wheel arch, sounding like rapid gunshots as Diamond floored the accelerator.

They sped away.

Diamond took their lives in his hands; he didn't slow down, didn't deviate, just pointed the car down what he hoped was the middle of the road and left Wheatley praying there wasn't a sudden bend in the lane up ahead.

"You came here in Houdini's car, right?" Diamond asked as they reached the end of the lane and started to skirt the film set, the lights of the abandoned car still shining. "Leave it. With luck they'll think you're still out there and waste time looking for you."

"Right."

"Next logical place to look for you is the boarding house, so that's out. Anything they associate with the film is out. That leaves my office. It may lack creature comforts but it's safe. Or safer, at least."

"Right," Wheatley said again.

Diamond slowed the car as they approached the town limits again. Even so, it felt too fast, especially as the buildings began to close in around them. There was no one on the streets. A quick glance at his watch told him it was almost one o'clock.

Diamond pulled the car to a halt alongside the feed store. The windows were dark. He led the way around the back, and up the iron rungs of the fire escape. Diamond fished out a set of keys—there were more keys on the key ring than any one man should need in a lifetime—and after a furtive look around, opened the door and led the way inside.

Wheatley didn't follow him. He waited outside while Diamond closed the blinds and turned on the banker's lamp on his desk. He motioned for Wheatley to come in and close the door behind him. Wheatley took the client chair—it was a battered old leather thing that had been rescued from the trash by the looks of it, very much in keeping with Diamond's seedy down-at-heel persona. Diamond uncorked his whisky bottle and poured the pair of them a healthy measure. Wheatley knocked it back in one and held the glass out again. It was only after knocking back the third that he realized how badly he was shaking.

"I'm not trying to frighten you, Denny, but any way you look at it, you're not safe here," Diamond said. "You need to hustle your ass out of here, get on one of those big swanky liners, and head home as soon as you can." Wheatley shook his head, but Diamond was like a dog with a bone. "This is a dangerous place, pal. You don't want to leave it too late to get out."

"It's already too late."

"The enemy's not at the door. We can get to the docks. It ain't over yet."

"Not what I mean. I can't go now. Not with Harry... Someone has to take this to the police...make them do something."

"The police? The only reason Martin and Ropes'll want to see you is to clap you in chains and throw you in the slammer. You're Public Enemy Number One right now, Denny boy, right up there with the likes of Lucky Luciano and the Five Points Gang. They're looking for a scapegoat, and you've got form thanks to that loser back in England and the guy who went overboard on your way here."

"So they just want to close the case rather than find out what's actually happening? Who's actually committing the murders?"

"Welcome to America, pal."

Wheatley felt sick. He looked at his empty glass, regretting the last drink and stared out into space.

"They are afraid what they might uncover," Diamond said. "They know this place. They know what happens 'round here.

They just wanna get out of Dunwich and Arkham, Innsmouth and the territories, and back to the Big Apple before they lose their minds. They ain't the first, they ain't the last. This place takes its toll. Better men than Martin and Ropes have gone the way of the dodo, Denny boy."

"You've met them?"

"Oh yeah, I had a little visit the other day. Verney's grieving husband let them know that I'd been doing a little digging on his behalf. Or to put it another way, the S.O.B. was only too happy to point the finger in my direction. Anything to take the heat off himself. And the long arm of the law was only too happy to try to put me in the frame—unlucky for them I was being threatened down at police headquarters for sticking my nose into something else they didn't like when her murder went down. Hard to argue with an alibi like that." He smirked. "Hoisted on their own petard."

"I can't believe they weren't interested in Harry's disappearance."

"Of course they weren't. Look at it from their point of view. Right now they're dealing with the murder of a pretty young actress. It won't take much for them to pin it on Collins. He fits the jealous husband role to a tee. Sending a private dick to spy on his wife when she was out with a known adulterer in Taylor Andrews? He's painted a big old target on his back. Doesn't matter to them that I didn't find any evidence that old Taylor was dipping the wick with his latest leading lady; as far as they're concerned I didn't find anything that proved she wasn't, either. Monk was in the frame for the murders, too, and he's gone missing, which isn't helping his innocence. They've got a nice neat case here; why would they want to muddy the waters by throwing in the disappearance of the world's greatest entertainer and draw every reporter in Christendom to their door?"

It made sense, of course, but that didn't mean he liked it.

"Monk's holed up in his house with his secretary," said Wheatley.

"He's not coming forward to make himself available to the police, is he? In their world that means he's got something to hide." The private detective sounded as if he was speaking from experience.

"He's not right in the head."

"I've seen some of his cast—tell me something I don't know."

"Something has spooked him."

"*Something*. You mean something like we saw tonight?" Diamond poured Wheatley a fourth drink, but was more generous with his own measure.

"Who knows? He's not talking. Last coherent thing I heard him say was—" Wheatley stopped himself. He had been about to say the dead god's name. But that wasn't right. Monk had shown them the reel with Catherine Beddows in the water, her mouth moving over and over again, the film silent but obviously shaping the name Glaaki. "I thought he was starting to get his head together...but when I went to see him this morning...it was like he'd suffered some kind of relapse."

"Any idea why?"

"Honestly? I don't trust the woman, his assistant. The first time we saw her I caught a glimpse of a tattoo on her wrist... It's the same mark we've found associated with Glaaki. I think she's one of them." Diamond listened intently, but said nothing while Wheatley related the story of the encounter, the missing manuscript, and everything else from the face at the window to the reel of film Monk had shown them from Beddows's screen test. He was trusting Diamond with everything he knew because there was no one else to trust and he couldn't do this alone.

"If the Servants of Glaaki knew I was here, they'd go through you to get to me, wouldn't they?" Wheatley said slowly.

Diamond took another slug of whisky and nodded. "Without a second thought."

Which meant they'd need to keep their wits about them—and four slugs of whisky was anything but wise. Too late to worry about that now.

"And if you weren't here, they wouldn't be interested in me."

"So being around me makes you a target," Wheatley realized.

"Yup, paints a big bull's eye on my back. You should leave. But not because of me. I can handle myself. But if I were you, I'd get out."

"But you're not me."

"Nope, and I know you've got this stupid idea about doing something heroic. Don't do it."

"If this place is so toxic why don't you leave?"

"Where would I go? Everything I have is here; this is where I belong. But you don't. Go back to England, to your friends and family. Face the law. If you're innocent like you say, this Tombe thing'll blow over. It's where you belong."

"What about Harry? He deserves justice."

"I'll kick up a stink about it. Martin and Ropes aren't going to like it, but I can be a real pain in the ass."

"I don't doubt it for a minute," Wheatley said.

Diamond grinned. "If they mess up, that will be their careers down the shitter, and if they so much as look like they are not up to the job, then other officers will be parachuted over their heads. The reinforcements will want reinforcements. Houdini's big news. High profile. Even so, without proof, without the body, then as far as they are concerned he's a Missing Person and that just propagates the mystery of The Great Houdini and keeps people entertained for years to come. They can live with that, because that's not their problem."

"You don't seem to have a lot of faith in the police."

"If they did their job properly I wouldn't have one, put it that way. I suppose I should be grateful. But there's one thing you get to learn doing this job, in this town, and that's trust no one. Not even your nearest and dearest."

"Hence the bachelor life?" Wheatley suggested, doing his own deduction. It wasn't difficult to tell Diamond was a lone wolf. No woman worth her salt would have put up with his hours, and his low-rent lifestyle.

"Put it this way, Denny boy, there are people in this town who have learned to keep their mouths shut and there are those who haven't. Unfortunately for most of us, it ain't as though they wear a sign around their necks to say which is which. Trust no one. That's my motto, and it's the best advice I can give you whether you are here or back home in England."

"Surely you can't think that their reach extends over there?" Wheatley said, suddenly frightened that he'd never be free of the horrors of the last few days.

"Who knows, pal? I've never even left the States, but I wouldn't want to bet my life on it. Trust no one."

Second Intermission

My body is no longer my own.

I know at last that the pain I have endured all my life has been worth every moment, every excruciating joyous moment of agony, it has all been part of the Plan. It has all shaped me into this, into what I have become, what I was always destined to be.

And now that I have given myself, an empty vessel for Him to use, other pleasures are mine. Pleasures the likes of which I could only dream of.

Here.

Under.

The.

Surface.

Here.

In.

The.

Dark.

Here.

In.

The.

Cold.

Here.

In.

The.

Great.

Emptiness.

Here.

In His place, only the blessed are welcome.

Here.

I am home.

In the citadel that He built deep beneath the water everything exists to demonstrate His glory.

I can breathe the water now. He has changed me. I no longer need the air. I could not have dreamed this place. Here is Everything. Here Everything has meaning.

This is His home. My home.

The stars brought to Earth a vastness crammed into a small place.

And in the heart of it He waited in the deep. For me. He slumbered in his labyrinth beneath spires grown out of the bedrock.

And all I feel is His hunger.

My hunger.

His hunger for me. My hunger for Him.

It is a gnawing that aches in my belly and scrapes and claws and tears trying to find its way out of me. Insatiable.

Slowly I am transformed again.

The muscles and organs of my earthly body shift and change beneath our skin until they are all consumed by this hunger.

I am just a hollow shell.

At last my skin splits. It cannot hold the liquid remains of my insides. The black oozes, drifting through the water around me. Ink. Blood. The last vestiges of me—the old me—drift away like manta rays in the deep. All that remains is me. The newly formed carapace that shines black and hard.

I am His messenger.

People will fear my presence.

Feature Presentation

Reel Three

Chapter Thirty-One

"Tell me how Houdini disappeared. All the details. Don't leave anything out. Anything you can remember might be important." Diamond said, tipping the bottle over his glass to ring just a few more drops from it.

"I've already told you once," Wheatley said, unable to hide his exasperation. "There's no point in going over it again. It won't change the facts."

"No, it won't, but it might make you *remember* something. The mind's like that. Things you think you remember, things you think you don't…they're all in there. The answer's inside you."

"You sound like some demented yogi, you do realize that, right?"

Despite his protestations, Wheatley repeated everything again, beginning at the beginning, from that first time they entered his room, Houdini taking a look outside and along the corridor, him being sent outside to look up at the building to confirm the escapologist's suspicions, the strange light in the window that shouldn't have been there if his was the last room, thinking he saw Houdini's shadow, the man not returning to the window to summon him, going back to his room only to find it locked from the inside and having to borrow the key from Ma Mocata. It was the same no matter how many times he told it.

There wasn't a single thing that was added or taken away from each new telling.

"We need a look inside the room beneath yours."

"We've already been inside."

The bottle slipped from Diamond's hands, catching the edge of the desk with a *thump*. Wheatley's hand snaked out and grabbed it before it spun to the ground. "Why didn't you tell me that before?"

"You didn't ask," Wheatley said, defensively.

"Tell me everything."

"There's a woman staying there. She's on her own. Her daughter's supposed to be with her, but the only thing in that room apart from her is a glass bell jar full of a dark liquid."

"The albino woman?"

Wheatley nodded. "Mrs. Whateley."

Diamond didn't seem interested in the jar, or what might be inside it. Wheatley was glad. He didn't want to have to explain why he thought it might contain the woman's daughter.

"The room. Describe it. In relation to yours—the same?"

"Larger."

Diamond nodded. "Confirming the hidden room then."

Wheatley nodded.

"We didn't get to spend long in there. We were interrupted."

"Interrupted?"

"We weren't exactly invited in. Mrs. Whateley returned from the bathroom about a minute after we let ourselves in."

"Breaking and entering was it?"

"The door was open, so there was no breaking involved."

"Okay, anything else? Anything strike you as odd. Wrong?"

"The room was larger than mine, like I said, but thinking about it, it still wasn't as big as it ought to be, not if it runs the length of the building."

Diamond leaned forward. "Now we're getting interesting, Denny boy. A secret room at the end of hers, too? Or maybe a stair linking them? That'd explain how they spirited Houdini away."

He thought about it for a moment or two, then remembered a detail that right up until that moment he'd dismissed as irrelevant. Maybe it wasn't, after all.

"There was a door into what I assumed was a walk-in closet in the corner of the room."

"Same side of the room as your hollow wall?"

Wheatley nodded.

"Bathroom?"

"One on each landing on the opposite side of the corridor to my room. The layout is same on the floor below."

"There you have it, then." Diamond rocked backwards and forward in his chair. "We need to get back into that room," he said. "That door's the answer. I'd bet my life on it. There's a staircase up to the secret room beside yours. It's a one-way wall—opens up from the inside. That's how they got Houdini out of there, and how they crept up on him. It's the only thing that makes sense."

It did make sense.

A one-way mechanism would certainly explain why he hadn't found it when he'd tossed his room.

He thought of the mystery stories he had read to pass away the hours during his post-war convalescence. "When is a locked room mystery not a locked room mystery?" he said.

"When there's a door that hasn't been found yet." Diamond said, raising his glass to his lips in satisfaction despite the fact that it was long since empty.

Chapter Thirty-Two

Diamond offered to drive him the short distance back to the boarding house, but Wheatley insisted on walking—not that he actually wanted to walk. It was all about visibility. The last thing he wanted was for Diamond to be seen with him, increasing the chances of the locals realizing they were connected.

He was the one at risk. He could cope with that.

He didn't want to drag the private detective any deeper into the mire than he already was.

And it was all a question of risks. He didn't believe they would attack him in the street; that didn't seem to be their style. If it had been he wouldn't have been able to walk in and out of his room with impunity. So he made the relatively short walk from the office above the feed store, clattering down the rusty old fire escape into the back alley. The fog was thicker than it had been a few hours ago, which gave him plenty of cover as he walked out onto the main street. It was so thick he couldn't see the signs above the shops or the storefront window displays.

There were cars parked on the side of the road, but they were few and far between. Dunwich wasn't a thriving metropolis; it was a small town, with that unmistakable small town everybody-knows-you're-a-stranger vibe. Wheatley stuffed his hands into his pockets and walked, head down, fast. His footsteps filled the fog. The effect was disorienting. He imagined getting lost in the fog, never finding his way out of it. It was cloying. Overwhelming. He could taste it at the back of his mouth as he breathed. The world was reduced to the tips of his hands; anything beyond that didn't exist.

He could hear things out in the mist.

But couldn't trust his senses.

Slithering.

Whispering.

Sighing.

He walked faster.

He heard footsteps. They could have been his own.

He heard voices.

One word, a susurrus sliding through the oppressive white: *Glaaki*.

Or was it in his head?

He couldn't trust his senses. It was as though the fog had robbed him of more than just his sight. At one point he realized he was walking down the middle of the road—not that there was any traffic. Only Houdini was mad enough to try and drive in this. Thinking about Harry only made him sad. He tried not to, but how could he not? Houdini was a force of nature, a larger than life character, and suddenly, he wasn't there and the world was a lesser place without him.

Wheatley realized he was crying; not deep, raking sobs, just slow, silent tears running down his cheeks, like it could have been the wind stinging his eyes. He wiped them away.

He turned the corner and saw the vague silhouette of Ma Mocata's Boarding House on the other side of the street. It was a grim, oppressive thing looming out of the mist.

The only light burning—apart from a dull glow just inside the front door—was a flickering flame in the window of the secret room.

He crossed himself.

That light had two effects: it diminished the threat of the fog and reminded him what the real danger was. The fog held no fear in itself; it was all about what it harbored and he couldn't believe there were worse horrors lurking within it than hid in plain sight.

The freaks.

They weren't what they seemed.

What had Monk said that first time they'd discussed his movie? Children of the gods? He shivered now, recalling the filmmaker's words. He'd seen the unholy thing beneath that freak's skin. Even if he didn't have words to name it for what it truly was...it was becoming more and more difficult to think of them as anything but monsters.

He shivered, wrapping his arms around his chest and holding himself tight.

He was going to find out where that damn door opened in his room if it killed him.

And he was going to find it before they came looking for him again. His life depended upon it. He needed to be on the front foot.

That meant going through the front door.

One step at a time.

He climbed the stairs in near darkness, pausing every third or fourth step to listen for any sounds of life. The place felt eerily empty. The seemingly ever-present radio played softly in the background. It was too quiet to disturb anyone who was sleeping—if anyone slept in this house of the damned.

Diamond had lent him a handgun.

Even though he'd sworn never to fire one again, it felt comforting in his pocket. It was funny how a lump of metal could infuse a man with a false sense of courage.

He amended his hope—now it was simply never to have to fire at another living soul. And soul was beginning to take on a fairly liberal definition of the word.

The hallway either side of his door was in silence. He could *feel* the presence of someone behind the walls, hiding in the secret room. It was like a weight laid upon the silence. He stood stock still, listening for the slightest sound. Nothing. He crept on a few steps beyond his door and pressed his ear against the wall. He couldn't hear anyone in there, so he went back to his door and slipped his key into the lock.

He opened the door.

Fear was something best dealt with by coming face to face with it.

There was no sound, nothing to indicate that there was anyone inside. *Here goes nothing*, he thought and stepped from one black space into another.

Wheatley struck a match, one spark lighting the blackness just long enough for him to find the oil lamp. He wished—and not for the first time—that the rooms were equipped with electricity; even a small town like this should have it piped into every home and business by now. It was increasingly difficult to live without the stuff, but isolated backwaters like this could be in the metaphorical, and literal, dark for years to come.

Once lit, the lamp gave off a gentle lambent glow of both light and warmth that penetrated the darkness rather than banishing it.

He slipped off his coat and looked around the room for any indication that he'd received visitors while he had been out. Nothing cried out to him, but he guessed that whoever it was that had been coming in and out during the nights had been down by the lake with the others. As far as he knew they could still be there, carrying out whatever weird ritual they believed would summon their god.

He couldn't believe he'd dismissed them as a group of deluded souls practicing mumbo jumbo; not dangerous, just mad.

What he had seen down by the lake had put paid to that. They might well be mad, but more than that, they were dangerous. And that wasn't even taking into account that they might be right. Wheatley didn't want to think about the implications of what he'd witnessed, but he couldn't help it. What if everything they believed was true? What if there was a cosmos of alien gods, and one of their number had fallen to earth? What if his own belief was flawed? What if the miracles of Christianity were parsed through the incredible power of alien deities and nothing to do with Father, Son, or Holy Ghost?

He shook his head.

That way lay madness.

The thing he had seen was no demon called to the outré, no goat-headed devil summoned from the depths of Hell.

It was a strange creature, that much was certain, an impossible one, he would have thought but for the evidence of his own eyes. But there had to be an explanation for its existence however bizarre, and perhaps that really was that it came from beyond the stars?

He took the tumbler and pressed it against the wall once more. He wanted to be sure no one was waiting on the other side. He couldn't hear anything. Even in this smallest of spaces the whole building seemed to be eerily quiet. In fact the only noise in the entire place seemed to be from from that solitary radio playing to one of the guests who was obviously unable to sleep. There was comfort in noise. It kept the influence of that *other* at bay—like bad things couldn't happen if Louis Armstrong or Bessie Smith could keep the devil away.

Wheatley ran his fingers over the wall, feeling every inch of the flower-patterned wallpaper. He worked systematically, feeling for the slightest change in the surface texture. Nothing. Not the slenderest crack. Not the shallowest declivity. Not the most meager bump.

But the door *had* to be there. It had to be in this wall. The freaks had come through the wall and taken Houdini. He was sure of it. There had to be a way through the wall, even if the main door was down in Mrs. Whateley's room directly beneath his. There had to be because the freaks had crept in under the cover of night to daub Glaaki's name on his wall, and all the reasoning in the world couldn't change that fact. They hadn't turned the key in his door, they'd come in through some hidden door, so it had to be there.

He found a stub of a candlestick in one of the sconces fixed to the dressing table. A thin layer of dust around the top suggested that it was quite some time since it had last been lit. Part of the brass fixture lifted out freely, giving Wheatley a slender iron spike to use as a handle. He lit the stub and carried it back to the wall, holding the flame close to it in the hopes that the naked flame would flicker, betraying the slightest breeze. Any such flicker would mean a crack. And a crack would mean he'd found the door. He was rather proud of his own ingenuity. He worked his way slowly around the very edges of the wall, all the way up to the ceiling and down to the carpet. The candle failed to flicker even once.

Although he had been reluctant to do it in the dead of night, he started softly tapping on the wall with his ear pressed to it, just as Houdini had done. He listened for any change in the sound his taps produced, hoping that the change in solidity of the sounds would reveal a change in the fabric of the wall. There were slight changes in tone, but nothing that made him believe he'd found anything substantive.

Like it or not, he was going to have to get into Mrs. Whateley's room downstairs if he wanted to get into the hidden room.

He stood for a moment with his cheek and one palm flat on the wall. Beneath his skin he could feel a change as the wall began to vibrate.

Chapter Thirty-Three

Heart racing, Wheatley pinched out the candle between finger and thumb.

The last ember hissed against his moist skin and died.

He moved quickly to the other side of the room and extinguished the oil lamp, plunging the room into absolute darkness.

He reached out for the key in the lock, fumbling for it in the dark. He wanted the door open if he had to leave in a hurry. Some instinct was waking up inside him, making him remember what it meant to survive; it turned him into a soldier once more. He remembered the gun Diamond had given him.

The pistol was still in his coat, which he had thrown onto the chair at the other side of the room. Retrieving it would mean putting the bed between him and the door. If the wall opened before he could cross the room he'd be caught in no man's land. If it opened before he could return, it would mean he'd be forced to fight, not flee. There was no way of knowing what was on the other side of that wall. No way of knowing if a bullet could even stop it, no matter how much more comfortable he would have felt with the gun in his hand.

His eyes began to adjust to the limited amount of moonlight creeping into the room. It was filtered by the fog; so much so that only the vaguest of outlines were visible, and the change of light was disorientating. For a moment the dimensions of the room seemed to shift, as though the room was somehow longer on one side than the other. It was an optical illusion that created shadows where there had not previously been any.

A faint glowing line appeared in one corner of the room.

It ran from the floor to the ceiling.

Wheatley found himself holding his breath, knowing he was about to see how the mechanism of the secret room operated. He almost smiled, realizing that the flaw had been in looking for a door in the wall; the entire wall was pivoting back. The whole thing was one giant doorway.

The thin light grew incrementally, becoming a single glow that seemed to move toward him—a lantern? He couldn't see what was behind the light. But *something* was.

One of the freaks? That weird Whateley woman with her damned bell jar clutched to her breast? Monk's assistant with her sleeves pulled back on the sign of Glaaki on her wrist? The *thing* that had dragged Houdini to his death in the lake?

No. None of those.

A ghost.

Standing in front of him, glowing in the light of the lantern in its hand.

Wheatley started at the apparition, trying to wrap his mind around its existence.

A visitation?

He stared at the ghost.

The ghost spoke his name.

"By God, Wheatley," it said. "You're a sight for sore eyes."

Chapter Thirty-Four

Harry!" He had to stop himself from charging across the room to embrace the escapologist—and that was exactly what the man was, at his core, he'd even escaped death. Wheatley was shaking as he grasped Houdini's hand. "I thought...I thought...that thing had *killed* you!"

"Rumors of my death have been at least slightly exaggerated it seems," Houdini said, bastardizing the words of Mark Twain. "Though, I must admit it wasn't as easy to wriggle away from them as I'd hoped."

"What happened? We saw you get dragged into the lake... We thought you were done for." Wheatley lit the gas lamp to light the room, keen to see his friend's face while he learned what had happened to him.

"We?" Houdini asked.

"Joe Diamond. He was there. He stopped me from charging in to try to save you."

"Ah, I knew I liked the fellow; he's a smart man. I'm so glad he did, Dennis. As fine a specimen as you are, I doubt your lungs would have been up to the task. As it was, I had to master my breathing for almost four whole minutes—an impossibility for most men, and longer than I've ever managed before! Remind me to thank Diamond for saving you from yourself. But, I assumed you knew I was still alive. You left my car for me?"

"What is it you say, 'Things aren't always as they appear'? Heh, we abandoned the car up by the studio, hoping the freaks would assume I was still out there and not come looking for me."

"A happy coincidence then."

"Very much so. You have to tell me everything," Wheatley said. "What happened to you? How did you get away? How did you get here?"

"All in good time, Dennis," Houdini laughed. "I promise. I'll fill you in on all the little twists and turns of my great adventure. But first, do you think I could borrow some dry clothes?" He held up his arms and Wheatley saw the way the material clung to him, and the puddle that had begun to form on the carpet by his feet.

"Of course."

The suit that Wheatley lent Houdini was far from a perfect fit, but it had the distinct advantage of having not been at the bottom of a lake in the last few hours. Even if the pondweed clinging to his wet suit could be removed, it was almost certainly beyond redemption.

"Better?"

"Much," said Houdini. "Well, we've got a few hours till sunrise, so why don't I try to fill you in on what happened?"

Wheatley perched himself on the edge of the bed beside his friend. "I couldn't sleep now if I wanted to," Wheatley agreed.

"Okay, from the top. I locked the door behind you and went across to the window to watch for you to appear in the street when something entered the room behind me. I caught sight of its reflection in the glass, but just a little too late to make much difference. They came in through the false wall." He indicated the wall which was still on its pivot. "Before I could react, I was chloroformed, which, let me tell you, is not a particularly pleasant experience. When I came round I was tied up in a chair. The knots weren't particularly challenging, but the old guy pointing a shotgun at me discouraged me from trying to slip them."

"I can imagine," Wheatley said. "Where were you?"

"Downstairs."

"Mrs. Whateley's room?"

Houdini nodded. "She didn't grace me with her presence, though. I heard you causing a commotion. I'm guessing you had trouble getting into the room?"

"Ma Mocata had a spare key. I traded an hour of your company sampling her moist Battenberg in exchange for it."

"Assuming that's not some quaint British euphemism, I'd say that's a small price to pay. I tried to make a noise, but all I managed to do was alert one of the freaks who tied my binding tighter until I could barely move."

Wheatley couldn't recall hearing anything unusual, but he had been more concerned about what had become of Houdini than any banging about downstairs, so it was quite possible he'd just been too preoccupied to hear it. "So what happened then?"

"One of the freaks stabbed me with a syringe. Whatever they gave me, it did the trick. The room started to spin. It didn't take long and I couldn't feel my legs, which is a most peculiar sensation, let me tell you. They moved me from here to an old house riddled with damp and decay. The place was falling apart."

"The Lake House," Wheatley guessed.

"Why do I know the name?"

"It was the address on the back of the business card."

"Right, the place where Catherine Beddows was lured to, probably on the understanding that she was to meet Monk. That makes sense. I'm not sure how long I was kept there—hours—and they kept up their incessant chanting the entire time. Interestingly, it wasn't just the one word this time."

"No?"

"They held pieces of paper like song sheets. I've had some time to think about it, and, if I were a gambling man I'd place my money on them being the pages of Monk's missing film script."

"Why would you think that?"

"Purely hypothetical, but the missing library book, plus Monk's assistant with her Glaaki tattoo, I wonder if she didn't feed him the pages, making sure he stumbled upon the ritual for his script even if he didn't realize what it was. What's more authentic than a genuine ritual?"

Wheatley couldn't deny the logic of that, but it was still a stretch.

"It was dark when I was taken outside—or at least I think it was—they'd put a hessian sack over my head. It reeked of hops. They fixed me to a post with handcuffs out by the water's edge, and started up with their chanting, that name, over and over again. *Glaaki, Glaaki, Glaaki.* If I never hear it again in my life, it'll be too soon. I heard this *click, click, click.*" He made a passable impression of claws clacking together. "And then the sack was removed, but I couldn't bear to look."

"We saw. Actually, it's difficult to explain *what* we saw. It had been a man. Something happened to him. He transmogrified into a black beetle *thing* with a hard slimy carapace and claws. We interviewed him. Daniel Mason. The chap with Proteus syndrome." Seeing Houdini's confusion he added, "The Elephant Man."

"Ah."

"We saw him change in front of our eyes." Wheatley wondered why he hadn't put two and two together before this moment. Proteus syndrome caused an overgrowth of skin, bones, muscles, fatty tissues, and blood and lymphatic vessels, but that wasn't the link to Glaaki's cult. Proteus was also the name of the Greek sea god who could change his shape.

"Quite an ugly brute now isn't he," he laughed.

"He wasn't exactly a head-turner before," Wheatley said.

It could have been denial, or Houdini really could have found a coping mechanism in humor, Wheatley wasn't sure it was really important which, but it was good that his friend did not appear to be suffering any obvious trauma after his ordeal. Actually, it seemed that he was in higher spirits than ever, but perhaps that was because he'd not only escaped the creatures but also won some kind of personal battle?

"They dragged me toward the lake. The closer I got, the more shapes I could make out in the water. There were things down there, under the surface; creatures that seemed to be half-man, half-fish. They had gills on the sides of their necks that opened and closed in a steady rhythm as they breathed. I don't know what they were. True Servants of Glaaki? Children of the god? They dragged me down into the lake. The beetle man followed us in. I lost sight of him under the water."

"We didn't see it again, so maybe it never resurfaced?"

"Who knows? The stuff down there under the water… I wouldn't be surprised."

"That's when I wanted to rush down, but Diamond stopped me, and before I could wriggle free of him that guy we saw at the University burst out of the undergrowth and charged down to the lake. While the freaks were tied up with trying to deal with him, we ran. Diamond didn't exactly give me a choice. I'm sorry."

"Don't be. He was right to get you out of there. It's all about survival, Dennis. We couldn't fight on if both of us were taken out of the picture. It was relatively easy to escape their bonds—even when the rope was secured somewhere deeper in the lake and it was dragging me deeper. I've been buried alive, I've escaped certain drowning nightly for almost four years doing that milk can stunt, I've been thrown into the Hudson in a nailed shut packing crate, I've survived the Chinese Water Torture cell, and I've escaped from straightjackets suspended from the dizzy heights of a crane constructing the New York Subway and the Library of Congress. This was nothing—in theory. The difference was it was real, not controlled. I had to get out. I had three minutes or so before I would have to breath. Three minutes isn't a long time to affect an escape. I saw lights down there. I could see faces in the lights. Dead people in the pondweed. I didn't really feel like joining them, but there was something about that luminescence. Like the lights were part of a living structure. I suspect that's where some of these creatures live."

"Diamond's been digging into the cult we're up against. One of their core beliefs is that Glaaki has made his home at the bottom of the lake."

"So maybe they're not stark raving mad after all. Put it this way, it's getting harder to believe that there's not a grain of truth in what they believe. They've probably been feeding whatever lives down there for generations; keeping its larder stocked up for whenever it gets peckish."

Wheatley shook his head. "Unbelievable. And they've been getting away with it?"

"Obviously. But, you know, that's how a lot of illusions work, too. The bigger the lie, sometimes the easier it is to pull it off. Think about it: look at what we've experienced in Dunwich. It's a small community. People don't say boo to a goose. Maybe that's because they're scared. They know what it means when someone goes missing. They don't want to ask questions because they don't want to be next."

"That's insane."

"No more insane than the alternatives. Imagine, in their place...what would you do to protect your own? Lure people in from other towns? If no one makes the connection to Dunwich, no one would come here looking for them. Meaning someone like Catherine Beddows, and yes, like you, Dennis, make the perfect sacrifice."

"People disappear all the time," Wheatley said, thinking aloud. "It's not always sinister—or doesn't appear to be. Some head for the bright lights of the city in the hope that they'll find streets paved with gold. Some run away to join the circus—" He stopped mid-thought. They looked at each other, making the same leap of logic. They had no evidence to support the idea, but it made a chilling kind of sense. "Darke's Carnival must attract all kinds of people looking to leave old lives behind. How many leave forwarding addresses?"

There was silence for a moment as each considered the implications. Then Wheatley asked, "What happened next?"

Houdini sighed before continuing. "Once they had secured me, the fish-men swam down toward the lights and left me. Slipping the cuffs was fairly straightforward, though getting the lock picks out of my pocket wasn't easy, given the circumstances. The cuffs were standard police issue, not even the newest sort, so there was no real obstacle there once I'd calmed myself. Indeed, the cuffs made me wonder if perhaps the long arm of the law isn't somehow complicit in all this—more so than just turning a blind eye. The hardest part of the escape was ignoring the dead floating around me. Their bodies were on anchor ropes just like me. I think I recognized at least one of them. The missing actress."

Wheatley swore under his breath. He'd been expecting the news ever since Houdini mentioned seeing bodies under the water, but confirmation was no less unsettling for being expected. "Why do you think that the bodies were like that?"

"As I said, basically they're using the lake as a meat locker. The water is decaying the flesh, but they're not rotting, not properly, and they're not hosting maggots and flies as they would left in the open air."

"So they're food for Glaaki, or his fish-men?"

Houdini nodded.

Wheatley couldn't quite believe how *accepting* he was of the notion. Only days ago he would have laughed off the idea as being some crazy deluded fantasy; now he was taking it in his stride as if it was perfectly ordinary and everyday.

"Out of the cuffs, you managed to slip away without too much difficulty?"

"I had to come up for air, of course, my lungs were on the point of exploding by then, but I managed to swim a reasonable distance before they did. It was a wonderful feeling, Dennis. Sincerely. It's so hard to explain, but I felt *alive*. I've not felt anything like it for such a long time." He could see Wheatley's doubt, so tried to explain. "So much of my work has become about showmanship—about faking tension and carrying off a smooth illusion. Every day I try to make things look so much more difficult, and dangerous, than they really are. I'll encourage the audience to hold their breath along with me when I'm doing a water escape because I know they can't hold it more than a minute at best, so when they gasp it's not just with amazement but fear. They're in my place, and in my place they couldn't do it. But this was real. This wasn't safe or controlled. It was do or die."

Wheatley nodded again. It made sense. But even so, it was strange to hear Houdini talking about what had happened to him as if it was just another stunt in which he risked his life.

Until a short while ago he'd thought his friend had been lost forever. He'd been wrestling with grief and self-doubt, and he'd been so bitterly angry at himself for not being able to save him—not even trying—and yet now he was listen to Houdini explain with some kind of perverse pleasure how he'd mastered the situation. He wanted to say something; to tell Houdini how he had felt being the one left behind, but now wasn't the time. Instead he listened intently to the rest of his story.

"When I came up for air, the first thing I saw was our hairless friend. He certainly had their attention. I dipped back under the water and swam some distance around the shore before I staggered out of the lake. No one was looking for me. Why would they be? I'd been staked out as an offering for their hungry god. I stumbled about like a blind man in that damned fog, of course. Did you notice how it curled back away from the lake? That gave me the creeps, I don't mind saying. Somehow I managed to find the track that led back to the film set without stumbling into any freaks, and was delighted to see you'd left my car there for me. Most considerate, I thought. Very typically English of you, to think about me like that. It would have been a long walk back for a man in a dripping wet suit weighed down by pondweed." He grinned at that.

Wheatley said nothing.

"Rather than risk drawing attention to my miraculous return from the dead, I parked on the outskirts of town and walked the last stretch. Plenty of people would recognize the car. I didn't want to risk anyone becoming suspicious. I got the worst of the weed off my suit as I drove, but fear I might have left a bit of a trail to begin with, before I realized what I was doing. There will have been some wet footprints from the lake to the car, some from the car to here, probably, couldn't be helped, and hopefully no one will see them."

"But why come creeping out of the wall like that? Why not just knock on the door?" Wheatley nodded toward the false wall that was still ajar. He'd heard as much as he needed to know about the great escape. Any more exploits and it'd start to sound like Houdini's latest, greatest, *Boy's Own* adventure story.

"The carpet," he indicated. "See how it's scuffed and worn down when you compare it to the other corners of the room?" Wheatley nodded. "Even before they drugged me and dragged me away, I'd worked out that the opening had to be through there. But it was only when I thought about it properly—about the dimensions of the room and how they related to the outer structure and the room below us. It struck me, they came and went with ease, but we couldn't locate so much as a draught. Why? Well, ask yourself this, why would they need to open the door from this side when there's a perfectly serviceable door downstairs? It was the last piece of the locked room puzzle to fall into place. I knew that the albino woman was at the lake with her cronies. I wanted to be sure I was right. It's a weakness of mine—I like to know I am right. Thankfully I didn't lose my picks in the lake, so getting into her room was easy. So, my friend, as you can see, it was no more than a trick."

"We came to the same conclusion—Diamond and I."

"I knew you would, sooner or later."

"So, what has been going on in there?" Wheatley pointed toward the secret panel.

"Best you come and see for yourself," Houdini said with a grin.

Chapter Thirty-Five

Houdini pushed himself up off the bed and picked up the lantern he'd brought in with him. He led the way into the secret room.

As it had been so hard to find a way in, Wheatley was now worried what perversities, what grotesqueries or madnesses he might find inside. What had the freaks so desperately wanted to keep so secret?

Wheatley grabbed the oil lamp and stepped through the crack in the wall, into the place where the constant chanting had emanated in the depths of the night.

The first thing he saw as he entered the room was the word *Glaaki* had been painted on the wall; not the single word that had been daubed on the other side of the wall in his bedroom. In here it had been painted on every possible space, over and over, in countless hands. Some of the painting was done in a vivid red that seemed barely dry, while some of the daubs were darker, almost brown and rusted. There were new entries and old ones; some so old that the paint or whatever had been used was dry and flaking from the walls.

The room was some kind of insane shrine, and it had

clearly been in use for a long time, if not since the building itself had been erected.

This was where they worshiped their god away from the lake. He couldn't find the words to express the way he felt seeing the writing, the mad scrawl of it all over every inch of the room, every surface. It was nothing short of insanity. The presence of the god's name was dizzying and claustrophobic.

"Quickly," Houdini whispered. "We don't want to be stuck in here when the freaks return."

He was right, Wheatley really didn't want that.

Houdini motioned down a flight of stairs—each step a bare floorboard seemingly built into the frame of the house—at the far end of the narrow room.

Dennis stumbled down them as quickly and quietly as he could.

Even so, each step groaned like the sighing and settling of the old house—but anyone who was aware of the hidden stair would have known exactly what the sound was.

Houdini came down behind him, close on his heels.

Below them, Wheatley heard the sound of someone entering Mrs. Whateley's room.

They stopped dead in their tracks.

Houdini pointed back up the way they'd come.

In little more than a heartbeat they were on the other side of the room and Houdini was pulling the wall back into place with his fingertips.

Wheatley couldn't see how he could possibly pull it completely closed as the sound of footsteps on the secret staircase grew closer.

When the wall was less than an inch from locking in place, Harry Houdini pulled his fingers away and drew two of his lock picks from a leather pouch in his pocket. He slid them through the gap, twisted them so they caught on the edge, and used them to hook around the plaster partition and pull it back into place.

It took him a second longer to free them, but the wall gave a reassuring *click* when it was in place.

Houdini fell back against it, grinning like the cat that had just had a particularly exciting adventure on its way to get the cream.

Wheatley prayed that whoever—*whatever*—was on the other side of the wall hadn't heard the click the mechanism made as it closed.

Chapter Thirty-Six

"We need to get out of here," said Houdini, slipping his lock picks back into their leather pouch, and that back into his pocket.

"Where?" It was getting light outside. Still foggy, but with that weird diffuse light that passed for daylight around here.

"This is all about the film, Dennis, everything is to do with the film. The two dead actresses, Edward, the dead technician, even the missing script pages with Monk's changes. Whatever that strange chant was, it was part of it. And then there's Monk himself. He's another casualty of this, but right now we're lucky, because unlike the others, he's still alive. And then there's the freaks. Mason, the guy who transmogrified—was that the word you used? Good word—into the beetle man, let's not forget that he was going to appear in the film. That was why he was on Monk's list and why we talked to him in the first place. There's only one man that can help us make any sense of this, and that's Ulysses Monk. But I doubt very much that he actually knows what is going on. Not all of it. But if we're lucky he'll have some of the core pieces we're missing and we can put it all together."

"I wouldn't hold out much hope. He wouldn't talk to me

when I went to his house. That assistant of his wouldn't let me near him. Something had scared the living daylights out of him again. I wanted to talk to him. I thought with you gone…he might know what I should do, but he didn't want to know."

"Well then, Dennis, we'll just have to make sure that we get him away from the delightful Tanith, won't we? Come along then, time and tide and all that. Let's go pay a visit to our erstwhile employer, shall we?"

Not only was the car parked on the very outskirts of town, it was parked in an alleyway out of sight from the main road, meaning they couldn't find it because, as they came to quickly discover, all of the streets looked distinctly similar in the fog. It took them an hour of walking from street to street before they found it.

The interior smelt of pondweed.

Strands of the stuff still hung from the clutch pedal.

"Sorry about the smell," Houdini said as Wheatley slid in and closed the door behind him. "But at least the leather's dried out," he joked.

They drove with the windows open, letting fresh air circulate through the car as they made their way through town. Not that it helped. The fog seemed to keep the odor wrapped inside. And it only seemed to worsen as the car warmed up.

Wheatley was glad when they pulled up outside of Monk's rented house because it meant he could breathe again.

Houdini craned his neck and pointed up at the bedroom window. A light was burning behind the drapes. "Looks like someone's up with the lark."

Wheatley wasn't surprised in the slightest. Monk had looked as though he hadn't slept for days when he'd seen him briefly yesterday—or was it the day before? He was beginning to lose track of how much time had passed. He wanted to blame the fog, one day looking and feeling exactly like the next, and the kind of lethargic depression that clung to it, but the truth was he was running on fumes himself.

But no matter how exhausted Monk had been, there'd been a manic edge to him that betrayed a mind incapable of sleep. Wheatley recognized the symptoms from the Great

War. There was far too much turning around inside his mind to allow him to find anything approaching rest. The best he could hope for was an absence of thought and quieting of the voices plaguing him relentlessly, demanding to be heard. The chances were that the light had been burning all night long.

While the light was unsurprising in itself, and the idea that Monk had worried away the night, awake, was almost expected, the fact that the front door stood open was neither.

"Wait," Houdini held out an arm to stop him. "I don't like the look of this." He said, easing the door open wider, so they could see inside the filmmaker's house.

Dennis followed him quickly inside.

They stood just inside the threshold. Houdini called out Monk's name. No answer. He called again. Wheatley pressed a finger to his lips, sure he'd heard something. A noise coming from deeper inside the place. It wasn't an answer. It was a whimper.

Houdini took two steps forward, moving toward the sound instinctively. Wheatley looked over the escapologist's shoulder. Something was wrong. In the semi-darkness he could see a man slumped at the bottom of the stairs, his throat and chest stained dark. Wheatley didn't need a light to know that it was blood. The whimpering came from deeper inside the house.

Houdini leapt forward, regardless of danger to himself, and rushed to the fallen man's side. Wheatley knew that there was no need for urgency. He had seen enough corpses to know when the last spark of life had bled away from a man.

"It's not Monk," Houdini said, the relief clear in his voice. "We need to find him."

"We don't have to look very far," Wheatley said, pointing to where he'd already seen the filmmaker, crouched in the darkness a few steps up the stairs from the corpse.

Monk rocked himself backwards and forwards, oblivious to their presence.

Houdini clambered over the corpse to get up the steps to reach his friend. Wheatley walked across to the middle of the lounge. The whimpering was louder. He turned, discovering the source of the sound; a figure standing in the shadows of the doorway to his left.

His first thought was that it was the woman, Monk's assistant, but he dismissed the notion immediately. The figure was too tall, too manly.

"Who's there?" Wheatley asked, startling Houdini, who was crouched over Monk protectively. He'd clearly been oblivious to the shadowy presence. He twisted to to see who Wheatley was talking to.

Wheatley felt his heart rate rise as the shadow moved, sure, suddenly, that it was one of the murderous freaks who had been standing in wait for them. Now he was about to peel away from the shadows and finish what the creatures of the lake had tried and failed to do.

The man stepped out of the shadows.

It wasn't one of the freaks.

But he was no less frightening for it.

Wheatley saw the cadaverous white-skinned man who had run into the arms of the freaks at the lakeside begging them to take him.

Chapter Thirty-Seven

Turn the switch by the door," Houdini said. "Now!"

Wheatley had forgotten that the house was equipped with electricity, unlike his room back at the boarding house.

The viewing machine that Monk had used to show them the film clip had needed power to operate it, which had obviously influenced his decision to rent this place rather than another more convenient for the film set. The electricity meant he could work well into the night if inspiration struck, review the day's rushes at his leisure, and, when he needed to, hide away from the rest of the world. It took a moment to find the switch, but then the room burst into light so bright it hurt his eyes. The cadaverous white-skinned man howled in pain and covered his eyes with his hands as though the light burned.

And that was when Wheatley realized he was as afraid of the light as Wheatley was of him.

"We should call the police," Wheatley said, knowing that meant getting past the strange man to reach the telephone, so that wouldn't happen. The man started for the door, shuffling forward with his hands still shielding his eyes as he attempted to push Wheatley to one side. The impact sent him staggering sideways, and as he tried to catch his balance, tumbling to the ground.

Wheatley dove forward, taking hold of the man's legs, fiercely determined not to let him escape even as the man lashed out, kicking and shrieking a weird ululating howl as he tried to wriggle free. Wheatley clung on to the man for grim death as he tried frantically to shuck free of his trousers if that could buy him his freedom.

"Help me hold him down," Wheatley gasped, as the man threatened to break free, but before he could, Houdini answered his call and was on top of him, pinning the man to the ground.

"Now, why don't you calm yourself down, my new friend?" Houdini said, calmly, smiling at the bald-haired monstrosity they'd pinned to the floor.

The man howled and spat.

They dragged him back into the room he'd been hiding in, and made sure that the door was closed behind them. They weren't about to give him the opportunity to run again.

While a flight was not an automatic admission of guilt, the moment they bundled him into a chair and turned the light on, and pulled his hands away from his eyes, Wheatley's opinion changed. Instead of suspecting the man was responsible for the corpse in the other room, he was convinced of his guilt.

Wheatley stared at the true horror of the man: at his long thin head with its sunken eyes set in deep harrowing sockets, at his ears which were a little too long, and his front teeth, yellowed and pointed, animalistic, and the blood smeared around his face. It stained the front of his clothes, too.

There was nothing innocent about the man. He was a very human monster, and that made him so much worse than the freaks out there in the fog.

"Watch him closely," Houdini instructed, leaving them for a moment to get Monk away from the body on the stairs.

Wheatley felt utterly alone.

"Dear God in heaven, what *are* you?" Wheatley muttered, unable to look away from the strange man as he cowered in the chair. The man looked...broken. He pulled up his knees to protect himself, assuming a fetal position. Wheatley knew the psychology of the move. It was defensive. He was protecting himself from an attack. Wheatley had no logical reason to be afraid of him, despite what he had done to the man in the hallway.

"Not what. Who," Houdini said, returning with Monk leaning against him for support. "I know him." Houdini helped Monk into a chair. Monk shuffled along, dragging his feet, barely functioning under his own steam. His body might be still working, but his mind had sealed itself off from the world.

Houdini crouched down to take a closer look at the frightened man, rocking back and forth in the chair. While he still looked utterly alien, the light and his fear banished anything otherworldly about him. He looked like a frightened child. "Now that I've got a good look at him, I know where I've seen him before. I didn't recognize him at Miskatonic University, but it's unmistakably him. An actor from Europe, somewhere, I believe. Not famous here. Not yet."

"An actor? So it was always about the film, just not in the way we feared," Wheatley posited. "We should call the police. Let them sort this one out. I'm sure that they'll be happy to find the victim and the murderer together in the same place. Nice and neat. Shouldn't be beyond even their powers of detection."

Houdini didn't move. He studied the man, ignoring Wheatley as he took matters into his own hands and moved toward the phone in the other room.

"I've seen him in a film," Houdini mused. "He looked like this... He was playing a vampire... What was his name?"

Wheatley held the earpiece to his ear and picked up the phone to talk into it. Before he could ask the operator to put him through to the police, Ulysses Monk screamed at him, "*Stop!*"

Chapter Thirty-Eight

All eyes turned to Monk.

Wheatley put the telephone receiver back into its cradle, cutting off the woman's tinny voice as she asked which number he required.

"Ulysses? Are you all right? What happened?"

"I've been better, Harry. But no police, please, not yet. At least not until I've told you everything. If you want to call them then, by all means."

Houdini nodded, but Wheatley was less easily convinced. "We've got a dead body in the other room."

"Let me tell you how that happened, please."

"If that's what you want," Wheatley said skeptically. "But it better be pretty damned good as far as explanations go. Well, first things first, do you know who this is?"

Monk looked at the gaunt man in the chair. His eyes had rolled up into the back of his head. Shock, he realized. "Of course," Monk said, like surely everyone should recognize the man. "That's Max. Max Schreck. He's a German actor. He's really quite remarkable, lives and breathes the roles."

"Of course," said Houdini. "*Nosferatu*! That was the film. How could I have forgotten? Staggering piece of work by F.W.

Murnau. A symphony of horror, they called it, didn't they?"

At the sound of his name and that single familiar word, the blood-smeared actor's eyes came back into focus and he sat forward in the chair. It was as though that word, *Nosferatu*, had brought him back to life. Perhaps it was the first word he had understood since coming to America?

"He barely understands a smattering of English," Monk said, seeming to read Wheatley's thoughts. "I brought him over here to work on the film with me. But…the poor man's head was turned inside out by that cursed film. He has lived as that character ever since he finished making *Nosferatu*."

"He believes that he is a vampire?" Houdini asked.

"And because of that he killed that man?" Wheatley asked, putting the pieces together. "He tore that fellow's throat out because he's convinced he needs to drink blood to stay alive?"

"Oh heavens no, he didn't kill Simon. It was one of the freaks who did that, not Max. Max stumbled in afterwards. He'd been trying to make contact but needed to be invited across the threshold."

"Simon?" Wheatley said, catching the dead man's name. "You know the dead man?"

"Of course," said Houdini. "I didn't recognize him." He moved his hand across his face. "The blood. He was a cameraman."

"Principal photography," Monk corrected, giving the man his proper position in the hierarchy of the film rather than simply saying what he did. "He's an old friend. We've been together every step of the way."

"If he," Wheatley pointed to Schreck, still talking about the man as if he wasn't there, "if he didn't kill Simon, then why is his face smeared with the dead man's blood?"

"He couldn't help himself," Monk said, sadly and simply. "There's a part of him inside that would never allow him to kill, just as there is in all of us, but drinking a dead man's blood must have proved irresistible. After all, he truly believes that he is a vampire—or more specifically he believes that he is *the* vampire, Dracula—and that he has drunk human blood for longer than he can remember. You have to understand that he is thirsty. He can't help it."

The very thought of it made Wheatley want to vomit. Even

if this man hadn't drawn the knife across the man's throat, he most certainly had defiled the corpse, and in such a disgusting manner. To fall back on some psychological nonsense about not being able to control his urges was bunk; the man was sick and he needed help—the kind of help offered by the doctors of Arkham Asylum. No amount of rest and recuperation was going to help cure him. He needed shock therapy to purge the delusion from his mind before his entire life was ruined by that lead role in *Nosferatu*.

And despite Wheatley's distaste for places like Bedlam, it was obvious it was a place of last resort for Schreck, and that it might offer his only hope of ever being himself again.

He should have pitied the man, but seeing him sitting there with the blood drying on his chin, it was difficult to.

"There's no need for the police to see him like this, is there?" Monk pleaded. "He's innocent, we can protect him. I'll tell them what happened to poor Simon, but can we keep Max out of it?"

Wheatley took another look at the man. He looked far more pitiful than he did threatening. It was obvious now that one of his elongated ears appeared to have become detached in the struggle. Wheatley could see the traces of stage makeup around it, and the dried glue that had held it in place. Just another illusion. If Monk said that the man was not involved—and Monk had no reason to lie—then they had to get him away before they called the police. His presence would make him a suspect, and his madness would surely find him arrested.

There was nothing they could do for Simon now, so delaying the call to the police would make little *real* difference.

"We have to get him out of here before the police come," Houdini agreed. "He's too convenient a suspect for them. And even if you deny it, they'll just say that you are protecting a friend. He's been lurking all over town, skulking around in the shadows, following people. It won't be too hard to pin all four murders on him. It's Arkham Asylum or we throw him to the wolves."

"Arkham," Monk said without the slightest hesitation.

Wheatley went upstairs in search of fresh clothing. They

couldn't very well take him to the asylum in his blood-stained clothes a few hours before reporting another murder. Even the Dunwich constabulary were not that dense.

While he was going through Monk's drawers, though, Wheatley found something he sincerely wished that he hadn't. A small metal box. It wasn't the box that disturbed him, though, it was what it contained.

By the time he made his way back downstairs, Houdini had made the call to the asylum, using his celebrity status again to ensure the patient got the best possible care.

They cleaned Schreck up as well as they could, which was only as well as he would allow them to, then bundled him into Houdini's car. They had argued about leaving the body of Simon Aron, the cameraman, alone, but Monk had convinced them that in all the time he'd been there, the only late night callers apart from his secretary had been Wheatley and the escapologist so the odds of anyone stumbling across the crime scene were slim. They doused all the lights, closed the interior doors, and locked the front door behind them, then walked around the house making sure that nothing of the murder was visible from the outside.

Schreck and Monk shared the back seat. They had a blanket that Houdini provided for warmth, and within moments of setting off, the steady rumble of the engine and the rocking motion of the car were enough to have both of them drifting off to sleep.

The journey was only a dozen or so miles, but progress was painfully slow until they breeched the shroud of fog and hit the open road. The drive ensured the pair managed to get some real rest before they reached the asylum, and gave Wheatley and Houdini time to think.

"What do we do with Monk once we've dropped off Schreck?" Wheatley asked. Houdini concentrated on the road ahead, hands at ten-and-two on the wheel.

"I'm not sure," he said. "We could leave him there, I suppose, a safe distance from Dunwich and the cultists?"

Wheatley nodded. It made sense. But…that place?

"As a visitor or inmate?" he asked, only half joking.

"Just keeping an eye on his friend," Houdini said. "It's better than taking him back to the house while there's a corpse in the lounge. The police will be tearing the place apart in the morning, looking for anything to link Monk to the murders. He's just started to get a grip on reality again. Too much excitement might tip him right back over the edge."

Wheatley couldn't really dispute any of the logic. It was a delicate balance. But it didn't seem fair to leave a vulnerable man in the line of fire, and that was exactly what he would be if they returned him to the house.

"I want to talk to him before we go back, though. I want to know why Simon was killed in his house. Why there and not somewhere else? I think Monk knows something he hasn't told us yet."

"You think he's holding out on us?" Wheatley couldn't imagine any reason why the man would, unless he had been too traumatized to recall precise details at the time. Now, at least, he seemed to be in a better state of mind than he had been, so if there were memories locked away inside him it made sense to try and get to them. The only fear was that Monk was teetering on the brink, and forcing him to relive those harrowing events might be all it took to push him one way or the other when his mind could fall so easily either side of the line of sanity.

Once inside the city limits of Arkham, finding the asylum wasn't difficult. They passed through the huge wrought iron gates and turned onto the gravel drive that curled like a lazy serpent all the way through lush grounds to the huge gothic monstrosity of the asylum's main building. Wheatley stared up at the old building, which wouldn't have been out of place in the wonderful Wren-esque architecture of Holborn with its dramatic lines and stark angles. It was almost Roman. But then, there was an element of madness behind the design of all great buildings, wasn't there? To see things a certain way—to see things differently than anyone else—wasn't that the definition of madness?

The tires crunched gravel as they pulled up in front of the huge double doors.

Ugly gargoyles leered down from on high.

The place really was like something out of a nightmare.

Houdini insisted on taking Schreck in on his own. It was his position that had managed to swing a few privileges, so it would be easier to ensure that the agreement was met if he had the opportunity to do it on his own rather than putting the orderlies on the back foot by going in mob-handed. Wheatley wasn't about to argue. He was in no great hurry to set foot inside a nuthouse. "Besides," Wheatley said. "If they see the state of you, who's to say they won't want to keep you in, too?" He winked, emphasizing the joke, but in the best humor there was always a grain of truth.

Houdini winced as he climbed out of the car and clutched at his side. He stood there for a moment, leaning against the car for support, then straightened up.

"You okay?" Wheatley asked, concerned.

Houdini felt out an area around his appendix, pressing down on it slightly and wincing again. Then it was like he pulled a mask down over the pain and Houdini the performer stood in the injured man's place. "Just a little tender. Nothing to worry about. Those freaks were a little heavy handed, that's all. I'll be fine when this is all over and I can rest up for a few days." He was making light of it, but Wheatley could see how much the injury pained him. It wasn't good. But he could see the man's fierce pride in action. He wasn't about to accept a helping hand. Wheatley let it drop.

Wheatley helped get Schreck out of the car, then settled back into the front seat to wait for Houdini to return. Monk showed no sign of stirring while Houdini was gone. Wheatley found himself drifting while they waited, his head lolling only to rest against the cold window and snap back upright. It had been a long night. He was only beginning to realize how desperately he needed to sleep. Despite being older, Houdini seemed to be a machine. He was an incredible specimen. He seemed to possess boundless energy and inhuman reserves of strength. The knock he had taken to his side was actually the first hint the man had shown of being mortal in all the time they'd been together, and even then his mind was sharp. Wheatley, on the other hand, was on the point of passing out into the arms of Morpheus when Houdini returned.

"Everything's sorted," he said, slamming the door behind

him. "He's in the best place." Wheatley wasn't sure if Houdini was trying to convince himself or stating a fact.

He nodded at the sleeping man in the back. "Been out cold the whole time you were gone. But I think that there's something you should know about your friend."

"Go on," Houdini said, turning the key over in the ignition and gunning the engine to life.

"When I was getting clothes for Schreck I found something hidden in a drawer. I swear I wasn't looking for it, but..." He shrugged and fumbled in his coat pocket for the metal tin he'd taken from Monk's room. He handed it over to Houdini. He opened it to reveal a syringe and the other trappings of an addict.

"Opium," Houdini said.

"You don't seem surprised?"

"I have spent enough time around addicts in my life... I've seen the signs with Monk, but stupidly refused to believe them, I suppose. I don't think he has been chasing the dragon recently, but there's no denying it explains so many things."

"We should keep a close eye on him, now that we know for sure."

"Indeed," Houdini said, slipping the tin into his own coat. "Looks like you could do with some shut eye, too. Try to grab a few minutes while I drive back. You'll thank me for it in the long run. I'll wake you when we get back to Dunwich."

Wheatley didn't need to be told twice. He presented his back to the side-door and was soon settling his breathing to the rhythm of the car. They were barely out of the asylum's grounds before he was lost in sleep. His dreams were fitful and unpleasant, filled with peculiar images of freaks and burning edges of celluloid, as though his life had become part of a film and it was shriveling away at the edges, melting through to the center, being consumed by fire. All that remained was an infinite blackness. And within it, the laughter of a dark and hungry god rang out.

It was the engine being turned off—not the car coming to a halt—that roused him.

Sweat clung to his skin.

He ground his knuckles into his eyes, trying to rub the

sleep away, and had to blink a dozen times until he could focus again.

They had reached the edge of the fog. It was like a solid wall of white ahead of them, reminding Wheatley once again of how it seemed to be concentrated on the small town.

Houdini was staring straight ahead, wrestling with a decision and not about to share it.

After a moment, he turned and reached over to the back seat.

"Time to wake up, sleepyhead," he said, nudging Monk gently to rouse him out of his exhausted sleep. "We need to talk."

Monk shifted slightly, struggling to bring himself fully back from the sleep he so desperately needed. He forced himself to sit upright, trying to focus on Houdini from beneath heavy-lidded eyes.

"Just a few minutes," Houdini promised him.

"What is it?"

"Why did Simon come to the house?"

"Simon?" He pressed his fingertips to his temple, trying to tease the memory out from the fog that had gathered inside his head. It was every bit as dense as it was on the road ahead of them. "He didn't. They brought him to the house."

"But why?"

"I don't follow?"

"Why did they bring him to the house? What was so important about it? Why not dump him in the Lake House, or on the set? Somewhere he wouldn't be found."

"They were looking for a piece of film. Simon had told them he didn't know where it was. They thought I might have it."

"And do you?"

Monk shrugged. "I had no idea what they were talking about."

Wheatley believed him.

"And that's what you told them?"

Monk nodded. The ghost of fear haunted his face once more. "That was when it happened. They grabbed Simon, pulled his head back and drew the knife across his throat. The blood… They just dropped him and left him to die on the floor. It was so…cold."

"So why didn't they kill you?"

"I don't know. I thought they were going to. I begged. But they just left."

"Curious," Houdini noted. "Perhaps ignorance saved your life?"

"Or something else," Wheatley said, meaning his relationship with his assistant, Tanith, the woman with the sign of Glaaki inked on her flesh. The others didn't pick up on it.

"Did they give you any idea what was on the film?"

"Not really. Simon said that it had chanting on it. Perhaps part of a ritual of some kind, but we haven't filmed anything like that so I don't know what they're driving at."

"But there was some kind of ritual in the script, wasn't there? In the new pages?" Houdini said.

"How the hell could you know that? You can't know that!" The pitch of Monk's voice rose in barely suppressed panic. "No one knows what's in that script, not everything. Pieces. Only pieces. That's the whole point, don't you get it. That's the only way that it will work. If people see too much... If they know...then the fear won't be real... You can't pretend fear...it needs to be visceral. You can't pretend to be a freak of nature... You can fake deformity, but to be a true freak, to fit inside the vision of my work, it has to be real... But even if it is real...that first encounter, your first exposure to the freak, that reaction cannot be replicated. The revulsion. The fear. It is primal. Instinctive. Beautiful." The man was rambling and Wheatley couldn't help but wonder how much of this was a side effect of the opiates rather than the things he had seen since his arrival in Dunwich? "It is the *fantastique*. The nature of the other. That is what captivates us. Film asks us to pull back the curtain, to make the viewer uncomfortable by showing them what they are genuinely fascinated by, and that, my friend, is the *difference*. We are obsessed by difference."

The filmmaker slumped back into the seat. Wheatley couldn't tell if he was energized by talk of his art or overcome by paranoia. It was a fine line. By the time Houdini started the engine again, Monk was staring out of the window, repeating phrases about the beauty of monsters, the infinite cosmos, the enemy out there, and Wheatley regretted their waking him. The filmmaker had nothing meaningful left to tell them.

"If it's film footage they are looking for, there are only two possible places it could be hidden: the house or the film set," said Houdini. "When Monk says it's not at the house, I think we have to believe him. After all, he showed us Catherine Beddows's test reel. If this missing film was ever there, it isn't any more. Think about it: his not-so-delightful assistant has had ample time to catalog every last piece of celluloid at the house, and they left when he said he didn't have it, so that only leaves the set."

"I've been thinking about that test reel," Wheatley said. "What if it wasn't? I mean, what if those few minutes of Catherine Beddows weren't from her audition. What if that was filmed when she arrived at the Lake House? There was chanting in that, wasn't there? Could that have just been a cut from the missing reel?"

Houdini made a moue. "Theoretically, I suppose. But Monk knew the test reel, he recognized it. This wasn't it. And who would have filmed it? Are you suggesting one of the freaks knows how to use a camera?"

Wheatley shook his head. "No. Edward. Wasn't that his name? The first technician that was killed. What if they killed him to silence him? If they'd cajoled him into filming the ritual for them he would know too much, wouldn't he?"

"And that would make him a liability. Good thinking, Dennis. Good to see that brain of yours hasn't lost its edge. And rather than rule out the possibility that there is an unknown piece of film out there somewhere, it actually increases the likelihood, doesn't it? So what's on that film? What secret was recorded that the freaks would prefer remained secret?"

"A ritual?"

"Not just any ritual, Dennis. *The* ritual."

"And the freaks want it destroyed because it reveals something they don't want anyone to see?"

"Evidence that they are responsible for at least one of the killings?"

"Quite possibly. More than likely, even."

"If they get to it first it will never be seen again no matter what it contains."

"Precisely. We need to recover this piece of film before anyone else gets hurt."

Houdini looked at Monk through the rearview mirror, then shifted in the driver's seat and winced as he did. Wheatley could see that the pain in his side was worse than he was letting on, but stubborn as ever, the man was determined not to let it slow him down.

"You should rest. Let me drive," Wheatley suggested.

"Later. We have to get to the film studio as quickly as we can, and of the two of us, I think I'd rather put my faith in my reflexes, wouldn't you?"

Wheatley looked at the wall of fog ahead of them, secretly glad he didn't have to try and negotiate the roads blind.

He nodded.

The filmmaker was fast asleep in the backseat with his head against the cold glass of the window.

Chapter Thirty-Nine

Wheatley clung on to the handgrip on the side door as they hurtled through the fog. Houdini wrenched the wheel around from side to side abruptly, causing the car to tilt precariously on its suspension. Wheatley *hated* not being in control. Even in normal visibility these tight country roads weren't built for these speeds. With visibility so poor it was suicidal.

It really did feel as though Dunwich was cut off from the rest of the world. The fog was so thick, cloying, and pulling at the car as they tore through it, it wasn't such a great stretch of the imagination to imagine a strange sentience behind it, especially as it had hung around for so many days now, and that the only break in it seemed to be around the lake.

As they approached the film set, Wheatley saw lights in the road ahead. It took him a moment to realize they were moving toward them. He heard something, too. A sound coming in their direction. It began as a deep rumble that was caught in the sound of the car's engine, but quickly grew into its own distinct harmonic. Wheatley didn't need to wind down the car window to know what that sound was. It possessed a rhythm that was so familiar to him now it had taken up residence within his brain. It was the slow and steady chanting of that word over and over again: *Glaaki*.

"What the devil is *that*?" Wheatley asked as Houdini slowed the car down to a crawl.

Slowly, through the fog up ahead, they saw the true nature of the lights: flaming torches and firebrands. They brought light, but more than that, they brought menace, fear, and the oppressive threat of violence, with them.

At first Wheatley thought the torchbearers were all freaks, but as they began to emerge from the fog he realized there was a mixture of freaks and ordinary townsfolk together. "Are they coming for us?"

The mass of bodies shuffled forward, the resonance of their chanting made all the more eerie by the weird atmospherics of the fog. The freaks in the mob looked savage. Unforgiving. Wheatley gripped the door handle tighter. There was nowhere they could go—but he could see Houdini itching to floor the accelerator and force a path straight through the middle of the mob. They moved weirdly, lurching stiff-legged from side to side and as they neared, Wheatley realized the townsfolk had a peculiar look in their eyes, like they weren't all there. It took him a moment to really grasp what it was—a deadness—and then it began to dawn on him the extent of the threat they faced. They were looking for blood. Theirs. Monk's. "We have to get out of here," he gasped. "Now."

Houdini didn't say a word. He slammed the car into reverse and stabbed his foot down on the pedal. The tires screeched, the engine protesting shrilly as they spun back. The smell of burned rubber filled the interior. Houdini didn't ease off until he had put some distance between them and the shambling mob of freaks and dead-eyed townsfolk.

The mob was little more than a dark smear in the fog before them, their lights diffuse and guttering, swaying from side to side. It was the chanting they couldn't escape; no matter how far they reversed, it seemed to be all around them, on every side, on every street.

They didn't have to move quickly. They were surrounded. All of the damned were converging on the fog-blanketed streets of Dunwich, and Wheatley and Houdini were trapped in the middle of them. "I guess we'll get to see how good an escapologist you really are," Wheatley said bleakly.

"Worst comes to worst, we can outrun them if it comes to that," Houdini said, grinning. "Besides, I don't think they're after us, look." He was right, the mob appeared to have altered its path and was weaving and stumbling through the handful of parked cars in the direction of the movie set, the workshops, and beyond them, Monk's office. "And if they'd wanted to kill Monk they had ample opportunity to do so at his house. Besides, as you so ably proved with your snooping, his blood is tainted by the opiates he has pumped into his veins. Tanith will know that. Monk is unclean. This mob isn't an ambush. I'm willing to risk my life on it. It's not even for us. As far as they are concerned I've already died once. But you, my friend, well, they *could* be looking for you, I suppose. A worthy sacrifice for their god, and all that."

"Thanks. I feel so much better now. This is getting too big for us, Harry. We can't stand up against an entire town. We need to get out of here while we can. Head for Arkham, regroup, get word to the police, and let them handle the mob."

"Fine in theory, but almost certainly too late to help the innocents of Dunwich who find themselves snared in this nightmare, Dennis. And before you say that's not our problem, consider this: there *is* something in that lake. These people are piecing together things that will lure it out of the water. That's what this ritual of theirs is, a summoning. They want to bring it to the surface. I don't know if it's a sleeping god. I don't really care. The freaks have gathered here for a reason, and it wasn't just the film that brought them to Dunwich. It was the thing in the lake. There's a reason we have that cliché: let sleeping gods lie," Houdini said, keeping a completely straight face. "Monk's film may have been the trigger, maybe gathering so many freaks in one place at the same time had some kind of effect, maybe they reached some kind of psychic saturation point, I don't know, but what they were doing at that old tumbled down house, their ritual on the lake side, the fish-men down there with the dead in the watery meat locker, they weren't *just* praising their god. They're trying to usher him back into the world above."

"So what do we do? We're just two people, and as you're so fond of saying, you can't actually do magic. Neither can I. So what does that leave us with? How do we combat a god and his mad followers?"

"Well what we *can't* do is loiter here in the hopes that the police will come and save the day. Even if by some miracle they were to ride into town, there wouldn't be enough of them to make any real difference to the outcome of proceedings."

"But we are only two men," Wheatley repeated. "Unless you're hiding an army in the fog there's nothing we can do."

"You're thinking like a fighter. We don't have to *fight* them. We've only got to beat them. If we can get into the office and retrieve the film, then we've got what they want, and that gives us the upper hand. Grab every damned fragment of footage we can lay our hands on, and get as far away from this place as we can. They're here for the same reason as we are. We just have to beat them at their own game."

"That's a hell of a risky assumption, though," Wheatley said. "What's to stop them just tearing us apart the moment we set foot outside the car?" He looked at the silhouettes gradually darkening in the fog in front of them. Darkening. Getting closer.

"Have you got any better ideas?"

"Apart from turning this car around, getting the hell out of here, and just letting them get on with it?"

"Brilliant plan. Anything else?"

"No, not really."

"Okay, well perhaps this is the point when we part company?"

"What do you mean?"

"You go your way; I go back in there."

"Why on earth would you do that?"

"That mob's going to tear the set apart. Everything Monk owns is in that place. Even if I can't get the film out, I can salvage some of his equipment rather than letting them smash it up."

"You'd risk your life for some cameras?"

The escapologist shook his head. "No. But I would risk it

for friendship. That's just who I am, Dennis. I can't expect you to understand, or demand you accompany. I'd like your help, but to be honest, I'm going in there with or without you."

"I can't let you do this on your own, Harry, and you know that."

"I never for a moment thought you could, old boy. Let's go raise some hell, shall we?"

"Or, preferably, sink it to the bottom of a lake once and for all."

"Good point. I like your suggestion better." And with that Houdini was out of the car and running toward the side lot where the set had been assembled.

Wheatley clambered out of the car, looking back once as Monk, unconscious in the backseat, muttered, "No, don't get out, we'll be right back," and slammed the door.

They ran hard, each of them struggling in different ways. Off the road, the ground beneath their feet was muddy. The mud sucked at their shoes. The fog-bound air burned Wheatley's scarred lungs. He had to suck in great labored breaths. In front of him, Houdini favored his injured side.

They kept ahead of the mob by moving fast. Houdini was right—or seemed to be. The freaks showed no interest in them. That would change once they reached the building—if they found the film reel, then as the Americans were fond of saying, all bets would be off.

Wheatley had learned something about himself today: he would gladly give his right arm for the chance to see what had caused all this mayhem. It wasn't just thrill-seeking. It was rooted deeper than that. It went beyond curiosity, too, into something fundamental. The core of his being; who he was. Maybe it was a ghost of the battlefields, maybe it had always been there. Or maybe this need for the truth had been woken by the murder of his friend and mentor, Eric Tombe?

"We need to get the underwater camera safe, if we can. It's the most important piece of kit here, worth a small fortunate, and knowing Monk, uninsured." He made it sound practical, but Wheatley knew what Houdini was thinking: the underwater camera would be the one they'd need if they wanted to record the truth of what lay at the bottom of Spring Glen.

The heavy wooden doors of the workshops stood open. There were lights on inside, but no one was home. The benches were abandoned mid-work, half-cut jobs still lying in the vices, as though the stagehands had set down their tools and just walked away. Maybe they had. With everyone doing multiple jobs it was more than possible that Edward or Simon might well have doubled as set carpenters. Great coils of rope and cabling were stacked in the corner along with tins of paint left over from the set design.

Houdini made his way quickly to the storeroom that lay toward the back of the workshop while Wheatley riffled through the accumulation of material looking for anything resembling a film canister. He was still empty-handed when Houdini returned a moment later with a silver case he was clearly struggling with.

"Here," Wheatley said, taking it from him. The escapologist seemed about to argue, but relinquished his grip on the handle with a nod of thanks.

Freaks and townsfolk alike moved closer to the open doorway.

They weren't just dark shadows now.

They had faces Wheatley recognized.

He shuddered. They needed to move quickly or they were going to be cornered. He didn't relish the prospect of having to fight their way out of the workshops. It wasn't that he was afraid of physical confrontation—he imagined they'd be able to push their way past the freaks without having to stand toe-to-toe with them, Marquis of Queensbury style. Already the first few were beginning to shuffle into the lot between the workshops, the offices, and the set itself.

Given a few more minutes it would become an impassable barricade.

Houdini raced across to a row of metal lockers against the far wall and started to pick the locks. Despite the pressure of the situation, the first lock popped simply and he pulled the door open.

A twisted face slammed up against the glass. That word whispered through the fog, was coiling around him: *Glaaki, Glaaki, Glaaki*.

"We have to get out of here, Harry."

The escapologist looked up from rifling through the contents of the second locker, and nodded. But instead of rushing back so they could go out side-by-side, he forced the lock on the third locker.

Wheatley couldn't afford to wait any longer, not if he was going to lug the heavy steel case containing the underwater camera out. He clutched it to his chest and went for the door, ready to use it as a battering ram if he had to. "Come on!" he yelled. He had to trust Houdini was following him.

He crossed the threshold, pushing his way through the handful of townsfolk who crowded around the door. They held their torches high in the air. One of them, a woman in a torn gingham frock, reached out to touch Wheatley. Her nails were bitten down and scratched across his arm as he tried to force her aside. The air stank of sweat and something else. Pondweed. Acrid, bitter.

Glaaki. Glaaki. Glaaki. The chant was low, incessant. He felt each word like a physical blow, deep in his gut.

He used the camera case like a shield as the first of the torchbearers swung their brands at him, deflecting the fire. The torches spat and sizzled, the heat coming off them staggering. They seemed to slice clean through the wisps of fog now. Wheatley put his head down and plowed on, driving a path through them.

When he looked up again, ten paces on, he found himself stranded in the center of a semi-circle that arced to either side of the doorway. Freaks. Surrounded by townsfolk. Where the normal people seemed somehow dead inside and lacking purpose, the freaks were coming alive in a way he hadn't seen before. The tension in the air was palpable.

There, stepping into the middle of the arc to join him was the transmogrified man, Daniel Mason, returned to his lumpen, twisted self. He studied Wheatley with his oversized head tilted to one side, too heavy for his neck to support. His lower body was twisted awkwardly, his hips side-on to his caved-in ribcage. It was a miracle his bowed legs could support his weight. As horrific and grotesque as his visage was, there was something incredibly powerful about it, too. He was their totem.

"So, what's worse, being cornered by Beetle Man or being cornered by Elephant Man?" Houdini said, coming up behind him.

"Six of one, half a dozen of the other," Wheatley said. The black humor was a defense mechanism. Laughing in the face of death. The man's transmogrification was burned indelibly on Wheatley's mind. He would never forget the sight of the man's skin cracking and falling away on that black carapace. But the fact that Mason had returned to his twisted human form from that other thing, that had to mean something, didn't it? He'd surely lost some of his power, hadn't he? Or had that thing he'd seen by the lakeside merely been masquerading as the Elephant Man? He couldn't imagine Mason had simply been able to put that skin back on like a cheap suit, could he? Was that possible? Or did he have to regrow skin?

Mrs. Whateley stepped out of the semi-circle to stand beside Mason. The albino woman clutched her precious bell jar to her breast with filthy hands. The dirt stood out like blood against her pale skin. She raised a trembling hand in their direction, leveling a crooked finger directly at Houdini. "He is the one," she rasped. "He belongs to our lord. He belongs to Glaaki!"

Mason dropped on all fours, his twisted musculature suddenly more mobile, like this was his natural stance, his weight spread more evenly across his limbs. His bulbous head came up to glower at them. He might have returned to his skin, but he was anything but human.

Slowly, deliberately, Mason crabbed closer, each limb seeming to move to its own rhythm as they sought to find their positions in the sequence of movement. One shoulder rose, the other fell, one hip dislocated, the other pushed it forward, Mason skittering forward, his fingers clawing at the gravel as he moved. His movement answered one question: the skin was held together with stitches. As the creature inside stretched and strained its legs extended, its monstrous body pushed at the skin, opening the stitches wider.

He raised his repugnant face to look first at Wheatley, then at Houdini.

The stitches across its back tore, revealing the slimy black carapace he had seen down by Spring Glen.

In a matter of seconds the rest of the bulbous and mis-shapen skin was sloughed free as the creature freed itself from its human disguise.

There was absolute joy on the faces of the freaks gathered behind it.

Glaaki. Glaaki. Glaaki.

The townsfolk looked on blankly, no longer seeing what was happening right before their eyes.

Chapter Forty

"Get back, Dennis. If this thing wants me let's not confuse it, shall we?" Houdini said. "I'll keep it occupied, you get back to the car and get Monk out of here."

"No. I said I couldn't let you do this alone and I meant it."

"Just for once do what you're damned well told, would you? I brought you into this and I will absolutely make sure that you get out. You have to get out of town, get to Arkham, talk to the police. Tell them everything."

The problem was he'd abandoned Houdini once before. He wasn't about to do it again, no matter how fiercely the escapologist protested.

"Sorry, old bean. We're in this together."

Where there was one monster there would be others. That was the only way to think. The man-sized beetle couldn't be the only monstrous thing hidden within the freaks. Just because others hadn't metamorphosed didn't mean they were incapable of transformation.

Houdini flashed him a manic grin.

"Then let's have it, my friend. Cry God for Harry, England, and Saint George!" Houdini roared.

"As long as one god's crying, we'll call it a win," Wheatley said dryly.

Houdini lunged into the Beetle Man's path, its mandibles clacking in time with the mad chant. *Glaaki. Glaaki. Glaaki.* It had never really gone away, though as the freaks circled them it had fallen to a murmur, like white noise in the background of everything. Wheatley saw villagers opening and closing their mouths adding to the hubbub, but clearly oblivious to the sounds coming from their mouths.

The Beetle Man raised itself up on its hind legs, mandibles snapping wildly at air. Those great claws swung out at Houdini. The escapologist threw himself to the left, hitting his shoulder hard on the gravel and rolling into a tight crouch. The beast missed him by a matter of inches. Houdini rose slowly from the crouch. The Beetle Man came on, snapping high and low, trying to cut his feet out from under him or take his head off his shoulders—it wasn't fussy.

The escapologist miss-stepped, catching his heel on a stone, over-compensated for the loss of balance, and fell back into the workshop as the Beetle Man skittered forward.

Glaaki. Glaaki. Glaaki.

It didn't move quickly enough to take advantage of Houdini's fall.

The man was up on his feet in the silence between clacks from the Beetle Man's jaws.

Wheatley lunged at it with the metal case, swinging it with all of his strength. The momentum nearly carried him off his feet, but for all the force he put behind it, the creature simply swatted him away. The impact sent Wheatley sprawling into the wall.

He gasped, the air driven from his lungs.

The metal case slipped from his grasp. It slid across the floor, coming to a stop at the feet of the albino woman.

Wheatley saw his chance to escape, but didn't take it.

He wasn't going to let Houdini die.

Not here, not now.

Houdini scrambled backwards, trying to put himself out of the reach of the creature as it moved inexorably toward him.

"Over here!" Wheatley yelled, trying to draw it away from

his fallen friend, then realized he had nothing to fight with. In a moment of panic as the thing's head rolled around to face him, he lunged forwards as though to try and retrieve the case. One of the freaks lunged, pulling it away from him. But Wheatley had never been interested in the metal case—in that moment of confusion he tore the glass bell jar from the albino's grasp and held it aloft.

Mrs. Whateley let out the scream to end all screams. It tore through every other sound. It owned every inch of the film set.

It cut the chanting dead.

Silence.

Just the *snick-snack* of the Beetle Man's constantly moving mandibles.

Every eye turned toward the source of the sound.

Wheatley didn't hesitate.

He had one chance.

As the Beetle Man launched itself at him, he hurled the bell jar toward its open maw.

The glass shattered on impact.

Mrs. Whateley's first scream had nothing on her second. She howled. She raged. Shrieked. Tore at her hair and face. Clawed at her skin, leaving bloody red weals down her cheeks. The beast wailed with its own pain, rearing up in agony. The noise emitted from its maw was soul-rending. It was unlike anything Wheatley had heard in his life.

It lashed around, contorting its already twisted frame into evermore agonizing shapes, teetering as its legs buckled, and toppling backwards.

It came down on its slime-glossy carapace and couldn't right itself. In that instant, Houdini launched himself at the creature.

Its legs thrashed wildly. A green viscous liquid oozed from the thing's thorax.

Wheatley saw the chisel buried all the way in to the handle, and then Houdini standing over the fallen child of Glaaki, his hands covered in the ichor.

Several of the freaks howled in unison, sharing the agony of the Beetle Man's death throes; others urged the townsfolk to attack, screaming and yelling as they rushed at Wheatley and Houdini. But their exhortations were lost amid the other cries. Whatever grim force had controlled them had lost its focus. The townsfolk stood rooted to the spot, transfixed by the horror of the dying creature. Its cries spiraled in pitch, until a single deafening *crack* heralded the first window to shatter.

That ear-splitting scream of glass and dying monster seemed to snap the albino woman out of the paralysis that had gripped her in the seconds after Wheatley had hurled her daughter at the beast. She ran screaming at him, flailing at his face with broken nails. She raked them across Wheatley's cheek, drawing blood.

Wheatley fought to hold her at bay.

Houdini—clothes smeared with the green-black ichor—stood over the remains of Whateley's daughter. It bore no resemblance to any sort of child he'd ever seen. It flapped and slapped on the gravel like a fish pulled fresh from the water, thrashing about, unable to breath.

Mrs. Whateley saw it, too.

She wrenched herself free of Wheatley's restraining grip and threw herself onto the shards of shattered glass from the jar, not caring as the glass sliced into her skin, to gather up her tiny deformed child in her shaking, bloody hands.

"Come on!" he screamed at Houdini. The escapologist pushed his way past the albino woman who was on her hands and knees cooing over the fully formed, living, breathing fetus, comforting her daughter as she let out her own high-pitched keening.

Wheatley stooped to snatch up the camera case and used its protection to barge an opening through the crush of bodies as the freaks gathered around them, closing ranks.

"Is there another way out of this place?" Wheatley gasped, turning frantically left and right, looking for breathing space as the freaks drove them back toward the workshop. "A window? A cellar? Anything?"

"I don't—wait, yes, there's a fly window, in the restroom. If we can barricade the door, we might buy ourselves enough time to make a break for it."

"Then let's stop talking!" Wheatley stumbled on the threshold, then roared and swung the case in great sweeping arcs like a demented loon. The freaks didn't back away, but as the corner of the metal case cannoned into the face of the first of their number, she fell, and took with her the two closest behind her.

That was all Wheatley needed to slam the door. Even as he was trying to force the bolt in place, Houdini wrestled with the nearest workbench, pulling it free of the mooring that anchored it to the floor, and dragged it over to barricade the door. "It won't hold them back for long," Wheatley said.

"Luckily, we don't need long," Houdini said.

They wove a path through the workbenches and machines toward the door that opened onto the prop cupboard—which wasn't a cupboard at all, but rather a huge warehouse storage area—running between the aisles of the monstrous and macabre, as well as the utterly mundane stuff of the movie world, as behind them, the freaks forced their way inside the workshop. Wheatley heard the crash of them bursting through the barrier. Wood buckled and burst as hinges twisted and split. The first thing through the door was that damned word: *Glaaki. Glaaki. Glaaki.* As the chanting swelled to fill the workshop and the weird hollow acoustics of the props warehouse, the freaks followed it in.

Houdini grabbed one of the struts supporting the high stacks of shelving and heaved with all of his might, toppling the structure as he ran beneath it. Wheatley barely ducked around the corner of the aisle before the entire thing came crashing down. It would buy them a few more precious seconds.

But only a few. The freaks came on, crawling over the debris.

Wheatley and Houdini reached the small door at the back of the warehouse that led to a cramped restroom with a single porcelain toilet bowl, and, more preciously, a narrow fly window that opened out into damp and foggy air.

Houdini clambered onto the cistern and forced the window open while Wheatley blocked the door. "I'll go first, so I can pull you out from the other side."

Wheatley nodded. A moment later the escapologist kicked upwards and wriggled through a gap that seemed far too small for his body, but somehow he made it through. His feet disappeared through the window and suddenly Wheatley was alone.

The freaks hammered at the door. He could smell their fetid stench through the thin wood.

Houdini's face appeared in the window. "We've got a clear run to the car. Come on, Dennis." He reached a hand through. Wheatley lifted the camera case up for him to take. It barely scraped through the transom with some serious pushing from his end. Houdini reappeared a moment later, offering his hand again. Wheatley grasped it and jumped, kicking and scrabbling at the wall, until he felt the fresh air on his face. He was suddenly terrified he was going to get caught in the window, too fat to wriggle through. Behind him, the restroom door splintered. Houdini heaved, and Wheatley was through the window and lying on his back, gasping as the window slammed shut on the leering, manic faces of the freaks that clutched at thin air.

They had come around behind the back of the mob, so their run back to the car was free. The stench of the dead Beetle Man was overpowering, even from this distance.

They half-ran half-stumbled back toward the car, the crunch of the gravel underfoot not enough to draw the attention of the mob. Houdini was really struggling with the pain in his side. Wheatley slowed, allowing the escapologist to use him for support. The injury was obviously worse than his friend was prepared to admit. "Almost there," he kept saying over and over to urge Houdini to keep going.

One of the car doors opened. Monk, looking more alert now, clambered out of the vehicle. "Quick," Wheatley shouted to him. "Give me a hand. We've got to get out of here before all hell breaks loose."

The filmmaker sprinted toward them and Wheatley started to hold out the underwater camera, grateful to be free of its weight, and knowing no matter how much it cost, it wasn't worth their having returned to this place. But instead of taking it from him, Monk ran straight past them—back toward the workshop and the warehouse and the freaks.

"Monk!" Wheatley yelled after him, trying to look over his shoulder to see what the idiot was playing at, but supporting Houdini's weight made it difficult.

Monk showed no sign of slowing down as he neared the buildings.

"We've got to get out of here while we can!"

"*No!*" the filmmaker yelled.

He couldn't chase the fool. The best thing he could do was to get Houdini into the passenger seat, then if Monk came back to the car they could go. Houdini was his priority. He didn't owe the director anything. If he wanted to put his life in danger, fine, but he wasn't about to die trying to save the moron. Wheatley put the camera case down and adjusted his grip on Houdini, reaching around his back, one of his arms across his own shoulders to help him into the car. Each movement bought a fresh wince of pain from Houdini. The relief when he was finally settled into the car was almost audible.

Wheatley slammed the car door—the sound resounded like a gunshot. Immediately in its wake he heard the incessant rise and fall, *clack clack clackity clack: Glaaki. Glaaki. Glaaki.*

Wheatley raced back for the camera case, yelling after Monk, but his name was lost in the rising chants of the mob.

They had to go. Now.

But something was happening back by the door of the workshop. Freaks were emerging, carrying cans of film.

Across the parking lot he saw a bonfire had been hastily dragged together and lit. The flames grew rapidly. The freaks shambled into the fog, toward the flames, clutching the canisters of film to feed the rising fire.

Someone was trying to stop them, running from freak to freak, clutching at the canisters in their hands, reaching into the fire and screaming in pain even as he tried to salvage lengths of film from the flames, but all in vain.

Monk.

The filmmaker was crying and yelling incoherently and scrabbling about on the dirt, but he couldn't stop the freaks from destroying his masterpiece.

Wheatley could smell the sickly sweet stench of burning flesh and knew it could only be from Monk's hands.

By the time Wheatley reached him, pulling him away from the fire, the filmmaker's hands were ruined, the flesh red, raw, and already blistered from the flames. His last fragile grasp on reality had slipped away with his film, fed to the hungry flames. Wheatley knew that it would be a long time before he found it again, if ever. He almost pitied the man, but not enough to let him get them killed.

The freaks continued to work with ruthless efficacy, emptying the contents of Monk's office onto the great pyre one piece at a time, always to the accompaniment of that damned word: *Glaaki. Glaaki. Glaaki.*

Then one by one, they faded away into the fog, only the eerie sound of their chant remaining, and soon that too was a thing of the past.

Wheatley grabbed Monk and dragged him away from the fire, kicking and screaming all the way back to the car. Arkham Asylum would welcome another inmate before the day was out.

But first they would have to answer to the police.

The two officers, Martin and Ropes, were standing by Houdini's car. They showed no signs of wanting to interfere with the mayhem that was being played out only yards away from them.

"Looks like we arrived just in time," they said.

"No, it looks like you arrived just a little too late," Wheatley replied.

"It depends on how you look at it, I suppose, Mr. Wheatley. You're under arrest for the murders of Collette Verney, Max Schreck, and Edward Sissons. If you'd be so kind as to hold your wrists out so Constable Ropes can put the handcuffs on?"

Chapter Forty-One

"Oh, enough of this nonsense," Houdini called through the open window. "You can't possibly be stupid enough to believe that Dennis here's responsible for any of this? For one thing, Schreck's not dead, so it's difficult to prove a case of murder against a living man, wouldn't you say?"

"How can you possible know that?" Martin, the senior of the two officers, asked. "The man was thrown overboard by Wheatley off the coast of New England."

Beside him, Ropes licked his lips.

Wheatley said nothing. He didn't need to. Houdini's laugh was abrasive enough for both of them. "Mr. Schreck is currently living in the lap of luxury in Arkham Asylum, very much alive, if not by the strictest definition of the word, well..."

"And you know this how?"

"Because, my dear fellow, I drove him there myself not two hours since, as Monk and Wheatley will attest. All you have to do is ask them. A well-placed inquiry using that newfangled invention, the telephone, will no doubt save you a lot of blushes, and some time. But let's not allow facts to get in the way of tasty allegations, shall we. And by facts I am referring to the timeline of events. Dennis wasn't even in the country when the first death occurred."

"Yes he was. He was on set when Collette Verney was murdered. We have witnesses placing him at the scene."

"Ah, but that tragic beauty was not the first victim of this killer. Catherine Beddows, a young, promising actress whose body is currently decomposing in the waters of Spring Glen, was. She was reported missing. Weeks before Dennis here arrived in our fair land. Indeed, without her unfortunate demise, Collette Verney would never have been cast to step into the role."

"Are you sure?" Martin asked, looking sick at the prospect of being proven so horribly wrong.

"Positive. And that means he couldn't possibly have been involved in the first murder. The likelihood of there being two separate murderers stalking this film is...unlikely, wouldn't you say? And before you answer that, yes, yes, I am completely aware of his unfortunate situation last year, the death of his dear friend back in England. The theory is sound, of course, in that he has been dogged by misfortune, but that, regrettably for you, does not make him a killer, no matter how much you might like it to. Now, perhaps we can put an end to this charade and get out of here before the mob decides they're not finished feeding the fire." He patted the side of the car.

"So, do you want to tell us what this is all about, then?" Martin asked, giving the scene the once over. He didn't move to un-cuff Wheatley, but neither did he bundle him into the back of their car, obviously undecided.

The fire was still blazing high, but the freaks were nowhere to be seen.

"Honestly, I'd rather do the explaining as far away from here as possible," Houdini said.

Martin looked across at the pyre, then over to the workshop.

The fog was still dense enough that the man didn't see the festering remains of the Beetle Man seeping into the gravel. Or had the freaks fed it to the blaze in offering? Wheatley couldn't be sure either way. He'd been ushered away by Ropes before he could get himself into a better position to see.

"We need to go to Monk's house; everything will become clear," Houdini said, biting back on another stab of pain. He was still in some discomfort.

"No one home," Ropes said. "That's why we were here. Looking for the elusive Mr. Monk."

"Well, you've found him, obviously," Houdini said sarcastically, indicating Monk, who Wheatley was surprised to see was now seated in the back of the police car.

"Indeed," said Martin wryly, a look of surprise flashing across his face as he saw Monk and then disappearing in an instant, "that's why we're detectives." He turned his gaze back to Houdini. "We've been trying to get hold of him for a couple of days, though. He hasn't exactly made himself available to help with enquiries. But then again, neither have you gents, have you?"

There was no annoyance in his voice, more like frustration.

A few of the townsfolk still wandered around the set, their minds lost to a place where they would be hard to find. Perhaps it was temporary. With luck it would be. But Monk was beyond redemption. He sat dumbly in the back seat, staring blindly into the middle distance. Occasionally his lips twitched. Wheatley didn't need to be a lip reader to know they were shaping the name of the dead god.

More cars began to arrive at the set. Backup for the detectives.

Ropes spoke to one of the policemen, making arrangements for Monk to be taken into custody while his colleagues dealt with the few distressed townsfolk still wandering aimlessly around. Monk was helped out of Martin and Ropes's car and into the new one. He didn't fight, didn't even seem to really notice what was going on, but merely followed along muttering to himself. The opiates couldn't be helping his condition. With the destruction of his life's work, something inside the filmmaker just seemed to have broken.

"We'll take both cars," Martin said. "If you'd be so good as to follow us?"

Wheatley held up his cuffs.

"Unlock them, Ropes," Martin instructed. "But consider this, Mr. Wheatley. The bulge beneath my left arm is my revolver. If it should even look like you are so much as thinking about making a run for it, I won't hesitate to use it. Do we understand each other?"

"Perfectly," Wheatley said, as Ropes popped the lock.

He rubbed at his wrists as they came free. Even though he had only been in the restraints for a matter of minutes he was glad to be rid of them.

They drove to the house, Martin and Ropes in the first car, Houdini and Wheatley following close behind. Wheatley and Houdini hadn't mentioned the body they knew was waiting for them in the lounge yet; it was very much a case of crossing that bridge when they were forced at gunpoint to, and not a moment before. Wheatley couldn't know Houdini's reasoning, but it all came down to showmanship—too much planning and their collusion would be obvious.

So they waited until they were at the door before Wheatley said, "There's a fourth victim inside. The film's principal photographer. We found him at the foot of the stairs, along with Schreck and Monk. It's a mess. Schreck's illness… It's hard to explain. You need to see for yourself."

"Just open the door, please, Mr. Wheatley," Martin said. "And stand aside."

He did.

The lounge was empty.

There was no body at the foot of the stairs.

No sign of blood.

Someone had cleaned the place thoroughly in the time since they'd left.

"It was…right…there," Wheatley stammered, adamant that they'd left a corpse at the foot of the stairs.

"And the fairies came in and cleaned up, I suppose, sir?" Ropes said, barely concealing his smirk, only to be chided by his superior office.

"Death is no laughing matter, Ropes."

Houdini remained uncharacteristically quiet. He had been reluctant to leave the comfort of the car.

"Could you have been mistaken?" Martin asked. "I mean, could the victim have been stunned insensate, come to his senses, and left under his own steam?"

"If there was a handy resurrectionist in the area perhaps,"

Houdini finally spoke up. "But barring a successful séance, Simon wasn't talking to anyone, never mind walking out of here."

"Then we have yet another curiosity here," Martin observed. "But unfortunately with no body and no signs of a struggle, there's no crime to investigate."

"But there was blood. They've cleaned the place, but surely there must be traces?" Wheatley said, realizing how desperate he sounded. Then he remembered something. "There was a rug here. In the hallway. It's gone. Find the rug and you've got your proof."

"Now, who do you think would have broken in and cleared away the evidence like that?"

"The freaks. The killers. That has to be what's happened. It's the only thing that makes sense."

"Of course they did, sir," Ropes said. There was nothing more annoying than being patronized, but, and this was the nub of the matter, if the policemen refused to believe the freaks could have killed a man and disposed of the body without leaving any trace of the crime, how could they possibly accept what they had witnessed on the shore of the Spring Glen?

If he tried to explain, even if he omitted stuff about the dissolving Beetle Man and his hideous transformation and only talked about the secret cult dedicated to the worship of a god they believed slumbered at the bottom of the local lake they wouldn't just laugh at him, they'd ask him where he was hiding his opium pipe.

All he could do was shrug.

The telephone rang, its bell shattering the near silence that had descended on the house. Martin looked at Ropes and nodded. Ropes picked up the receiver.

"Hello, who is this, please?" he asked. He listened then placed his hand over the mouthpiece, looking confused. "It's for Houdini."

"Who is it?" Martin mouthed.

Ropes shrugged.

"Would you like me to take over?" Houdini asked, reaching for the receiver.

Martin nodded, so Ropes handed it over.

"This is Houdini," he said into the handset, then stood in silence as he listened to the person on the other end. He didn't betray any emotion, merely saying "Thank you" at the end of the call and handing the receiver back to Ropes.

"Who was that?" the detective asked.

"My agent. I need to be in Montreal by the end of the week for rehearsals."

"Ah, of course. The show must go on and all that," Martin said, with a hint of irony in his voice. "Well, I'm sure that there will be no need to keep a busy man like you hanging around longer than we absolutely need to. It's not as if we can't find you if we need you, now is it?" Houdini nodded in acknowledgment. There weren't a lot of places in the world he could hide without being recognized. "As to you, Mr. Wheatley, we must reluctantly accept that you weren't in the country when the unfortunate events began, and while I don't necessarily believe that means you can't be involved in the latter ones, it does mean you are innocent of the earlier crimes. I would, however, be grateful if you left a forwarding address when you leave town should we need to talk to you."

Wheatley was about to object, argue that he couldn't leave without seeing this through to the bitter end, but he was already beginning to suspect that he could live in Dunwich for the rest of his life and not get to the bottom of things. This place was unlike anywhere he'd ever been. It had already substantially shifted his worldview—he certainly wouldn't be so quick to dismiss the outré from now on. There were more things in heaven and earth than he'd dreamed of in his philosophy thus far, it seemed. He nodded. "Of course."

"I'm assuming the lack of a body rather interferes with your promised explanation?" Martin looked at Houdini.

"I'm not sure you'd believe me if I tried," Houdini said.

"How about you let me be the judge of that?"

Houdini shrugged. "The long and the short of it is I don't think that first detective was so wrong. The blame almost certainly lies at the door of the freaks, but not those of Darke's Carnival, as he suspected—they're just circus acts—but the genuine freaks. Abominations of nature. Monk was keen for us to weed out the afflicted from the poseurs; as word of his film spread it brought in plenty of folk looking to cash in on curious little deformities, but that didn't make them true freaks, not like the others."

"Go on."

"I believe that Monk stumbled upon something. You understand the nature of his film?"

Martin nodded. "To some extent, yes."

"I believe that while he thought he was creating a work of fiction, he was being influenced into making certain decisions that actually hark back to a darker tradition of long forgotten rituals and—"

"Rituals? As in magic?" the policeman scoffed.

"Not at all," Houdini answered smoothly. "Are you a good Christian man, officer?"

"Of course."

"Then you yourself observe certain rituals in keeping with your faith. The Sunday service? The simple act of prayer itself, these are all rituals. The Eucharist, partaking of the flesh and blood of Christ, baptism, there's nothing magical here, but these are rituals."

"So you think the murders are some sort of ritualistic killings?"

Houdini nodded.

"That's an angle we haven't considered," the policeman admitted. "But none of the victims have been found in any sort of ritualistic setting. Surely that would discount that theory?"

"That depends on the faith in question, for instance if you believed there was an ancient creature at the bottom of Spring Glen, your ritual might be to stake a body out down there once every six months or six years or whatever you believe its feeding cycle to be, as an offering. That doesn't mean there is a creature down there. Superstition is a powerful thing."

"Is that what you believe is happening here? Superstition driving a killing spree."

"Yes," Houdini said simply, leaving no room for argument.

"Can you prove *any* of this?"

"No," Houdini said, equally succinctly. He could tell them

about the Lake House, but that would only lead to more questions, more delays, and he obviously wanted to get out of this place as quickly as he could. Perhaps he would let them know when he was out of town, maybe he wouldn't. It was apparent he still felt that the police didn't really believe what he had been telling them anyway, and Wheatley agreed perhaps ignorance was the best state of affairs.

"Well, there's nothing to be gained from standing around here contemplating our navels," Martin said after a moment. "I think, perhaps, we should return to the set. If someone was influencing Monk, that is certainly one place to begin our search. Perhaps we'll strike it lucky and unearth some evidence that substantiates Mr. Houdini's more outlandish suppositions?"

"Of course," Houdini said. "And if you happen to be in the region of Detroit on the 26th, I've got a performance on at the Garrick. You'd be my guests, of course."

"That's mighty kind, I'm sure, but I doubt we'd be able to make it."

"Consider the invitation open, anyway."

They made their farewells. Houdini didn't say another word until the glow of the police car's rear lights disappeared in the fog.

"What now?" Dennis asked.

"Now, I make a slight confession."

"Why doesn't that sound good?"

"That call back at the house wasn't from my agent, it was from the asylum."

That was unexpected. "Something I should know?"

"Schreck has escaped. He attacked two of the orderlies, biting chunks out of their throats, then threw himself out of a first floor window. It seems he expected to transform…"

Wheatley shook his head. "Why don't they have bars in place to stop the inmates—patients—residents or whatever the correct name for them is, from doing just that?"

"It's uncommon for someone to defenestrate themselves from the head of the asylum's office. Not even the head himself, though he was, I believe, the last man to go out through the window, almost a decade ago."

"Have they reported it to the police?"

He shook his head. "Schreck was there voluntarily, not under orders. The orderlies accept the risks as one of the hazards of the job."

"What will happen to him? Will he be able to cope out there?"

"He was surviving before we intervened."

Wheatley wasn't sure what "surviving" really meant in this context, in a place like Dunwich, for a man who thought he was an immortal bloodsucking fiend. It didn't exactly fit within any definition of normalcy. No one could know what was going on in the actor's mind, or how he'd interpret the sickness of the character trapped inside there with him. It was like some form of multiple personality.

"That doesn't change the question, I suppose: What now?" Wheatley repeated.

"Back to the boarding house, I think. See if any of our friends have returned home, or if they've flown the coup."

They made the short drive back to the boarding house. It was eerily empty from the moment that they crossed the threshold. It felt like an entirely different place. They knocked at Ma Mocata's door, expecting to have to pay their penance in the form of a slice of slightly stale cake, but their knocking failed to elicit a response.

They made their way up to Wheatley's room, climbing the stairs slowly, as Houdini was still suffering and needed to lean a little more heavily on the banister with each flight they climbed.

Wheatley stopped on the first landing and listened for a moment, but even the ever-present radio had fallen silent. That was probably more disturbing than anything else. The place was deserted.

"They've all gone, Harry. Each and very one of them."

"Indeed, even the redoubtable Ma Mocata, it would seem."

"I just—" Wheatley shrugged. She'd fooled him with her homespun promise of cake and her "number one fan" routine.

"It would have been impossible for the freaks to come and go without her being part of it, my friend. Don't be hard on yourself. She fooled everyone."

He opened the door to his room. There was no sign that anyone had been in there since they'd eased the fake wall back into place after discovering Glaaki's shrine, but, in reality why should there have been? The people who had plagued him almost since the moment he had arrived in this godforsaken place weren't interested in him. It had never been about him, despite the message on his wall. It had always been about Houdini and trying to get to him through Wheatley.

"I know I keep saying this, Harry, but what now? Do we just give up and go home?" Wheatley already had one eye on his suitcase—which was perched on top of the wardrobe waiting for him to pull it down and start packing with all haste—as he asked this.

"No, no, no, my friend. Not when things are about to get interesting. Now," he said with a grin that belied his obvious discomfort, "we get that wall to move again."

Wheatley hadn't even realized that Houdini had left one of the bent slivers of metal wedged into the narrowest of cracks where the fake wall met the real one, preventing the mechanism from completely locking into place.

If any of the freaks had seen it there, they would have known that their secret lair had been breached. But, equally, if one of their number had crept into Wheatley's room, the pick would have fallen to the floor when the aperture had been opened. It was still wedged in place, a third of the way up the wall, meaning no visitors.

Houdini didn't hesitate. He slid the metal pick up the wall toward the middle, until he located the catch that kept the wall locked in place. He made it look easy, with concise, deft movements. There was a click that seemed louder than it reasonably ought to have been. Wheatley felt his heartbeat accelerate, his pulse kicking like a mule. In seconds Houdini eased the wall back just far enough to allow them passage into the hidden room.

"Abracadabra," he said with a flourish. Another wince, caused by moving a little too quickly and pulling at the muscle in his side. "Down we go, into the heart of darkness. There's a mystery waiting to be solved once and for all."

"What are we hoping to find?"

"No idea, but I'm sure we'll know when we find it. If we're lucky, they'll be the answers. We may never catch the perpetrators, but I for one would like to get to the bottom of these killings, wouldn't you? We know so much, and so little really, just enough to be sure they weren't random. And that means there has to be a reason driving them: Why did they happen now? Why these victims? What is the connection with the film? Everything we think we've worked out up till now is purely guesswork, really."

Wheatley followed Houdini inside.

There had been no noticeable change in the room.

The walls were still daubed with Glaaki's name. Wheatley honestly believed it was burned into his brain; he would never be able to forget it, no matter how hard he tried. He would hear its echo in his sleep from now until the day he died. Save for the writing on the walls, there was little else to show anyone had been in the room recently.

He noticed a pair of candle stubs that had burned down to the nub.

Houdini lit one of them and led the way down the staircase to the albino woman's room.

Even though he knew the place was deserted, Wheatley found himself creeping down the stairs with exaggerated caution. The treads creaked with every single step.

It was only when they reached the door that opened into the albino woman's room that Wheatley realized the staircase continued downwards. Houdini pointed down. Wheatley nodded. There was no point in wasting time searching Mrs. Whateley's room; the freak would have salvaged anything of a personal nature before she fled.

"This where they took you?"

Houdini shrugged. "Probably. I remember different things, different places, the effect of the chloroform, no doubt. Nothing fits together in here." He tapped his temple. "There's only one way to find out what's down there," he said, then started down, holding out the candle to get the most from its meager light. Wheatley followed him down.

They passed another door.

This one was locked.

Wheatley tried to piece together the layout of the old building—this one almost certainly opened out into one of the downstairs guest rooms, perhaps even Ma Mocata's apartment. They carried on down. The steps changed from wood to stone as they descended, the new staircase carved out of the rock that the town was built upon. The middle of the steps had been worn smooth by generations of use. These steps almost certainly predated the boarding house. Perhaps they belonged to some sort of smugglers' cavern network or slave railroad?

Nothing could have prepared him for what he found when the stairs finally came to an end, though.

They stepped out into a huge cavernous chamber.

It was impossible to grasp the sheer enormity of the place; the tiny light from the candle barely broke the darkness. Houdini crossed the stone floor, reaching for a sconce set into the wall. He lit a reed torch from the tiny stub of candle before doing the same to another, then another and another until the whole room was filled with flickering light.

Wheatley could only stand there stunned by the sheer jaw-dropping magnificence of the place; the open space could easily hold a thousand people—more, two, three thousand. It was huge. At the far end of the chamber he saw a great stone altar.

"I remember this place," Houdini said. "I remember the altar. I remember the weird acoustics of this place when they started chanting. I thought I was going to lose my mind."

Dennis barely registered what Houdini was saying. He was enthralled by the sight of the symbol that adorned the wall behind the altar. There it was again, the sign of Glaaki. This place, this temple, was a focus of worship for the Servants of Glaaki who had gathered together here for generations to call his name.

He caught sight of something white on the floor behind the great stone table—realizing as he did that the stain on its perfection was almost certainly blood, marking it out as a sacrificial altar. He shuddered, then bent over to retrieve what turned out to be one of the missing pages from Monk's script. Wheatley held it out to Houdini, who took it over to one of the torches to be able to better read it.

"Oh my God!" he said before he'd even finished reading the first paragraph.

"What's the matter? What is it?"

"It's the scene by the lake. But it's not. I mean, it's what happened to me by the lake, exactly, but in this the sacrifice is a woman."

"Catherine Beddows?"

Houdini nodded, biting at his lower lip as he skimmed the rest of the text on the page. "This is it. This is the proof that Monk stumbled upon the ritual that was supposed to summon Glaaki from the bottom of Spring Glen. It was real enough. But," Wheatley noticed Houdini's fingers begin to twitch, like he was tapping out a subconscious rhythm, thinking, sorting through ideas, until he said, "Why sacrifice a woman? That doesn't fit."

"Doesn't it? They murdered two actresses."

"Exactly, Wheatley! Exactly! They *murdered* two actresses. That's precisely what doesn't fit. Why would they kill them if they were going to be sacrificed beside the lake anyway?"

It was a good question.

"Unless they were killed because they were not right for the part."

"The part?" Wheatley asked.

"The sacrifice. They weren't fit for the purpose. And if that's the case, then surely that means someone else knows more about the ritual than Monk, doesn't it?"

"Perhaps there was only ever going to be one soul fit for the role of sacrifice. We are talking faith, perhaps it's preordained. Damn it. I hate when I'm wrong." Houdini jabbed a finger at a line on the page. Wheatley tried to read it in the candlelight. Between lines of dialogue there was a single camera direction that caught Wheatley's eye: *Close up of symbol on woman's wrist.*

"Monk's assistant? You think she's the sacrifice?"

"Obviously. We've completely misjudged the woman, Dennis. She's the key to all of this. She bears the sign of Glaaki. She's in danger. I don't know why I didn't see it before. I was so convinced she was on the side of the devils. Damn it. I don't even know where to start looking for her."

"Yes you do. If they've taken her you know exactly where to look."

"The Lake House," Houdini said, following his reasoning.

"That's where they held you. That's where they held the others."

Houdini nodded. "That's assuming they've got her. And if they have, I pity the poor woman. We've got to get her out of there and help her get as far away from here as possible."

Chapter Forty-Two

The world had changed by the time they emerged from the underground chapel. They were tired beyond words, running on no sleep for nearly two days, and desperately hungry.

It was the morning after a horrific nightmare come true. The fog had lifted completely. The world seemed to be waking up from the grip of a particularly grim, oppressive dream.

Wheatley and Houdini drove to the Lake House as though the Devil himself had ridden out and was hard on their heels. The place, though, was every bit as deserted as the boarding house, though they did find signs that it had been used to hold someone captive; the ground floor was filled with the detritus of deprivation and suffering, waste and filth. They stood in the middle of it, in Wheatley's case trying to imagine what had happened here, in Houdini's remembering.

They checked the place top to bottom.

She wasn't there.

They were out of ideas. It was going to take a lucky break to find her. The only places either of them had ever seen her were the film studio and Monk's house, and there had been no sign of her at either.

"The only positive is they haven't got her," Wheatley offered, closing the door behind them.

"Or they've already finished their ritual and she's long gone," Houdini countered.

"Do you really think that?"

"I don't know. I'm beginning to think I don't have any of the answers, Dennis. Because every time I think I'm beginning to understand this town, Dunwich goes and surprises me anew."

"She must have somewhere—a place of her own? Somewhere off-set?" Wheatley said, not allowing the escapologist to brood on yet another failure.

"We're chasing ghosts, Dennis."

"We can't think like that, Harry. For the first time we're ahead of the game: we know who their sacrifice is, and look at the water, that damned place, it's placid, and even the fog's lifted its thick, oppressive pall. Do you think that she's already down there? I don't. Not for one minute. There's no freakish party going on by the water's edge. Rituals take time. They need the alignment of the moon, they need portents and God knows what else to be in place. You don't raise a sleeping god in twenty minutes during your coffee break."

Houdini laughed at that. "Perhaps you're right my optimistic friend, perhaps you are right. Just this once it wouldn't be bad to be proved wrong, at least."

They were back in the car with no idea of where to go next. Tanith had been an ever-present in the background since they'd arrived in town, but when he tried to think about where she might have taken refuge, he realized he knew next to nothing about her beyond the fact she seemed devoted to Monk. At times he had thought there were sinister undertones to the relationship, but he'd come to realize that it was more of an obsessive attraction than anything else. He tried to think like a woman obsessed, hoping it would help.

"She would have wanted to be close to the set, I think, perhaps one of the trailers? Close enough to Monk, to always be at his beck and call."

"And the place will be deserted by now, unless the police are still picking through the wreckage."

"Unlikely. They'll have got out of there as soon as they could and with the footage destroyed and Monk incapacitated, I can't imagine the actors are being paid to hang around. They'll be out there touting for work already, and they won't find any around here."

A sudden tap on the passenger's side window interrupted their conversation. Unbidden, Joe Diamond opened the door behind Houdini and climbed onto the back seat.

"Welcome to Ghost Town, USA, gents," the private dick said, leaning forward in the gap between the front seats. "Creepy, isn't it?"

"Where have they all gone?"

"Arkham, Innsmouth, Kingsport, maybe further afield. Who knows? It's a big old world out there."

"The carnival people?"

"Gone, too. There were cars and trucks heading out of here for at least a couple of hours, a mass exodus. I have to say I'm kinda hoping we'll never see them again."

"So what's the word?"

"Our friendly neighborhood law enforcers are trying to lay it all on that strange-looking guy we saw take a dive into the lake the other night."

"They're barking up the wrong tree with Schreck," Houdini observed.

"You know the guy?"

"We've met. He's a troubled soul, for sure, but he's no killer. And I've told them as much."

"Then let's hope he manages to keep himself out of jail. But between you, me, and the Model T here, I don't think they are in the mood to go looking for someone else to blame."

"But he didn't do anything," Wheatley said, remembering all too well his own collision with the law. Innocence, it seemed, didn't matter if your face didn't fit or the evidence stacked up the wrong way.

"Bit of bad luck then, wouldn't you say?" Diamond said matter-of-factly. "It's all about perception. They need the locals to feel safe. That means someone has to go behind bars. If the freaks really were behind the killings, well, they've split town, so locking your man Schreck up will work just fine. The killings will end and it'll look to all the world like they got the right man."

Wheatley didn't like the sound of it, but he knew all too well you could plead your innocence until you were blue in the face and it wouldn't matter a jot if no one listened.

"Monk had an assistant up at the film set," Houdini said. "We think she might be in danger."

"You got a name?"

"Tanith. That's her first name. But that's all I've got."

Diamond said nothing for a moment, clearly thinking.

"Give me half an hour," he said at last, then opened the door again without giving either of them the chance to reply. "I'll meet you at Rosie's. If I can find your girl, you're standing lunch."

Wheatley watched Diamond hurry across the road in the direction of his office. If anyone could find the woman, it was the PI. And it'd be worth more than a cup of coffee and a slice of Rosie's famous pie if it saved her life.

They had time to kill. And Wheatley couldn't remember the last time he'd eaten.

Houdini insisted they drive to the diner despite the fact that it was only a couple of blocks away on the pretext that they might need to leave in haste, and time had a bad habit of being of the essence when you were least prepared. Wheatley didn't argue, but suspected it had more to do with his injury. "You should get yourself checked out," he said, not looking at Houdini.

"As soon as we're through here, my personal physician will give me a thorough physical, worry not." But he did worry. He would have been happier to drive over to Arkham while they waited for Diamond to work his magic. The body wasn't something to be messed with and he had been warned often enough that he needed to take better care of his own. You only had one of them and his was his livelihood. Unless you were the Beetle Man, and even then having a second hadn't helped him.

They slipped into a booth and Rosie appeared in a few minutes with menus, a smile, and a brimming pot of hot coffee. She poured out cups, suggested that the apple pie was, quite honestly, to die for, and left them to their conversation.

The coffee tasted good. Really good, actually. But only served to remind Wheatley how little he had eaten over the last few days.

He called Rosie over. "Bacon, eggs, sunny side up, sausage, the works. I could eat a horse," he said with a smile.

"And how about you, honey?" she asked Houdini.

"The same," he said.

Both men stuffed their faces, eating as though their bellies thought their throats had been cut. It wasn't just food, it was survival. They were alive. It was as simple as that.

But when the pie came later, Houdini did little more than pick at it. Wheatley continued eating with gusto. "Something on your mind?" he asked between mouthfuls.

Houdini shrugged. "It could be something or nothing," he said.

"Tell me about it."

"I was thinking about that room, back at the Lake House, where they held me."

"What about it?"

"I don't know…that's the thing… Something just didn't feel right about the place."

"In what way?"

"Look at the subterranean chapel, at the hideaway behind your room, the sign of Glaaki was all over those places, but it was nowhere to be seen in the Lake House."

It was a good point.

Before Houdini could elaborate, Diamond came through the door and slid onto the booth beside them.

"Looks like *Cherchez la femme* has brought you some results," he said, snagging a piece of toast from the rack. Rosie appeared with coffee. She was like the genie of the caffeine lamp.

"You've got something for us?" Wheatley asked, laying aside his flatware.

"It took a few calls, but yeah, looks like I found her. Knowing her name might have helped, but there aren't that many Tanith's in the vicinity. You can thank me later. Right now, I do believe a meal or two is on you." Diamond was like a kid with a secret he was itching to tell.

Houdini produced a folded ten dollar bill from his pocket and spread it out on the table between them.

Diamond reached to take it, but the escapologist covered it with his hand.

When he lifted it again the bill had disappeared.

"Nice trick," Diamond said.

"What have you managed to find out?"

"Don't trust me, eh?" Diamond pulled a small notebook from his pocket. Wheatley knew full well it was his own version of showmanship; the private dick could remember everything he'd written there.

"The girl's name is Tanith Jugg, so it's hardly surprising she didn't exactly shout about her family name. She's a New York native, but that's as much as I found out about her past in the time I had."

"Hardly worth ten bucks," said Houdini.

"Oh you can have that for nothing. That's not the good stuff."

"So what did you find?" The note reappeared in Houdini's hand. He ran his fingertips across the edge, making it alternately rigid and then limp.

"Miss Jugg has a ticket booked on a ship leaving Kingsport this evening, heading down the coast." He tore out the piece of paper with the details scrawled on it, and placed it on the table where the ten dollar bill had been a few moments earlier.

Houdini picked it up and left the cash in its place. "Good man."

"If you're ever in the need of quality investigative services, gentlemen, you know where to come."

"That we do, Mr. Diamond," Houdini said, slipping the note into his pocket and sliding out of the booth.

"Take me back to Ulysses's house, please, Dennis," he said as they reached the car. "There are a few personal things I need to collect. I have a feeling I won't have another chance."

"What do you mean?" Wheatley felt like he was being abandoned.

"I need to be in Montreal in a few days."

"I thought you were making all of that up? When you spoke to the asylum on the telephone?"

"If you are going to tell a lie, my friend, it is always more convincing if it comes wrapped in the truth. I have a show in Montreal that I need to rehearse for. If Miss Jugg makes it onto her ship this evening, there's nothing to keep me here. My work here is done."

Wheatley's own passage was booked for late next week. He shouldn't have been surprised. Houdini was a man of multiple commitments, and not one to break them. He didn't fancy the idea of seeing out the remainder of his stay at Ma Mocata's Boarding House though, not if he was going to be alone. He'd have to make alternative arrangements, maybe down in Kingsport.

He didn't even leave the car while Houdini went inside Monk's house to recover his belongings. A few moments later he reappeared at the doorway, struggling with his bag. Wheatley clambered out of the car to help him stow the bag in the trunk before they headed for Kingsport. They had more than enough time to get there, so they swung by Ma Mocata's to collect his own bags, then left Dunwich in the rearview mirror for the last time.

The dockside was already teeming with people by the time they reached Kingsport.

It didn't seem like all that long ago Wheatley had debarked here, but coming at it this way it was another world. They were surrounded by a sea of faces. It was going to be nigh on impossible to find her in the crowd if she didn't want to be found. He wondered if it would be possible to have an announcement made, telling her to meet them at some prearranged point. Of course, even with an announcement there'd be no way of knowing if she actually heard the message, especially if she was already onboard.

Passengers lugging trunks and struggling with suitcases bumped against them as they stood in the middle of the chaos, trying to spot someone in authority who might be able to help them find her.

The ship was considerably smaller than *The Dunwich Ghost* but still appeared to be taking a lot of cargo as well as passengers down the coast to Boston, and on to New York, with any number of stops in between.

Houdini slipped away, leaving Wheatley stranded in the

middle of the mob. It might have been a very different crowd to the one that had come at them up at the film set, but last night had changed him. Suddenly the constant press of the people, the noise, all of it came together with claustrophobic intensity. It didn't matter that there wasn't a freak amongst them. He felt panic swell up inside him. He pushed past a man, trying to open up some space around him so that he could breath, and started calling out Harry's name over and over as he stumbled forward, bumped and shoved by people thinking he was trying to force his way on board and jump the queues.

Wheatley pushed through the mob, eyes fixed on the Harbormaster's office, which appeared to double as the ticket office.

And then he spotted two of the freaks pressed close to the harbor side and his heart nearly tore free of its muscle walls and came out of his mouth, it hammered that hard.

"Have you spotted her?" Houdini asked, seeing his fear and confusion as he came up behind him. He had been so caught up in watching the freaks he hadn't seen the escapologist approach.

"Not yet."

"Her baggage hasn't been checked in, but he confirmed she's definitely booked on board."

"And you?"

"I've procured passage as far as Boston, so this is it for us, my friend. I'll be able to get a train directly to Montreal from there. It's been an experience to remember, wouldn't you say?"

It was hard to argue with that.

"What about your car?"

"All yours for as long as you need it. When you're finished with it, park it here and I'll arrange for it to be transported to New York ready for my return."

It wasn't going to be easy to say goodbye, even after spending such a short period of time in each other's company, given the distance and knowing that they were unlikely to ever meet again. Wheatley wasn't quite sure what he was supposed to say. That he'd never forget their adventure? That sounded a little crass. That he'd treasure their time together? That made him sound like a fussy old woman. So instead of speaking, he spotted a packing case that had been left unattended and clambered up on top of it to get a better view of the crowd.

He scanned the faces, not expecting to recognize the woman. It was just an excuse not to have to fill the last few minutes of their friendship with platitudes, or worse, truths.

And then a woman in the press of people turned slightly, and he caught sight of her familiar profile.

"I see her!" he cried, then realized his voice had carried across the quayside, drawing the attention of the freaks by the harbor wall. More heads turned in his direction. And then they turned in *her* direction.

There were more freaks in the crowd than he'd realized.

They began to push their way through the crowd toward him—and Tanith.

Monk's assistant looked up, seeing him perched on the trunk, and after making eye contact for a moment raised a hand in recognition. Wheatley scrambled down from the trunk. "Come on, Harry, they're here. They're hunting her… We've got to get her onboard before they can get to her." He snatched up the escapologist's bag and forced a path through the press of bodies, barging people out of the way until they stood face-to-face with Tanith Jugg. She looked terrified. And with good reason. The freaks were closing in on them, forcing their way through the crowd.

"Thank God!" Houdini said as they reached her. "We have to get you out of here. I don't think you realize just how much danger you might be in."

"Oh, I think I do," she said, eyes wide like saucers as she turned frantically left and right. "They are everywhere I look."

"Don't worry, we're here now. We won't let them hurt you, will we, Dennis?"

Wheatley glanced around. More and more faces were looking in their direction; strange faces. Even though he did not recognize half of them, he knew that each and every one of them were freaks even if their disfigurements and abnormalities were well hidden.

"Come on, follow me," Houdini said, and started to push his way toward the gangplank. She clutched his hand like her life depended upon it. "Were you still at the studio when they started burning the film?"

She nodded her head, but kept looking back over her shoulder toward Wheatley and the freaks, keeping her voice low, little more than a whisper. "I was hiding. I managed to slip away when the police arrived. I knew they were coming. Simon Aron, the principal photographer, begged me to hide a can of film. He said that he had filmed it himself, without Monk's knowledge. The next thing I knew he was dead and the freaks were tearing the place apart."

"Did you get the film?" Houdini pressed, matching her low tone, pulling her closer through the throng to be sure that she could hear him and that their words wouldn't travel far.

"Of course. But I'm afraid that if I take it on board with me they will take it from me somehow."

"I'm traveling as far as Boston," Houdini said. "I can make sure that we are safe until then."

"I would feel safer if the film was out of their reach, though."

"Then let me take it," Wheatley offered. "I can spirit it away from here while all eyes are on you."

"It makes sense," Houdini agreed. "Don't let anyone see you take it. If it's important enough for someone to die trying to protect, then we need to make sure that he didn't die in vain."

Tanith agreed and as the three of them huddled closer, she extricated the metal canister from her carpetbag and slipped it inside Wheatley's coat. It was like some complicated three card trick. They kept talking about nothing in particular, a little louder than they had been speaking before, trying to cover their nerves as they edged toward the gangplank.

When embarkation time arrived, Tanith gave no more than a simple smile of goodbye. Wheatley and Houdini exchanged a bear hug and a slap on the back that spoke volumes. In just a few days they had gone through so much both together and apart, but here they were, at the end.

Wheatley stood on the quayside as the crowd thinned, watching the railings around the deck but neither emerged for one final wave, unlike many of the other passengers. It was only as the ship moved away from the quayside that

Houdini and Tanith appeared at the stern, waving to him. Behind Houdini he could see the freaks gathering.

Wheatley did the one thing he could do that might make them safe.

He reached inside his coat and pulled out the canister of film he'd taken from Monk's assistant. He held it aloft and used it to wave back to Houdini, making damned sure the freaks were aware that the film they were looking for was no longer in Tanith's possession. He had no idea if it would keep the pair safe, but it couldn't hurt them.

Wheatley stood on the harbor watching until the ship grew so small it was impossible to make out the shapes of the people on the deck. Houdini would make it to Montreal in time for the performance and he would make sure that Tanith Jugg was safe and as far away from this place as she could get.

They'd won.

He turned the canister over and over in his hands, trying to see what could possibly make this particular reel of film so special. Of course, there was nothing remarkable about the can. Anything special had to be on the film itself. That meant he had to watch it if he finally wanted to discover the full extent of the mystery. He could only think of one place where he could do that: Monk's house.

Chapter Forty-Three

Wheatley couldn't quite believe what he was seeing flicker across the screen.

Monk's paraphernalia included a projector, but he had decided on loading the reel of film into the viewer as Monk had done before. It had taken him a couple of attempts, but finally the machine had illuminated the celluloid and brought it to life.

The slightly jerky black and white image was filmed from a single viewpoint which didn't appear to quite capture everything that was happening, as though only the center of the action was being focused on while other things were happening just beyond the reach of the lens. Things and people drifted in and out of shot, but the cameraman had been either unable or unwilling to change its perspective.

Wheatley perched himself on a rickety chair to watch the unfolding scene. He'd poured himself a glass of whisky, the bottle on the floor by his feet.

The center of the scene concentrated on the body of a woman staked out on the ground. Spring Glen was unmistakable. This was the same spot where Wheatley had watched Houdini tied to the post before being dragged into the water.

The shadows of two men ranged over her, but the men themselves remained out of shot.

It took a moment or two for Dennis to realize that the woman restrained on the ground was Catherine Beddows, Monk's original leading lady.

It appeared to be a scene from the film, yet Monk had made no mention of any footage with Beddows beyond the test reel; and as far as everyone—save Houdini and himself—was concerned, she had failed to arrive in Dunwich, yet there she was on the screen in front of him. This was a far cry from the excited face he had seen on the test reel; she was petrified, tears and thick lines of black mascara staining her face, but there was no doubt that it was her.

In the background he saw four figures emerge from the water. Their rubber suits give them the appearance of some weird underwater creature, but as he watched and they came into sharper focus, Wheatley began to wonder if these weren't actors after all. The longer he watched, the more he became convinced that this was not part of the film at all—this was a recording the cameraman had made that captured a ritual like the one performed on Houdini when the cultists offered him as a sacrifice to their underwater god. They weren't actors; he was sure of that now. But there was still a strangeness about them that marked them as being different and yet clearly closely connected to each other in some way. Their faces seemed a little too long, a little too thin, and their eyes were too far apart as if they were almost at the side of their heads.

The focus shifted slightly, and the surface of the water rippled and bulged as though something else was moving in the lake.

The two figures who had been casting their shadows on the actress moved into shot.

They watched the movement as intently as Wheatley himself was at this point. For a moment they looked across at someone else just beyond the edge of the screen, as though asking permission.

Wheatley had expected the two men to be freaks.

They weren't freaks at all.

He saw the familiar faces of Martin and Ropes, the two policemen so keen to lay the blame at Max Schreck's feet and close the investigation down as quickly as they possibly could.

And even then it wasn't the presence of the policemen—or the proof of their mendacity—that provided the greatest surprise; ghosting across the screen he saw another woman. She had her back to camera, but he recognized her. It wasn't until she returned to her original position he was sure, though, as Tanith Jugg raised the knife in her hands.

Images came and went; strange visions of things that shouldn't exist. Tanith ignored what was happening in the water. Instead she looked directly toward him, her mouth opening and closing as she spoke, but the room remained in silence save for the hum of the motor and the click of the spools as they turned.

Wheatley tried to concentrate on what she was saying, moving his mouth to match the word she was saying.

He had expected the word to be Glaaki, but his lips moved again and again until they fell in sync with hers and he realized that she was calling *his* name.

But how could she have known that he would be watching?

How could she possibly have known in advance that this would fall into his hands?

He wiped away the sweat from his forehead.

He took another mouthful of whisky, swallowing it straight down despite the fiery burn at the back of his throat.

He stopped the reel, leaving her face at the center of the frame locked in the middle of saying his name.

What did this all mean?

There was only one person he wanted to speak to: Houdini.

He needed to warn him that he hadn't been wrong after all; Tanith was not the innocent she made herself out to be. Far from being a victim or a bystander in this, she occupied center stage. She was the High Priestess of the cult.

He knew what was going to coming next; Tanith was going to kill Catherine Beddows before she was dragged down into the water.

It fit with the pieces of the puzzle, even if he was making some connections that there was no real evidence for.

Despite this knowledge, he started the film flickering again.

Tanith Jugg showed no sign of harming the actress who still lay on the ground, unmoving.

Tanith looked back at the water.

Wheatley saw the grey mass rising in the water.

Tanith stepped aside to allow whatever it was see their offering.

Was this thing, this unspeakable thing, really Glaaki?

Was there truly a slumbering god at the bottom of Spring Glen?

Water ran from the back of the beast.

Strings of slime slid from its rigged back.

Wheatley tried to find words that would describe this creature—a monstrosity which appeared to be at home underwater but had supposedly traveled here from the stars; a giant gastropod in constant movement, its edges undefined, continually changing. It slithered and crawled from the water, oozing up the bank until it reached Tanith. It raised itself upright, wrapping part of its flesh around her, and covering her in the slime that it secreted.

Its very touch sent the woman into paroxysms of pleasure.

She was joining with it in some way; communing with a god.

Coupling.

For a moment she was gone, disappeared inside him, before his flesh slid away and revealed her again.

She looked directly at the camera.

This time she was chanting the name of Glaaki over and over again. There was no mistaking that.

Even in the silence of the film Wheatley could hear it inside his head. He could hear the chants of the others on the lakeside that night, of those not even in camera shot.

And he joined in with them, his lips moving.

At last he *understood.*

He tore the film from the machine, feeling a sudden searing pain inside him that cried out for release.

This wasn't just some piece of film that had captured the ritual—it made the viewer a part of it!

Anyone seeing this could be drawn in just as easily as he almost was.

They wanted him to take it home to England so that more unsuspecting souls could be drawn into their hellish cult, worshipping that *creature*; spreading its perfidious influence ever further from its lair.

Well, that wasn't happening. Not if he had anything to say about it.

It had to be destroyed.

Wheatley unraveled the film and threw it on the floor.

He tried desperately to tear it into shreds, but it wouldn't split. He dashed the remains of his glass of whisky over it. He might not be able to kill the thing itself—not if it truly was a god—but he could deny it fresh blood.

There was panic in his head, it was almost as if he was no longer in control of his own actions.

All he could think about was destroying the film.

He had no care for the consequences.

He poured the rest of the bottle of whisky over the coils of celluloid, and then threw a match onto it.

Flames sucked the air from the room.

Even before he had backed out to the door the fire was out of control.

In moments the entire room was ablaze.

The whole house about to be engulfed.

He stumbled down the stairs and out to the car.

By the time he was behind the wheel the building was a raging inferno.

Wheatley glanced back in his rearview mirror a single time as he drove away. That fire was going to consume everything. There would be no trace that the film had ever existed. He was glad he'd had the presence of mind to gather his belongings from Mocata's and had no need to return to Dunwich. He drove for the town limits, and kept on driving on the road to Arkham. He would check into a hotel and hide away until it was time to board his ship and go home.

As he drove away he could still hear the roar of the flames and in it, mocking him inside the snap and crackle of the flames, the sound of that one word repeated over and over again. *Glaaki, Glaaki, Glaaki.*

End Credits

About the Authors

Steven Savile

Steven Savile has written for Doctor Who, Torchwood, Primeval, Stargate, Warhammer, Slaine, Fireborn, Pathfinder, and other popular game and comic worlds. His novels have been published in eight languages to date, including the Italian bestseller *L'eridita*. He won the International Media Association of Tie-In Writers award for his Primeval novel, *Shadow of the Jaguar*, published by Titan in 2010, and has been nominated for the British Fantasy Award on multiple occasions. *Silver*, his debut thriller, reached #2 in the Amazon UK e-charts in the summer of 2011 selling over fifty thousand copies in the process, making it the #26 bestselling ebook of 2011 in the UK (Bookseller Jan 2012). He wrote the story for the huge international bestselling computer game *Battlefield 3*, which sold over five million copies in its week of release, and he served as head writer on the popular online children's game *Spineworld* which have over one million players. His latest books include *Tau Ceti* (co-authored with International Bestselling novelist Kevin J. Anderson), the novelization of the computer game *Risen 2: Dark Waters*, and *Each Ember's Ghost*, his first novel for Fantasy Flight Games.

Steve lives in Stockholm, Sweden, and has done so for the last 15 years.

Steve Lockley

Steve Lockley spent far too many years working in banking and insurance but now writes full-time. His first novel *The Ragchild* written with Paul Lewis was nominated for the British Fantasy Award for Best Novel. He is responsible for more than a hundred short stories and writes the popular *Sally Reardon Supernatural Mysteries* series with Steven Savile.

With Mike O'Driscoll, Steve was awarded the BFS Special Award in 1995 for their work on the horror convention *Welcome to My Nightmare*. He has also served as a judge for the World Fantasy Awards.

Steve lives in Wales with his two children.